also by sarra manning

LET'S
GET
LOST

LET'S GET LOST

sarra manning

dutton books

DUTTON BOOKS
A member of Penguin Group (USA) Inc.

Published by the Penguin Group

Penguin Group (USA) Inc., 375 Hudson Street, New York, New York 10014, U.S.A.
Penguin Group (Canada), 90 Eglinton Avenue East, Suite 700, Toronto, Ontario, Canada M4P 2Y3
(a division of Pearson Penguin Canada Inc.)
Penguin Books Ltd, 80 Strand, London WC2R 0RL, England
Penguin Ireland, 25 St Stephen's Green, Dublin 2, Ireland (a division of Penguin Books Ltd)
Penguin Group (Australia), 250 Camberwell Road, Camberwell, Victoria 3124, Australia (a division
of Pearson Australia Group Pty Ltd)
Penguin Books India Pvt Ltd, 11 Community Centre, Panchsheel Park, New Delhi - 110 017, India
Penguin Group (NZ), Cnr Airborne and Rosedale Roads, Albany, Auckland 1310, New Zealand
(a division of Pearson New Zealand Ltd)
Penguin Books (South Africa) (Pty) Ltd, 24 Sturdee Avenue, Rosebank, Johannesburg 2196, South Africa
Penguin Books Ltd, Registered Offices: 80 Strand, London WC2R 0RL, England

Library of Congress Cataloging-in-Publication Data
Manning, Sarra.
Let's get lost / by Sarra Manning. — 1st ed.
p. cm.
Summary: As she acts out the role of "Mean Girl"—at school, with her father and brother,
and even with her new boyfriend—sixteen-year-old Isabel comes to a dead end and finally
confronts issues related to her mother's death.
ISBN 0-525-47666-0 (alk. paper)
[1. Behavior—Fiction. 2. Interpersonal relations—Fiction. 3. Emotional problems—
Fiction. 4. Death—Fiction. 5. Guilt—Fiction.] I. Title.
PZ7.M315653Let   2006
[Fic]—dc22   2006003866

First published in Great Britain in 2006 by Hodder Children's Books, London

Published in the United States by Dutton Books,
a member of Penguin Group (USA) Inc.
345 Hudson Street, New York, New York 10014
www.penguin.com/youngreaders

Designed by Irene Vandervoort

Printed in USA   First Edition

10 9 8 7 6 5 4 3 2

Dedicated to my mother, Regina Shaw

The memory of you emerges from the night around me.
—"A Song of Despair"
Pablo Neruda

With love and thanks to Jane Davitt
for cheerleading and beta-reading,
Sarah Bailey for never doubting me,
and Annakovsky for the name.

"It's always tempting to lose yourself with someone who's maybe lost themselves."
Angela Chase, *My So-Called Life*

LET'S
GET
LOST

1

I knew the party was going to suck. Parties usually do, but I still had this half excited, half scared fluttering in my tummy, like there was a baby bird in there, flapping its wings and trying to take a left just under my rib cage.

I had a bath and exfoliated and shaved and moisturized, then I tried to figure out what the hell I could do with my hair. I'd had this disastrous experiment with a pair of scissors and, well, it had said Starry Night on the box and I'd been hoping that when I'd finished (after getting black splotches over every towel we possessed) I'd look like a mysterious girl from a French film who had lots of lovers and spent a lot of time in cafés debating the meaning of life. Instead I ended up looking like a total goth. I had to hack six inches off, leaving me with a ragged bob that was more Amélie than Emily Strange. In the right light.

There still wasn't even enough hair to scoop into a ponytail, so I fashioned two bunches and fixed them with sparkly hair bobbles that I found lurking in the back of the bathroom cabinet. I sort of liked the finished effect in a strange way. It was edgy. It was striking. God, it was really time to book myself a hair appointment.

But that was merely the tip of my style dilemma as I stood in my daisy-patterned underwear in front of my bulging wardrobe and tried to decide who I wanted to be that night. I love to explore the possibilities of transforming myself from a lanky sixteen-year-old into somebody thrilling. I could do the Kate Moss boho thing. Or my Topshop version of Marissa Cooper. Rock chick was so very last year, and what had I been thinking when I bought that vintage lace dress with the rip under the arm?

I took a deep breath and padded into my parents' bedroom. If I'd stopped to inhale, which I didn't, I knew I'd still be able to smell the faint aroma of Calvin Klein's Eternity. I really don't know how *he* can bear to sleep in here every night, which is why he usually passes out in the study.

All her clothes were neatly arranged by color. A rainbow array of dresses and skirts hanging there with no place to go. I was doing them a huge public service just by rifling through the rails. Eventually, I found a plain black dress, which I don't think I ever saw her wear. It was regulation-issue, with three-quarter-length sleeves that fashion magazines would describe as understated and chic. Maybe I could do understated and chic, I thought as I wriggled into it. It was meant to hug my curves, but I didn't have much to hug, so it kinda skimmed over them and ended up somewhere just above my knees, which was odd because she'd been taller than me. But then I'd grown a lot over the summer. I dug a pair of fishnets out of one of her drawers, which accessorized perfectly with my pink kitten heels, and stole some smudgy gray eye shadow from the dressing table.

I looked older, which was good because it meant that I might actually be able to buy cigarettes and wine without having to get into this whole thing about my date of birth and who the prime minister was on the day I was born. All I needed was some cold, hard cash to give to the nice man in the liquor store.

Getting money from my dad is a finesse job. Luckily, I have finesse coming out of my arse. I barged into his study without knocking, marched across to his desk, and held out my hand. "Give me twenty pounds," I snapped. "I need twenty pounds. Give it to me. Now!"

My father is not like other people's fathers. No sir. When they made him they broke the mold, probably after orders from on high. He teaches American literature at the University, which is why my little brother, Felix, and I are named after characters from Henry James's novels. I tried reading *Portrait of a Lady* once to show willing because the heroine, Isabel Archer, is my namesake. It's about the only time in the last two years that he managed to look even faintly pleased with me. But I gave it up after the first chapter. I mean, God, would it have killed Henry James to use a comma or, like, a period occasionally? I saw the film with Nicole Kidman in it, though. And what kind of freak names their only daughter after a poor girl who has to marry some misogynistic prick who's only interested in her money? My father, that's who.

Right now, he was contemplating his glass of red wine, but he looked up and blinked slowly, then blinked faster as he took in my stylish little ensemble. "What on earth are you wearing?"

"Clothes," I explained, not wanting to get sidetracked from the mission. "Twenty pounds, Dad."

"Are you going out somewhere, then?" he inquired archly, like he'd invented the rhetorical question.

"Yes. It's Friday night. I'm going out, I'll be home before eleven. Now give me twenty pounds."

"There's no need to be quite so shrill, Isabel." He gave me one of his piercing looks, but after sixteen years they've lost their effectiveness. "And why should I give you twenty pounds?"

"Fine," I said, like it was no big deal. "I'll just go out and when it's time to come home, I'll walk the dark streets just as the pubs are emptying out because I haven't got any money for a cab. I'm sure I'll be all right. And even if I'm not, well, at least you've managed to save yourself twenty quid."

I hadn't even finished my Oscar-worthy speech before there were two crisp ten-pound notes fluttering on my outstretched palm.

"Now will you stop yammering and leave me in peace?"

"Consider it done," I said, backing out fast before he had a chance to change his mind. "Have fun with the dead Americans."

"Don't be late," he warned me, but I could tell that his heart wasn't in it, and he was already reaching for his glass before I closed the door.

We sent Nancy into the liquor store to take advantage of their "four bottles for twelve pounds" promotion because she could easily pass for twenty-one. All those tanning sessions had given her skin this orange leather look you don't see on most sixteen-year-olds.

"Get the Sauvignon Blanc," I demanded as I rummaged in my bag for some liquid eyeliner, because Dot was looking way too vanilla to get through the door of even the lame student party we were going to crash.

As I brandished the brush at Dot and grabbed hold of her chin so she couldn't get away, I could see Ella pull a face at Nancy. "Can't we just get some Bacardi Breezers?" she whined.

"Why do we have to always get wine? There's never a corkscrew at these parties and ..."

"Are you twelve? Do you want some candy and ice cream to go with your Breezers?"

"Ow! You nearly had my eye out!" Dot yelped, and I was forced to turn away from Nancy and Ella, who were still griping about my choice of alcoholic beverages.

I could have compromised and told Nancy to get a bottle of vodka and some mixers, but I've learned from bitter experience that it's best to squash any imminent signs of rebellion immediately. "Sauvignon Blanc," I repeated implacably. And then, because a good leader is a benevolent one, I conceded ever so slightly. "I guess you could get just two bottles and you could have red wine, if you wanted."

Nods, grudging smiles, Dot still whimpering about conjunctivitis as I attempted to make her eyes a little less piggy with a couple of sweeps of eyeliner: I guess we were good to go.

I was right about the party. *El muy sucko.* It was wall-to-wall University students back for the start of the school year. As we trooped into the lounge with our carrier bag of clinking bottles, I actually heard one girl say to her friend, "So, I was all like 'Mummy, you don't understand, I'm a free spirit.'" God, I loathe students. They're so up themselves.

I separated from the others immediately because Ella had already spilled red wine over herself and none of us were going to get any sweet boy action if we clumped together. I snagged a bottle of the Sauvignon Blanc and wandered into the kitchen to find a corkscrew. There was the regulation group of people in there talking about some lame TV program because they had zero personalities and nothing else to bond over. This boy with a gross birthmark on his face tried to come on to me as I wrestled with the cork, but I made it perfectly clear that I was way out of his league and he called me a "stuck-up bitch" and went back to banging on about *Doctor Who*. As if I'd ever be interested in a port-stained geek.

Clutching the bottle in my hand, I moved through the party, taking it all in, listening to the *thud, thud, thud* of industrial techno and occasionally getting told to fuck off as I interrupted people getting off with each other or rolling joints like they were wild desperadoes living on the edge of the law.

It was really hard not to die from sheer boredom. There was a girl crying on the stairs because she'd had a row with her boyfriend; a couple getting horizontal on the sofa and a small group of spoddy boys standing in a puddle of their own drool watching them; a queue for the toilet that stretched across the landing; and someone throwing up in the sink. Just like every other party I've ever been to. I really needed to find some classier places to hang out.

There was a child safety gate across the stairs, but I climbed over it and sneaked up to the third floor. Most of the doors were locked, but as I tried the last handle, it opened and I found myself in a junk room filled with boxes and crates. It smelled kind of funky, so I tugged up the stiff window and leaned out to take greedy gulps of the cold night air before I hauled myself up onto the windowsill and sat there with my legs dangling out, drinking the wine and wondering why I'd thought coming here was going to break life's never-ending cycle of extreme suckitude.

I was about halfway down the bottle and pleasantly buzzed when the door behind me slammed against the wall. After I'd managed not to land with a splat in the front garden and break my spine in thirty different places, I peered over my shoulder into the dark room.

"Sorry. Didn't mean to startle you," said a slurred voice, and then the room was flooded with light from the single bulb that dangled precariously from a fraying cord. I put my hand up to shield my eyes.

"Thanks for nearly killing me," I grumbled. "You're not meant to be up here, anyway."

"Neither are you," he said, staggering toward me so I could get a good look at him. Hair. He had a lot of hair and a really big nose. Whatever. And why was he still talking? "I just fell over that gate. Wouldn't have the gate if they wanted anyone in here."

I shrugged and turned back to gaze at the sky so he could get a super-sized portion of cold shoulder. Unfortunately, he was too drunk to notice.

"What are you doing?" he asked, coming up behind me. "I don't think sitting on the sill is safe."

I rolled my eyes and took a swig of the now lukewarm wine. "I'm just enjoying the quiet," I said pointedly. "That was a hint, by the way, for you to either leave or shut the hell up."

He shuffled away, then there was a creak as he sat down. "You're really rude," he mused, like stating the obvious was his life's vocation.

"You're really annoying," I replied in a bored voice. "Feel free to piss off at any time."

There was a gasp of outrage, then he finally shut up. I tried to concentrate on the feeling of the rough wall as I drummed my heels against it and wondered how many stars there were in the sky, but he'd killed the mood.

I twisted around so I could look at him. He was slumped on a rickety chair, staring right back at me. He had the most amazing eyes. They were the exact same shade of gentian blue that was my favorite color in my paint box when I still used to go to art class.

I think I must have been slightly drunk because I told him that, and he sat up suddenly and asked how my course was going.

"What the hell are you talking about?"

"I wish I'd decided to do the Foundation Art course, too," he said mournfully. "I hate philosophy."

"Blah, blah, blah," I chanted, and took another mouthful of wine. "Earth to dickhead, you've got the wrong girl."

"Can I have some of that?" he asked politely, because he was either way drunker than I thought or had skin like a rhinoceros. With a sigh, I leaned over and passed him the bottle. He had long fingers and the most bitten nails I've ever seen. "God, you've changed your hair," he exclaimed. "It looks cool. Very hard-times chic."

In the end, it seemed easier to go along with his addled thought processes. Also, being someone else, someone who hung with drunk boys with gentian blue eyes, was more fun than I'd had all week.

"I fancied a change," I said casually, toying with the end of one of my bunches. "So, when was the last time we saw each other? It's been a while."

He furrowed his brow and twisted his lips. He had very pouty lips. "I think it was Glastonbury. You were with Dean. But you broke up, didn't you?"

I hid a smile and shook my head. "Yeah. I dumped him. He

was such a loser. Not very good in bed, either." Then an awful thought struck me. "You and me? We've never done it, have we?"

He gave a sudden bark of laughter. "Jesus, Chloë! If we had, I'd be really offended that you didn't remember. You're in a weird mood tonight."

"Guess I've had too much to drink, just like you," I said carefully, and wondered who Chloë was. He seemed to like her.

"Hey! Do you remember when we got off with each other?" Gentian boy stretched out his legs and made no attempt to give me back the wine. He was wearing jeans and a beaten-up pair of Jack Purcells; the rubber on the soles was almost worn through. "You tasted really sweet and you said you'd been drinking coffee with lots of sugar in it, and I thought all kisses would be that sweet, but they weren't."

There was no stopping him. He went on and on about this party he'd been to with the mysterious Chloë and how they'd had too much to drink and ended up making out behind the sofa. He seemed very hung up about it.

In the end, all I needed to do was insert the odd "yeah" or "hmm" into the conversation to keep him happy. He wasn't going to be winning prizes for academic excellence any time soon.

It was getting cold, so I closed the window, then decided to get the wine back before he drank it all.

". . . and you said it was complicated because of Dean, but he was seeing Molly by then, anyway . . ."

As I walked toward him, he leaned back so he could gaze up at me with a slightly dazed expression on his face.

"Give me back my wine," I ordered in my most imperious voice, which is pretty damn imperious. It's, like, imperious to the power of a hundred. I gestured at the bottle, but he suddenly seized my hand and pulled me onto his lap. It sounds like a really suave maneuver, but in actual fact, I landed in an ungainly heap on top of him.

I struggled to get up, but his hands were clamped around my waist. "I forgot how pretty you are," he murmured, and then he tried to kiss me.

"Hang on!" I yelped, and then his hand stroked the back of my neck and really it had been so long since someone touched me. That's my excuse and I'm sticking to it. I wound my arms around his neck and bumped my nose against his as he tried to capture my lips.

"Just one little kiss," he begged, and he shut his eyes. Then I kissed him.

I'd never really put the moves on a boy unless it involved spinning the bottle and two minutes locked in a stinky cupboard under someone's stairs. Usually I just suffered some guy lunging at me and shoving his tongue in my mouth at the same time that he tried to shove his hand down my top. But his lips were so soft as I cupped his face and planted tiny little kisses against that pouty, defenseless bottom lip of his. I bit it gently and his eyes snapped open, then he was kissing me back fiercely. But no matter how desperate the feel of his mouth on mine, his hand was still painting circles along my neck.

After a while, we came up for air and he gasped, "I could die from your kisses." He was really weird.

"Maybe you're better off dead then," I told him softly, and he kissed me again. I didn't mind it when our tongues got involved, usually it's pretty rank, but he didn't try to do a spin cycle in my mouth. He just stroked the tip of his tongue along mine and one of his hands crept up to tilt my head back . . .

"Isabel! God, there you are, I've been looking for you for ages."

I took my mouth away from Gentian Boy long enough to say, "Huh?" at Nancy, who was standing in front of me with her hands on her hips.

"We're going. This party's dead," Nancy grizzled, and then realized that I was wrapped around someone. "If you can tear yourself away, that is."

Gentian boy seemed in no hurry to let me go. His hand tightened around my hip as I tried to disentangle myself, while Nancy stood there, looking like she'd sucked down a whole bag of lemons.

"Let me up," I hissed, and he blinked a couple of times before relaxing the death grip.

"Who's your friend?" Nancy demanded, edging toward the door in case the boy made any sudden moves. Like, he'd look twice at her.

I realized that there wasn't an agony aunt alive who could give you advice on how to handle the correct etiquette when you've been sucking face with a boy you don't know who thinks you're someone else.

"Nobody," I muttered, running a hand over my hair to smooth it down.

"I'm Smith," he supplied, pulling at his faded green T-shirt. "Where do you know Chloë from?"

Nancy flailed her arms, making her bangles rattle furiously. "Who the hell is Chloë? She's Isabel, you idiot. Jesus, I can't believe you'd get off with my best friend and not even get her name right. Wanker!"

I stared at the floorboards, and hoped some handy portal

would open up and transport me to another dimension where I hadn't just strung along some drunken boy with beautiful eyes simply to get some touch. Sometime between the stairs and here, I'd obviously turned into a ginormous slut.

When I eventually summoned up the courage to look at him, Smith, which was just the most stupid-ass name ever and his parents must have really hated him, was looking bewildered. But when he saw me glance at him, this sudden grin lit him up from the inside.

"Oh, Isabel," he whispered so that I was the only one who could hear him. "You've got some explaining to do."

But I didn't. I just grabbed Nancy's hand and dragged her the hell out of there.

2

I'm not too clear on what happened after that. I had a really vague memory of being sick in a toilet that I didn't recognize, then wiping my mouth on one of those tragic crinoline ladies that sit on top of loo rolls so no one gets offended by the sight of naked Kleenex Velvet. Whatevs.

Right now I was curled up on the doormat with my keys still in my hand, which really made no sense at all. Though you've got to respect a finely tuned homing instinct—but I guess crawling up the stairs to my own bed, was just one step too far.

It was a superhuman effort to lift my wrist so I could squint at my watch (it was just past two-thirty), which nearly killed me, and I collapsed back on the floor with a tiny little sigh. I was tempted to stay there for what was left of the night because it felt like someone had sandpapered the inside of my head.

But I could imagine the sour scene that would unfold if Dad came down and found me curled up against the draft excluder, so I crawled up the stairs, thought about getting undressed, and decided to collapse face down on my bed instead. All that alcohol and puking had really taken it out of me—someone could have started drilling for oil underneath my pillow and I'd barely have stirred.

It's the summer that Felix was born so I'm seven and she's wearing her white summer dress with the roses on it, stretched tight over her swollen belly.

The sand shifts beneath our feet as she holds my hand and leads me down to the water's edge. I've got my red bucket with me, and every now and again, we stop so I can crouch down and pick up a shell or a stone, worn smooth and shiny by the relentless lapping of the waves, and drop it on the growing pile with a satisfying crash.

"What a clever little girl you are, Belle," she says approvingly, and I dig into the depth of the bucket and pull out the prettiest shell, an orange periwinkle, and place it in her palm. I never speak in these dreams, but she does all the talking for us. "Thank you, baby," she murmurs, and then she straightens up and looks out to sea, a hand over her eyes to shield them from the glare of the sun, her dark hair glinting in the brilliant light so it almost looks alive.

"You stay here, Belle," she tells me, dropping my hand and pressing down on my shoulders, so I plop down on the sand and watch as she begins to wander toward the water, her gaze on the ground, searching for something.

The tide's started to come in, and she doesn't seem to notice it covering her feet with its frilly white edges, and I want to call out. Want to warn her, but when I open my mouth, nothing happens and I can't move, either. All I can do is watch her wade into the depths so the skirt of her dress billows around her so there are roses floating on top of the water.

My bucket is filling up with tears and it's getting hard to see her through blurry, sticky eyes—just the top of her head bobbing on the water remains. I scrub at my eyes with my fists, and when I can see again, she's gone and I can scream now, even though there's no one to hear, no one to help, and I can't stop the noise, can't stop screaming until I'm hauled to my feet and he's shaking me hard.

"What did you do to her?" he shouts, and he's blocking out the sun so all I can see are the shadowed, angry lines of his face. "Stop making that bloody racket and tell me what you did!"

I crashed back into consciousness, sitting bolt upright and screaming again, even though my throat felt rubbed raw, as I saw him glaring down at me, Felix peering out from behind his back with an anxious expression. Big faker. Underneath that whey-faced, wimpy little body clad in Superman pajamas for extra cuteness is a violent thug. When it's not the middle of the night and his big sister is screeching like a banshee, he spends the daylight hours punching, pinching, and flaunting his bodily functions in my face.

"For God's sake, Isabel," Dad barked. "You're hysterical. Stop it this instant."

My mouth snapped shut so suddenly that I bit my tongue and couldn't help the whimper that escaped from my mouth, which just made his jaw tighten up.

"Is? Are you okay? You sounded like you were being attacked by killer zombies." Felix sidled out from behind Dad and pulled a disgusted face. "Urgh! You're all sweaty."

The black dress was clinging damply to me and I'd pulled the bottom sheet off the mattress.

If it was possible, Dad was looking at me with even more distaste. "I think this is an object lesson in the consequences of going to parties and no doubt drinking yourself into oblivion," he intoned darkly. "And please don't go to bed with your shoes on again, you'll rip the sheets."

"I had a bad dream," I muttered, and then shut up. He was giving me a careful, assessing look that was painfully familiar. Like, when I'm just about to give away the triple-word score on a game of Scrabble, or I've told one too many lies, dug myself a great big pit and all he has to do is apply some gentle pressure so I fall right in.

But he decided it wasn't worth the effort. "Oh, go and have a shower, Isabel, and then get back to bed. You've wasted quite enough time with your melodramatics as it is."

I couldn't sleep after that. I listened to the sounds of the night; a car speeding up the road, the angry yowling of a couple of cats, and the hum of the streetlight outside my window, but none of it was loud enough to drown out the buzzing in my ears, and in the end, I gave up on sleep, rolled over, and switched on the TV so I could watch old black-and-white films without the sound on, until the sun started creeping in through the curtains, leeching all the darkness out of the room, and I could sleep.

3

School was meant to be this big deal now that we were doing A-levels. Like, we were suddenly adults because we didn't have to wear the revolting bottle-green uniform and had permission to go into town when we didn't have lessons. That was the general idea, but as I sat on a hard-backed wooden chair in Mrs. Greenwood's office with Ella, Nancy, and Dot, she was doing her utmost to make us feel like naughty Year Eights.

"I absolutely do not want a repeat of what happened last term," Mrs. Greenwood said sternly, eyes scanning our faces for signs of contrition. I could feel Dot practically shaking beside me, but I faced down Greenwood's bifocal glare. "I will not tolerate bullying, and the prolonged campaign you waged against certain members of your form was inexcusable." She tapped her pen sharply on the desk. "We had to call in a guidance counselor! And all mobile phones now have to be left with your teachers before first bell."

Ella choked back a giggle at that, while Nancy wore a faint expression of confused pride that her Nokia antics had had such far-reaching consequences.

"As you know, the subject of suspension was mooted, but in

light of subsequent events, the governors felt that the matter should be left to die a natural death . . ."

There was a collective gasp, and Mrs. Greenwood dropped her pen. "I'm sorry . . . Isabel, that was a very tactless way of putting it . . ."

I gave her my most serene smile. "Don't worry about it, Mrs. Greenwood. It's fine. I didn't even notice . . . much."

She inclined her head in a gracious nod. "So, despite no action being taken last term, I'll be watching the four of you very closely. Unfortunately, we haven't been able to split you up because Isabel's father felt that she needed the support of her friends at such a difficult time."

There was another titter from Ella, which Mrs. Greenwood quelled with a pointed cough before blathering on for a few more minutes about how the younger pupils looked up to us blah, blah, blah, and we had to apologize to Lily Tompkins yadda, yadda, yadda, and finished with a rousing chorus of "Year Twelve privileges can easily be revoked, you know."

I couldn't wait to get out of there and scrub her monotone drone out of my head, but Mrs. Greenwood motioned for me to stay behind.

I turned around to see Dot close the door with a shrug and a "what can you do?" expression before swiveling around to find Mrs. Greenwood doing the head tilt. I was so sick of the head tilt because it was always a prelude to, yup, here it came. . . .

"So, Isabel, how are you holding up?" she asked, concern dripping like honey from every syllable. "Really."

"Okay," I said, studying the hangnail on my index finger.

"I've spoken to your father about this wonderful family therapist I know who does a group session with teenagers in a similar—"

"I'm not going!" I yelped immediately. Sit in a room and listen to a whole bunch of sad sacks whining about how depressed they were? I got enough of that at home.

"That's what your father said. Though he was a little less strident." She smiled thinly. I could imagine exactly how that conversation had gone. "But if you change your mind . . ."

"All I really need to do is arrange a time to re-sit my Maths GCSE."

That totally took the wind out of her. I think she thought we'd have a cozy little chat and I'd break down and confide in her about how sucky life without a mother was shaping up but, hello, never going to happen.

Instead, she looked down at my school folder. "Well, you have an excellent academic record, and we have high hopes of a place at Oxford for you, but if you feel that things are getting too intense, you should let me or your form teacher know."

"They won't," I stated firmly. I had a perfect A-grade for well, everything, and it was going to stay that way. "I just want everything to be normal, like it was before."

"Isabel, I'm afraid that nothing is going to be like it was before," she said softly, fingers tapping out a quiet tattoo on the desktop. "You've lost your mother."

People kept saying that all the way through summer. All the well-meaning relatives and neighbors trooping through the house with food that tasted of the Tupperware containers it had been stored in. And that was how they phrased it, "lost your mother," like I'd left her on the bus and she was propped up in a corner of some Lost Property Office waiting for me to claim her.

Mrs. Greenwood was still waiting for me to prostrate myself on her office carpet, so I shuffled around on my chair. "I'm going to be late for French," I reminded her, and she gave this gusty sigh that fanned through the papers in my case folder.

"Fine," she said, straightening up from the head tilt and losing the "I'm your friend, not just your headmistress" expression pretty damn quick. "Fine. And though it might not have been your phone that that *disgusting* picture was sent from, I'm under no illusion as to who was behind it. You're on your last promise, young lady."

I could feel her eyes boring into me as I walked out of the room and shut the door with just enough force to let her know that she hadn't totally whipped me.

I walked into class as the register was being called. There was a moment of perfect silence as all heads swiveled to see my entrance. And for once, it wasn't to see what the most popular and feared girl in the school was wearing or what color I'd dyed my hair. They thought I'd changed over the summer because life had crapped all over me and that they'd be able to see it on my face. Like the tracks of all the tears that I didn't cry would have worn grooves into my cheeks.

The minute you show any sign of weakness, they start circling around you like sharks who've just smelled blood in the water. So I pasted on my trademark supercilious smile and sauntered over to the empty seat next to Ella. There was an audible sigh of disappointment.

The fierce whispers trailed behind me for the rest of the week. I was kind of used to that. Not because I was the prettiest girl in school or the funniest or even the cleverest. Those A-grades were the result of serious slog and staying up past midnight with ink-stained fingers and a mound of boring textbooks.

No, my place at the top of the school pecking order, heading up the inner clique of all inner cliques, is a result of being the biggest bitch to ever stalk down the hallowed halls of Brighton School For Girls.

The way I see it, school is like one of those documentaries about big cats on the Discovery Channel. It's maul or be mauled. It's not fair. It's not right. It just is what it is. I spent two years of middle school having my lunch money stolen and my clothes, hair, and teeny, tiny, almost unnoticeable lisp mocked by a bunch of girls who were bigger and uglier than me. So when I got to senior school, it was beyond time to reinvent myself.

I'm the queen of the rumor. Of the veiled insult. Of the nudge and a wink and a smirk. And that's how I rule the school. I have my three little minions. I decide who's on the shit list for that week, and they make that poor girl's life a misery, and the rest of the school follows suit. Maybe they're not big cats, but stupid, mindless sheep.

It's not like I enjoy it. It's just what I do to get myself through school. I can't wait to leave, to head off to University and be someone else. Because my whole queen of mean shtick is exhausting. I can't let my guard slip or show my true face for even a second. And I've paid such a high price for my status that I wonder whether it's really worth it.

But then I remember how it feels to sit at the loser table in the canteen. Or what it's like to have to skulk in the cloakrooms until everyone's gone home in the faint hope that this won't be the afternoon that I get chased through the streets. How it feels to have someone shove your head down a toilet and then pull the chain—not that I'd ever go to those kinds of extremes—and so I do what I have to.

And what we did to Lily Tompkins—she *so* had it coming. She'd been shooting her mouth off about Nancy getting knocked back by one of the boys from the local grammar school. I don't even know all the details. Just that if I hadn't nipped it in the bud, she'd have weakened my power base. So when Dot saw her disappear into the bathroom at a party with Nancy's brother's friend, who always wears a baseball cap back to front, like he's so bloody ghetto . . . well, she brought it on herself.

I'd sidled up to Nancy, who was staring at the heir to her heart while he macked on some giggly blonde. "I'd love to know what Lily's doing in the loo with Pimp My Ride," I'd muttered. "Maybe she's showing him where her navel piercing went septic. I can't think of another reason why he was peering down her top."

I didn't tell Nancy to go charging in there, though taking a picture on her camera phone had shown initiative I didn't know she had. "God, I wish Dot was here, she'd love to see that. It's so very Paris Hilton," I'd said when she showed me the surprisingly clear picture of Lily on her knees.

In a lot of ways, I was entirely blameless. It wasn't my idea to send the picture to everyone in Nancy's address book, who all promptly sent it on to everyone in *their* address books. Lily had the photo sent to her before she'd even come out of the bathroom, surreptitiously wiping her mouth with some toilet tissue. But even if she hadn't seen it, the fact that everyone was making "gobble gobble" noises might have clued her in.

She'd stormed out in tears and took, like, five junior Disprin and went to hospital and had her stomach pumped because she's such a drama queen. My last week at school was all letters home and disciplinary warnings and then the meeting that never happened. So if Lily was on my shit list before, now she was right there at the top with her name in six-foot-high letters.

I'd been keeping my head down for the week—I was still coasting the wave of my newfound notoriety as "The Girl Who Lost Her Mother™"—which meant people stayed away from me if they knew what was good for them, so I was a little surprised when Lily herself came tripping over to our table Friday at lunchtime.

I lifted my head from my plate of wilted chicken salad, gave her a bit of my patented evil eye, and went back to talking to Dot.

"It's blue with this tiny geometric print," I explained, trying to describe the skirt I was planning to buy on the weekend. "It's Marc Jacobs via New Look."

"Sounds cool," Dot said, slanting her eyes over at Lily who was shifting from foot to foot.

"It is, but I don't know if I've got anything that goes . . ."

"Isabel, can I talk to you a minute?"

I could hear Lily perfectly, but I carried on extolling the virtues of the skirt to Dot, like it was the finest example of haute couture.

"Look, Isabel, I think we should try to clear the air or something."

Dot smiled thinly. "Hey, Is, did you just hear this weird squeaking noise?"

I've spent years perfecting the nonchalant shrug that I gave. "Maybe it was just your imagination."

Lily must have had a total death wish because she pulled out the empty chair next to me and sat down. Worse than that, she touched my arm. I stared at her stubby fingers curled around my sleeve and very gently shook my wrist.

"What happened last term . . . We both did stuff . . . Y'know, and I thought . . ." She was giving me nothing but word salad, before she exhaled angrily. "Isabel, I'm trying to apologize!"

"Are you going to manage a complete sentence before the bell goes?" I rested my chin on my hand and watched her bottom lip tremble. "What exactly do you want to apologize for?"

I could see her mentally count to ten, though she got stuck around five. "I thought we could forget what happened and I wanted to tell you this all week, but well . . . I'm sorry about your mum."

"What about her?" I asked flatly. "What are you sorry about?"

She laughed nervously and looked at Dot for some clarification but Dot was staring at her bag of crisps like they were about to break into song.

"I'm sorry about your mum," Lily repeated. "About what happened."

"You should be," I said gently. "'Cause, if you think about it, it was your fault really."

It was really fascinating to watch the color drain out of her face as if someone had adjusted her contrast button. "That's a terrible thing to say," she gasped, her pink lip gloss even more garish against her blanched skin. "I thought you'd be different."

I knew she did. Everyone did. They wanted me soft and weak so they could stop being scared of me. They were going to have a long wait.

"Well, I'm not," I said, feeling my top lip curl with disdain and that bitch-goddess tone edge into my voice. "Business as usual. Now why are you still sitting there?"

Lily scrubbed her hand over her eyes, which were leaking tears, as usual. "Your mum died!" she screeched, ensuring that everyone in the canteen was now giving us their undivided attention. "And if you weren't such an evil cow, then you'd be upset about it."

I put my hand to my heart and made an "ouch" face, like I was bothered. "Listen, sweetie, so I'm one parent less—that doesn't change the fact that you gave that baseball cap-wearing twat a blowjob and everyone knows you're a skeevy ho. *Sucks* to be you, huh?"

She was rooted to the spot, opening that famous mouth of hers as wide as it would go. Didn't look like she was going to be moving anytime soon, which just made it easier to nudge my half full can of Diet Coke with my elbow as I got up so she was drenched in a sticky deluge of brown droplets that soaked into her white top.

"You should really wear more black," I advised her, gathering up my jacket and bag. "Doesn't show the stains quite so much, does it?"

"You bitch," she breathed as if she couldn't quite believe she'd just had a Diet Coke shower.

Dot bumped her shoulder as she brushed past. "I should totally go and see Mrs. Greenwood and tell her what you said about Is's mum," she hissed.

As I slowly made my way through the canteen, it occurred to me that I had something to thank Lily for because now the other girls weren't sorry for me. They were looking at me as if they were scared that it would be their turn next. And that, I knew how to handle.

4

One minute it was all still and silent, the next the curtains were being yanked back with a deafening swish so that the room was flooded with retina-burning light.

My hands groped for the pillow so I could pull it over my head, but Felix was already bouncing on the bed. "Get up, Is! It's nine, I've been awake for ages."

I felt fragile and *English Patient*-y. Dot had come over after school yesterday and totally outstayed her welcome. First she'd freaked out because all we had in the fridge was a jar of artichoke hearts and some moldy cheese so she wouldn't be able to keep her Diet Coke levels topped up. Then she'd wanted to TALK, or rather she'd wanted me to talk about my feelings and shit so she could coo sympathetically. In the end, I'd had to push her out of the front door and shut it before she'd had time to register what was going on, her aggrieved little face peering at me through the frosted-glass panel.

And it had taken me hours to persuade my body that it wanted to snuggle down and get some sleep. I'd even hauled the Henry James out of my bedside drawer to see if his turgid sentence structure would make me drop off. Eventually, I'd flicked on the TV and watched late-night poker until the cards had gone blurry.

I opened one eye in time to see Dad snap off the TV, which was emitting static, and then turned over so I could get a few more minutes snoozing in.

Alas, it was not to be, as I felt hands snatching the covers off me as I made like a ball and whimpered, "On fire? Are we on fire?" I was sure I could smell burning, but that might just have been the dream I was having before I was so rudely awakened. This time she'd walked into our old house in Alfriston, and as she disappeared through the front door, the whole building burst into fierce flames.

"No, Isabel, no one's on fire," he bit out, and what do you know? He'd actually managed to shave, though he had a wicked-looking nick under his chin. "Is it too much to expect you to get up at a reasonable hour?"

I didn't say anything. I certainly wasn't going to raise the issue that medical research proved that teenagers needed to have long lie-ins.

"I'm going to have a shower," I mumbled, swinging my legs over the side of the bed and waiting for the dizzy feeling to stop. Then I swiped at Felix, who'd picked up my pillow and was trying to whack me over the head with it. We really needed to start cutting down on his sugar intake.

"I had the most appalling woman—your friend Dot's mother—on the phone," Dad said querulously, as I rubbed a big piece of sleep out of the corner of my eye. "She was remarkably shrewish for a Saturday morning and informed me that I had no food in the house and that you and Felix were on the verge of malnutrition." He sniffed contemptuously, as if the lack of five pieces of fruit and veg every day was beyond his control. "But then I tried to do some washing, and we have none of those strange little ball things."

I felt like . . . well, like I'd managed two hours sleep punctuated by really horrible nightmares and he just. Would. Not. Shut. Up.

"I've been using washing powder, in the drawer . . ." I mumbled vaguely. "I'm going back to bed. I feel like crap."

"Isabel." He has this special way of saying my name like he can't even bear the sound of it. "You're to have a shower, get dressed, and then we're going to the supermarket."

"Come on, Is, it'll be fun," Felix cried, and gave me an expectant look that roughly translated as "Please, for the love of God, don't leave me alone with him."

"Fine, whatever . . ."

And obviously his mission in life for today was to work my last nerve, because Dad gave me his most condescending smile (I think it might have been a personal best) and said, "A little less petulance, please."

As trips to the supermarket go, and they don't really rate too highly on my list of fun things, it started off all right. Since . . . well, he never drives unless he really has to, he decided that we'd walk to Waitrose, even though Felix and I did try to point out that lugging heavy shopping up the hill was unpaid child labor.

"Nonsense, it will be good for you," he scoffed, setting off down the road at a brisk pace. I clamped my iPod earbuds in so I didn't have to listen to Felix crapping on about all the stuff he craps on about.

There was a tense moment when Dad became slightly baffled by the whole concept of shoving a pound coin into the slot before you could take a trolley, but he adapted pretty well, and soon we were freewheeling around the fresh produce aisle like we were born to it.

I wasn't exactly sure who was going to be cooking all the squash and leeks and broccoli that he was blithely selecting while Felix pulled agonized faces at me behind his back. But really, I didn't want to do anything to break the fragile peace treaty, so I concentrated on fruit because you just eat it as it comes and it stops you from coming down with a severe case of rickets.

It wasn't until we hit aisle 18—crisps, nuts, and snacks—that our family bonding excursion turned ugly. I innocently snatched a variety pack of Walkers from the shelf, but you'd have thought I was trying to do a trolley dash through the cigarette kiosk.

"Oh no," he hissed, tugging them out of my hands. "I'm not having junk food in the house."

Felix already had his arms full of Wotsits. "But we can't live just on vegetables," he exclaimed, his voice rising with indignation. "Mum always let us . . ."

It was kinda weird to hear him say the "M" word, like someone swearing in church. None of us had said it out loud in weeks.

"I beg your pardon?" Dad demanded, permafrost coating every syllable.

"I didn't do anything wrong." Felix's bottom lip was trembling like a kite on a windy day. "Why aren't I allowed to . . . ?"

"Just leave it." I gave him a warning punch on the shoulder.

"Obviously potato snacks are right up there with crack cocaine and, oh, I don't know, drinking yourself into oblivion every night."

Dad grabbed hold of the trolley, his knuckles white as he gripped the bar. "Is there something you'd like to say, Isabel, or are you happy to continue with your barbed remarks?"

And the thing is, I never know when to keep my mouth shut. I don't. I can't. I never could. So I shrugged, and I knew the smile I was wearing was so smug that if I'd seen it on my face, I'd have wanted to smack it right off.

"Nope, just y'know, if a couple of bags of salt and vinegar are going to bring down Western civilization, then I guess we won't be loading up on bottles of red wine, either."

Apparently, discussions about the huge amount of booze he guzzles were forbidden, too. His eyes narrowed so much, it was a wonder he could still steer the trolley round the corner. "You really are incredibly obnoxious," he hissed, glancing over his shoulder at Felix, who was trailing miserably behind us. "Oh, go and get your sodding crisps, then."

I watched Felix drag his heels away. "I get that you pretty much hate my guts, but don't take it out on him," I said.

That got me another flinty glare, as he practically hurled a bottle of fabric softener into the trolley. "I do not 'hate your guts,' Isabel. I just find you rude, willful, and thoroughly unpleasant."

Felix was padding toward us, clutching a multitude of variety bags, chin set like he was expecting another argument, not realizing that the first one hadn't finished.

"I can see I've been entirely too lenient with you, Isabel,"

Dad continued. "But these tantrums have gone on long enough and ..."

I turned to him and gave him the calmest smile I could muster, which threw him. "Oh, piss off," I said, and flounced away.

It was really liberating, the acting out or whatever you want to call it. Like, I'd drawn a line between us, one that had been there, anyway, but we didn't have to tread around it anymore.

My foot was poised to step off the curb so I could cross over Western Road and head down to the beach, when his hand came crashing down on my shoulder. God, I bet he wished that they'd never made spanking illegal.

"How dare you talk to me like that?" he spluttered. "Apologize at once."

"Get your hand off my shoulder," I told him pretty reasonably, considering it felt as if he was trying to mold my collarbone into a new and exciting shape.

He let go of me and we stood there, staring at each other. I wondered if he could even really *see* me as anything other than the shopping list of adjectives that summed up what a major disappointment I was.

"I'm still waiting for that apology, Isabel."

A guy pushed past us—and something in the way he held himself, the way his hair looked like it had had an accident with a vat of perming lotion, seemed familiar, even though I couldn't see his face. It was that boy, Smith, or whatever his name was, from the party.

"I don't have time for this," I told Dad, and walked away. I knew he wouldn't come after me again—that would actually have required some effort on his part.

Smith walked fast with a loping gait, almost bouncing on the soles of his sneakers, and I liked that he was so free, so unaware, not knowing that I was looking at him. Like, when you're on the bus and you stare into someone's front room and you see them watching television or slumped on the sofa, and it's like you're taking a tiny piece of them home with you.

He ambled into a couple of charity shops and rifled through piles of battered vinyl records and tattered paperbacks. I loitered by the racks of musty-smelling polyester dresses—I was going for this whole melting into the walls vibe, but I just looked really shifty, if the suspicious attention I was getting from the blue-rinse brigade manning the tills was anything to go by.

I hadn't been able to get a good look at him before. It had been dark, and there had been huge quantities of alcohol involved, but daylight softened out the slant of his cheekbones and the hard lines of his jaw, so he looked less thuggish. Didn't do anything to lessen the effect of his nose. If you were being kind you'd call it aquiline; if you weren't, you'd call it beaky. And I could see those lips that I'd kissed—how they looked as pillowy as they'd felt. His hair was still ridiculous, he'd obviously never got intimate with a pair of straightening irons. But what I liked about him (and I *did* appear to like him, even though he had a stupid name and needed to stop kissing girls at parties because he thought they were other girls he'd kissed at other parties) was his serenity. There was something utterly calm about him, no matter how fast his elegant hands leafed through records or pored over books. It was as if everything was out of focus except him.

He brushed past me on his way toward the door, and I pressed myself against a rail of coats. I waited for the door to shut behind him, then cautiously slunk out in time to see him disappearing into the newsagent's next door.

Luckily, I could pretend to read the ads for exotic Swedish massages while I peered through the window and watched Smith buy a packet of cigarettes and some chewing gum. As he was walking down the length of the shop, I realized my cover was about to be blown, so I dived into the nearest doorway, which happened to be a hardware shop and looked with feigned interest at the display of screwdrivers and oooh, power saws. Imagine the damage I could do with one of them.

At first I thought it was the wind brushing against me, but then it happened again, someone was tapping me on the shoulder. Even before I turned around I knew it was him.

I'd forgotten how blue his eyes were. I wanted to compose sonnets in my head about ocean depths and cloudless skies because I was obviously suffering from severe sleep deprivation. He was frowning at me, this little furrowed line popping up between his eyebrows.

I felt like I'd finally been caught shoplifting. My cheeks were burning traffic-light red as he fixed me with an intractable look. "Are you following me?"

There wasn't really much I could say in my defense, and besides, talking suddenly became this really difficult art that I hadn't quite mastered. I just shrugged and shuffled my feet instead, focusing my attention on my scuffed-up ballet flats.

"Well . . . ?" Smith prompted.

I wound a strand of hair around my finger for a bit until he tapped his foot impatiently. "Go and find someone else to annoy."

I finally looked up and he was all I could see. I could already feel my mouth getting ready to form the words, though my brain was trying to slam the brakes on. "I don't want to," I said, and my feet weren't moving away, so it must have been true.

The faint ghostly blur of a smile danced across his mouth. "Can you only speak in monosyllables?"

"Yeah." If I couldn't be quiet then monosyllables seemed like the way to go. And less is more. Maybe he thought I was mysterious and enigmatic—and I might have been until my stupid stomach let out an ungodly roar to remind me that it hadn't had anything to eat since the moldy cheese omelet I'd made last night.

That hateful, stupid blush flared up all over again as if my whole body had been immersed in Deep Heat. But Smith just laughed.

"Seems like your tummy has plenty to say even if you don't," he said, and smiled at me properly. It was the kind of smile that could knock a girl into the middle of next week, if I was that kind of girl, which I *so* wasn't.

"My tummy never knows when to shut up," I replied as my belly let out another gurgle just to remind me that it was righteously pissed.

There was a moment's pause. "Well maybe your tummy would like me to buy it lunch," Smith offered casually. "You could come, too, if you like."

It was strange walking along the street with him. Like, if people saw us they'd automatically assume that we were together. In reality, I was actually racking my brains for some amusing conversational gambit and coming up empty. Smith didn't seem to mind and when we crossed the road, he gently held my elbow as if he thought I might suddenly plunge headfirst into the oncoming traffic.

I've been mauled by boys for the last two years. It leaves me cold and worrying that I'm a freak because a sweaty hand on my tits and a tongue tickling my esophagus does nothing for me. But Smith's hand on my elbow made me tingle all over.

When we got to the other side of the road, I tugged myself away from his touch, as if it was radioactive. He didn't say anything, but then he kept this six-inch distance away from me at all times, as if he was worried I was going to go off on this sexual harassment rant. I knew, I just *knew*, that he wished that he'd never invited me along for lunch. I could see the fricking words hovering above his head.

But it was all right when we got to the café. The smell of bacon and freshly ground coffee made my growly stomach kick up a notch, as we snagged a table in the corner. There was the whole menu thing to deal with, but after the waitress had taken our orders, it was just the two of us and the condiment tray.

"So what's your name again?" Smith asked, tearing the cellophane off of his cigarettes.

"Isabel," I answered unwillingly. "It's a stupid name. But everyone hates their own name, I suppose."

Smith was rummaging in his jacket pocket and eventually pulled out a box of matches. "Why do you think I use the name Smith?" he commented cryptically. "Anyway, Isabel seems pretty not stupid to me."

That was easy enough for him to say. I decided to turn the tables. "So, Smith isn't your real name?"

He shook his head and grinned. And really he should do that more, because it creased his face into a pleasing pattern of white teeth and smile lines. "Nope, surname, and before you ask, I'm not gonna tell you what my first name is."

I was intrigued. "Why? Is it a state secret?" I asked as the waitress brought our coffees.

Smith nodded solemnly, but his eyes were dancing with mischief. "I could tell you ..."

"Yeah, yeah, but you'd have to kill me," I finished neatly for him, and took a cautious sip of my coffee.

"Are you making sure that the five sugar cubes were enough?"

He really thought I was a freak. "Well, it's just I need a sugar rush to get me kick-started."

Smith grinned again and looked pointedly at his watch. "It's lunchtime."

"Exactly."

There was another pause, and I sipped at my coffee and tried not to notice how he was looking at me. I knew there wasn't enough concealer in the world to get rid of the dark circles under my eyes, and there hadn't been time to do anything with my hair but try to scrape it back into a tufty, scraggly ponytail. I was wearing Felix's Sea Scouts T-shirt and school cardie with my jeans because they were the only clean things I could find. If I'd been some fashion bitch, I'd have called it androgynous chic, but it's hard to pull that off when you're a gawky sixteen-year-old.

"You never told me why you were called Isabel," he said gently, leaning forward. "I got the feeling there might be a story there."

"Isabel Archer. She's this character in a Henry James novel," I added, even though he probably didn't have a clue who Henry

James was. There still didn't seem to be much evidence that he was packing a big old brain in that not-so-pretty head of his.

"*Portrait of a Lady?*"

"Well, yeah," I spluttered, taking one of his cigarettes and lighting it. "Have you read it or have you just seen the film?" I didn't wait for him to reply. "My Dad's a professor of American literature and he was having this big Henry James thing when I was born, and it's the most depressing book ever and Isabel just gets, like, totally suppressed by this guy she has to marry, and why would you call your daughter after some character in a book who's miserable and hates her life?" I finished off with this angry exhalation of breath that gusted the napkins across the table, then I closed my eyes.

Why couldn't I just sit across the table from a moderately cute boy and be normal? Like, ask him questions about himself and giggle when he cracked a joke and generally be charming and witty and like ninety-nine percent of the rest of the girl population. Instead I was, well, being way too much like *me*.

"I'm sorry," I muttered so quietly that I didn't think he heard me, but he gave me a contemplative look and then leaned closer.

"Can I trust you to keep a secret?"

"What kind of secret?" I asked him suspiciously.

"The secret kind of secret. You do know what a secret is, don't you?"

"Yes," I snapped, and his eyebrows shot up. "Please . . . will you tell me? See, I asked nicely."

He let the suspense mount for about ten seconds, staring at me just enough so that I was beginning to get wigged out all over again before he relented.

"I'm named after someone in a book, too," he announced in a hushed voice, looking furtively over his shoulder, which was a touch too overkill-y.

"Yeah? Who?"

"You ever read *To Kill a Mockingbird?*"

I stared at him in disbelief. "No way! Oh, my God, did your parents name you Boo? That sucks."

He gave a throaty little chuckle. "You've just ruined my punch line."

"Whatever." I rolled my eyes. "So what's your name, then? Let me think. Jem? Scout? It can't be Calpurnia . . ."

He remained admirably stoney-faced while I threw names at him.

"Atticus? You kinda look like an Atticus, now that I come to think of it," I mused, and his nose twitched almost imperceptibly, which must be an occupational hazard when it's that big. "Atticus! I don't fucking believe it!"

"Keep your voice down," he hissed, reaching over to tap my arm. "It's not something I want to see on the front page of *The Argus.*"

I crushed the end of my cigarette in the ashtray. Really mashed it down hard because I hate it when they keep on smoldering. "That's a big name to live up to."

"My parents were all into anti-apartheid and banning the bomb, and I think they had this deluded idea that I'd go into politics and make the world a better place." He smiled faintly.

I clapped my hands in glee. "Like, hey, come on, help us fight racism, little baby Atticus." I giggled. "Did you have an Anti-Fascist Action logo on your onesie?"

Anytime soon, I was actually going to shut up, but Smith

didn't seem to mind. Or else he was hoping that day release would soon be over and I'd go back to the psych ward.

"You're really pretty when you smile," he said, tilting his head. "You should do it more often."

He didn't say it like it was some line to get me to drop my knickers, but I still had to clamp my mouth shut not to snap a reflexive denial. Instead, I looked around for the waitress because really, how long does it take to shove some cheese on a jacket potato and nuke it?

And just once, something in the universe went my way, because two steaming plates appeared at the serving hatch so I could turn to Smith, who was drumming his fingers noiselessly against the tabletop, and mutter, "I think our food's coming."

It took every last scrap of willpower I had not to lower my head and shovel the food into my mouth. I managed to cut myself delicate, girl-like bites and not make any embarrassing moaning noises as my taste buds suddenly kicked into life.

Every time I looked up, our eyes met, and he'd open his mouth like he was trying to think of something to say and I'd shoot him a vague smile and carry on eating.

Eventually, short of licking a few crumbs of potato and a bit of stringy cold cheese off my plate, I was done. He'd been super nice to me and bought me lunch, so I started to think of how I could extricate myself politely.

"So what kind of music do you like?" he asked abruptly.

"Different things. The Shins; Babyshambles, though Pete Doherty is so tragic; everything ever recorded by Belle & Sebastian. Maybe a little Destiny's Child for some light relief." I dug my iPod out of my pocket so I could show him my eclectic song stylings.

"Cool . . . cool . . . I can't believe you like him," he sneered as he saw my Bright Eyes playlist. "Camera Obscura? I'm impressed. Wanna swap?"

"Wanna swap what?" I asked, but he was already pulling out his iPod.

"I'll let you have mine for a week," he explained, scrolling down my playlists and wincing. Probably because he'd just seen the McFly album. "You take mine. I do this all the time with my mates."

"You sure this isn't some elaborate plan to stick me with your broken iPod?" I asked warily, and he gave me another of those elastic grins.

"God, you have serious trust issues. Look, I'll even keep my own headphones because they're a little on the gross side," he said, whisking them away before I could see any ear gunk.

"Well, how do I know I'm going to even like what you've got on yours?"

"How do you know you won't?" he replied with a mild smile.

I pouted, but I let him place his iPod in my hand, even though this whole scheme seemed a little dubious. "But what if I break it? Or, like, drop it if I have to run for the bus and what if—"

"Stop having so many what ifs and give me your phone number so we can arrange to meet next week and swap them back," he continued imperturbably.

"I'll have to give you my home number. I don't have any money to top up my phone." I frowned. "I so need to get a job."

"I thought you were a student," he remarked, still spinning my click wheel. "How old are you?"

I didn't even break a sweat. "Eighteen, and you?"

"Oh? Just turned twenty. So what's your number, and is it Isabel with an 'a' or an 'o'?"

He put my number into his phone, and I shifted his iPod from one hand to the other. It seemed imbued with unfathomable significance. All those songs—the ones he listened to when he was sad and the ones he listened to that reminded him of girls—that he played again and again; they were the soundtrack to his heart. And then there were the songs he played that were fast and frantic, and he'd crank up the volume and bounce down the street. Songs let you see into someone's soul.

I was just telling him that he wasn't to call me during the day under, like, pain of death—mine if my dad answered the phone and someone with a penis inquired after me—and he was giving me another one of those slightly bewildered looks when there was a bang on the window, which made me jump out of my skin.

Smith looked up and waved, and then this mass of people descended on us in this great swarm of hand slappings and greetings.

"Smithy! What the hell happened to you last night?"

"We were just talking about you."

"Have you got that tenner you owe me?"

There were all shapes and sizes of boys and girls, rocking the emo look and generally acting like they were way too cool for school. And in the middle of it was Smith, leaning back in his chair and just generally being loved. He was *popular*? WTF?

I don't think he even noticed as I quietly gathered my stuff up, including his cigarettes, and got to my feet, slipping around the back of the crowd of his adoring subjects.

But as I reached the door, I heard this tiny girl with the most perfectly straight bob I've ever seen, say in a piping voice, "Who was that?"

I paused, hand on the doorknob, in time to hear Smith say vaguely, "Oh, just some girl."

5

I spent the next week being really pissed off about being dismissed as "just some girl."

He could have said that I was "this girl I met at a party a couple of days ago" or "this girl who I trusted enough to confess the godawfulness of my real name" or "this girl who's intense and quixotic and I made her swap iPods so I'd have a reason for getting in touch with her." But no, I was "just some girl." Like, I'd just happened to be a girl who'd been sitting across from him in a random and inexplicable way.

I was tempted to flush his stupid iPod with his stupid whiny complaint rock songs on it down the loo. But then again, I did want to listen to Postal Service and Modest Mouse, and being taken to the small claims court for willful destruction of someone else's property would be distinctly unfun. Even, if that someone totally deserved it.

The two bright spots on my storm cloudy horizon were that when I got back from the café, the supermarket shop had been a surprising success and the kitchen was awash with food products. Including a veritable hoard of junk food. According to my infallible intel, once Dad had got back from disowning me he'd let Felix put anything he wanted in the trolley. Talk about inconsistent parenting.

And the other bright spot was that Dad wasn't talking to me. Which suited me just fine. It was all, "Felix will you tell your sister that her ratty tennis shoes are not an ornamental feature and she's to remove them from the hall at once?" and "Felix, please let your sister know that she's not to use my bottle of 2000 Pavie Decesse St. Emilion in her spaghetti Bolognese."

I could have joined in. But there wasn't anything I wanted to say to him. And it meant that it gave me a Get Out of Jail Free card to sneak the odd twenty out of his wallet because what was he going to do? "Felix will you ask your sister if she's been stealing money from me?" I think not.

We'd managed to go a whole week without even exchanging pleasantries about the weather, and by Friday evening I was congratulating myself on a job well done, as I finished up this kick-ass chili, which had everything in it except raspberries, which were for dessert. And then the phone rang.

Felix was already halfway there when I yanked him back by his belt and, from the unearthly yowling noise he made, I think I managed to give him the mother of all wedgies.

"Get off me!"

"Step away from the phone, then," I said warningly, not like I was expecting a call from anyone special. Just someone who'd probably given my iPod to one of his loser friends.

I picked up the phone with one hand and shoved Felix as far away as I could with the other.

"Hello?" It was probably one of Dad's students quaking in their boots about some late deadline request that he was going to get all pissy about—they were the only people who ever rang. Certainly wasn't going to be . . .

"Isabel? It's Smith. We need to meet, don't we?"

"Oh, hey, yeah." God, just kill me now.

He snickered softly. "You're doing that monosyllabic thing again."

I glared at Felix, who was leaning against the fridge and mouthing "Who is it?" at me, like the phone ringing was some big event.

"Hang on," I muttered, and then put my hand over the mouthpiece. "It's for me. Go away now!"

"But, Is . . ."

"Just fuck off."

Felix gave me the finger as he sidled out of the room, and I put the phone back to my ear. "You still there?"

"Yeah." He sounded like he was waiting for me to get to the point.

"How's my iPod? Is it still in one piece?"

There was this tense silence. I could actually feel my blood pressure start to rise.

"Yeah, about that. Does it generally do that weird thing when you try and pause it so—"

"What weird thing?" I didn't know my voice could get so shrill—all the dogs in the neighborhood must have been going into a complete frenzy. "I knew this was a bad idea."

"Isabel. Isabel. I'm joking," he said very gently. "It was a joke."

"I knew that," I huffed. Like, what? He thought I didn't have a sense of humor. "I was laughing on the inside. Kind of."

"So, anyway, do you want to meet up tonight?"

I tried out this sigh, which was meant to convey the message that I was a busy girl with a packed social schedule who couldn't commit to times and places just like that. "Well, I'm meant to be going to The Cellar with my friends," I said vaguely. "And I have this whole dinner thing first."

He didn't reply at first, and I could hear a muffled sound in the background, like he was talking to someone, before his voice came back, just a little distracted. "Cool. That's where my friends are gonna be, too. Does eight sound okay?"

It wasn't okay. I didn't want him anywhere near the Trio of Evil, but I suddenly became aware of this determined sizzling noise. "I have to go," I yelped, all my attention now firmly focused on the stove. "See you at eight."

I didn't wait to hear his response, just clicked the phone off and rushed to the saucepan.

The rice was simmering away gently, and I was mentally discarding one outfit after another as I shoved green leafy stuff into a salad bowl, when Dad and Felix appeared, even though one of them hadn't officially been invited to dinner.

Dad gave the bowl of chili a wary look as I put it down on the table. But he didn't say anything, and I got another plate out of the cupboard and placed it in front of him.

We had to listen to this really long-winded account of the diorama of a veldt that Felix was making for geography, and Dad was smiling and nodding and offering his services and his atlases, and Jesus, you'd think he was down to the final five for Father of the Year or something.

Then he looked up at me and said quietly, "Felix, will you tell your sister to stop playing with her food and actually eat it," and we were right back on track.

Felix thought about it for a nanosecond. "Isabel, stop playing with your food and actually eat it," he parroted back gleefully, and when Dad wasn't looking, I managed to whap the back of his hand with the serving spoon. He had no sibling loyalty, the little sod.

The minute that Felix finally stopped shoveling food into his mouth, I leaped up.

"You can clear the table, that's fair, right?" I told him. "There's raspberries in the fridge for dessert."

They were still in the kitchen when I came downstairs twenty minutes later. After much deliberation, I was wearing a little pink summer dress with a sweetheart neckline and a scalloped hem that was far too winsome without adding jeans and a stompy pair of boots for extra edge. The ensemble didn't exactly scream über sophistication, but I'd pinned this DIY construction-paper corsage I'd made in art class to my shoulder and concentrated on my makeup.

There's this trick to looking older, and it's not about piling it on so you end up resembling a teen whore. 'Cause older girls have got over the novelty of wearing makeup and they have, like, these little signature things they do. After I'd put on enough concealer so that I didn't appear to have bruises anymore, I stroked a sliver of shimmery green powder just above and below my eyes in this casual, "oh, I really don't bother with too many products" way. Then I slicked on some Stila Cleopatra lipstick from my last little crime spree in Boots and gave up doing anything with my hair. Really. I just shoved Felix's beanie on my head. It was a look. I think.

I almost got to the front door undetected, even had my jacket on, but I had to stop and retrace my steps to the kitchen, where the iPod was perched on the table. Felix and Dad were diorama-ing and I could just tiptoe in and snatch . . .

"Where do you think you're going?"

I shoved the iPod into my pocket. "Oh, so you're actually talking to me now, are you?"

Felix rolled his eyes and made a zipping gesture across his mouth, but he could just piss off.

Dad gave me a smile that was entirely devoid of humor. "Actually, Isabel, I asked a question that I'd like you to answer."

"Out, I'm going out," I called over my shoulder, beetling toward the front door before we could get into the details. "And the others are sleeping over, so don't barge into my room without knocking in the morning."

"Come back here immediately." His voice got louder with every word, so I knew he was on his feet and about to get all judge, jury, and executioner on my arse.

I whirled around. "No! Don't even think about it," I hissed as he took two more steps nearer to me. "I'm going out, and there's not a single thing you can do about it. You lay one finger on me and I'll totally—"

He stopped my invective mid-flow by suddenly leaning his forehead against the banisters, hands clutching at the wood like it was a life raft. He looked, I don't know, defeated, which I guess meant I'd won.

But as I slammed the door so hard behind me that the glass in the panel rattled, the funny thing was that I didn't feel like a winner.

6

I had to run all the way to The Cellar so I'd only be a little bit late, as opposed to spectacularly late. It started to rain as I sprinted down Trafalgar Street, skidding on the slicked pavement and only slowing down as I hit Gloucester Place, so I didn't get too out of breath.

I could see Smith waiting outside the steps that led down to the club; he was all hunched up as the rain came down faster. I picked up my pace as I saw him squint at his watch and tried to think of some excuse for being late that didn't involve Part 317 of the ongoing row with my paternal signifier.

When he saw me coming across the road, he lifted up his hand and smiled, like he was pleased to see me. Or pleased to get his iPod back. Or relieved that soon he'd be inside where it was toasty warm and there were no raindrops dripping down his back. Or none of the above.

"Hey," he called. "I was just about to give up on you."

"I had this thing," I said, just a mite tetchily. "I'm sure I told you I had a thing."

"I thought this was the thing you had," he protested as I reached his side. He leaned forward, head down, like he was about to kiss me on the cheek, which threw me, so I took a hasty step backward because he was taller and leaner and actually better looking if you got used to the nose, which I didn't think I ever would, and smelled much nicer than I remembered. I needed a second to just take it all in.

"I had a dinner thing, too." It was like I'd become Miss Inarticulate 2006.

"You're doing the monosyllable thing again," he teased, like we were friends who had an in-joke about my inability to string a coherent sentence together.

"Well, yeah, I do that. A lot." I shut my eyes in despair, and when I opened them, he was gesturing down the steps.

"Look," he shouted over the rain, which was starting to upgrade to a full-on gale. "Do you want to go in? I've got a spare plus-one."

I peered at the shadowy depths of the entrance to see if my least favorite doorman was lurking, all ready to mock my attempts to pass as an eighteen-year-old. He didn't seem to be on duty.

"I was meant to meet my friends . . . yeah, whatever . . . okay."

The Trio of Evil could fend for themselves, I thought as I followed Smith down the steps and let him pull the door open for me. There was a mousy girl standing there, holding a clipboard with a sheet of names on it, who didn't look like she was going to give me any trouble.

"I'm on Duckie's guest list. Smith, no, just Smith, and I've got a plus-one."

I stood there with my hands in my pockets and tried hard to look nonchalant, as if it was my right, nay my privilege, to be the plus-one for the achingly hip boy in the achingly hip, retro trackie top, who was on the guest list for the most achingly hip local band. I wasn't convinced that it was working too well and then, out of the corner of my eye, I saw the bouncer bearing down on me.

I quickly shifted so I had my back to him, but he'd obviously read up on sneaky behavior exhibited by obviously underage girls.

"How old are you?" he bellowed at me from across the foyer.

"I'm eighteen!" I said, like it was so painfully obvious that he must need glasses. I had signature eye shadow for crying out loud!

"What's your date of birth?" he shouted in my face, like that was going to outfox me.

I didn't try anything fancy, just stuck two years on the original date. "August 8, 1987. And my star sign's Leo," I added helpfully because, yeah, it seemed like a really good idea to antagonize the angry man.

He didn't believe me, I could tell. He was examining me intently as if I had the year of my birth etched into my skin with a laser.

"You don't look eighteen," he announced eventually. "You look about fifteen, tops, if you ask me."

I didn't even have to fake my indignation. "I am *not* fifteen."

"ID," he said blankly, holding out his hand.

"Why do you always pick on me?"

"ID," he repeated, and I was already fumbling in my pockets in the vain hope that I'd have some kind of legally binding document in there that would exonerate me.

Instead, I got Smith's arm suddenly curling around my

shoulders. "She's with me," he told the age Nazi. "Is there a problem, Frank?"

Of course, he *would* know the bouncer and be doing some idiotic knuckle-bumping thing with him, when a simple handshake would do.

"No problem, dude. Just that your girlfriend's under eighteen and she's not coming in."

"I am not his girlfriend," I said scathingly, which got me another bewildered blue-plate special from Smith. "We're just ... like, whatever. And I am eighteen."

His arm tightened around me and I tried to smile in a mature manner. "Look, she's eighteen. Take it from me."

There was one fraught moment of possibility, then Frank the wanker gave a bark of laughter. "Is that what she told you? Yeah, right. Look, go in, but if I see her drinking anything alcoholic, I'm chucking you both out."

Smith was all big with the thank-yous, like he'd granted us some amazing favor, but I just turned on my heel and stalked inside.

"God, I get that all the time," I backtracked when Smith caught up with me. "It's so embarrassing."

"Yeah, it must be." He nodded, then paused. "You are eighteen, aren't you?"

"Oh, don't you start," I whined. "I'm eighteen, just drop it. Please . . ."

He held his hands out in front of him. "I'm dropping it."

"Good."

We elbowed our way through the crowd, and I didn't know why they were so high and mighty about who they let in because the place is a total pit. All low ceilings and sticky walls that left this black gunk clinging to you. The air was thick with this damp fug and everything smelled hot and smoky, like there was a weird chemical being pumped into the atmosphere—it made me tense and excited at the same time. I could feel something slowly unfurling at the base of my spine and floating its tendrils through my body so that when Smith took my hand and tugged me toward a group of people sitting in the last booth along the back wall, my fingers tingled again.

I realized that we were heading toward people whom I didn't know but whom I was going to have to talk to, which was my absolutely least favorite kind of people in the world. Well, except for old people who crap on about the war.

"Shouldn't we go to the bar?"

"What? No, come and meet everybody," he exclaimed eagerly, like . . . like . . . like . . . He was a big, friendly, shaggy dog who'd got a dead bird in his mouth that he wanted to show his master. Which made me the dead bird in that scenario and as analogies go, it felt a little too close for comfort. Especially as we tripped nearer and I could see that "everyone" was a motley collection of scenesters, who looked like they did overtime appearing in mobile phone ads lounging elegantly around grimy clubs.

"This is Isabel," Smith said by way of greeting, and I limply waved a hand at them as he went through this collection of names that left no impression on me. There were a few nods in reply and I thought the worst of it was over, but then Smith pushed me onto an available five centimeters of seat. "Drink?"

"I'll come with you." I tried to get up but his hand was on my shoulder, keeping me rooted to the sticky vinyl.

"No, stay and get to know everyone. What do you want?"

I couldn't get through this in a state of stone-cold soberdom. "Get me a vodka and Diet Coke, and make it a double," I said decisively, as if I'd drunk enough alcohol in my time to have a preference.

To his credit Smith didn't remind me that both our arses were on the line if one teeny sip of liquor passed my lips. He just rummaged in the back pocket of his jeans and chucked a packet of cigarettes at me. "Thanks for nicking mine last time, by the way."

"Don't mention it," I said breezily, waving him away because the quicker I got a drink in me, the quicker my social ineptness would transform into something approaching scintillating. That was the plan, anyway.

I think the reason why cigarettes are a good thing—apart from speeding you off this mortal coil a few years before your time—is that they give you something to do when you're sitting with eight close, personal friends of a guy you don't really know.

I shuffled around on the bench so I had my back to the girl sitting next to me, and concentrated on snaking a cigarette out of the packet, tapping it against my palm, and then lighting it. Which took all of ten seconds, and then I could get on with smoking it and wishing that my hair didn't look like it had had a collision with a hedge trimmer because my head was getting awfully hot underneath my hat.

"Where do you know Smith from?" the girl sitting opposite me suddenly asked, and I realized there were eight pairs of eyes studying me with feigned disinterest.

"From around," I muttered.

I'm really good at closed sentences. There was nowhere to go after my reply, so I twisted my lips into a grimace-y smile that got me a blank look back and tried to telepathically communicate with Smith to get the drinks and get back to the table stat. My Jedi mind tricks were for shit because he was gone ages, and by the time he finally returned, my leg was jiggling uncontrollably against the table edge and I was halfway down my second cigarette.

I don't think I've ever been so pleased to see anyone. He sat down on the table in front of me and handed me my drink. "There you are."

"Thanks," I said, and took an enthusiastic gulp, wincing slightly as the vodka burned on the way down.

Smith turned to the girl who was sitting next to me. "Isabel's dad teaches American literature at the University," he said, like it was a good thing. "What's his name?"

"Dr. Clarke," I said flatly, and she shuddered with this ophidian wriggle of her shoulders that made her glossy red hair shimmer underneath the lights.

"I have him for my Modern Classics module," she gasped, and pinned me with an accusatory look, like it was all my fault. "He's . . . well, quite sarcastic. . . ."

"He's a tosser, you mean?" I supplied sweetly, and she gave me a tentative smile as if she didn't know whether I was joking or not.

"You're so lucky you're in Cultural Studies," she said to Smith whose knee was bumping against mine, until I moved my leg away so he couldn't feel me shaking.

"Oh, I forgot you were a student." It came out a tad more venomously than I'd intended.

"You do realize that you said that the way someone would

say, 'Are you a child molester?' or 'Do you like Girls Aloud?' But yeah, I am. Is that a problem?"

I hated students and the way they filled up our answerphone with their academic crises. Or came over for these once-a-month suppers with Dad where they spewed all this pretentious crap out of their mouths in the hope that he'd be impressed.

I knew my face was twisted up in an expression of utter horror, but I blanked my features down and took a generous swig of my drink. "I'll get back to you on that, shall I?"

Smith laughed and reached over so he could pull my hat down over my forehead. I forced myself not to jerk away, even though my forehead was starting to get sweaty, and he cupped my cheek with his hand. "You're a piece of work, you really are," he said, and he sounded dazzled by the concept.

It's so stupid how someone touching you—just their skin on your skin—can make you feel all sorts of things that you don't want to feel. His fingers were stroking my face, and it made me want to brush my head against his shoulder. So I stood up. "I have to go and see someone."

The only someone I had to see was my reflection in the bathroom mirror. I looked a state. The concealer was wearing off and I was all shadows and smudges, like an out of focus photograph, the green eye shadow and the red lips garish points of color in my pale face. And that vodka on an empty stomach? Really not helping.

I locked myself in an empty cubicle and sat down with my head in my hands, because I was kidding myself if I thought I could do this. When your representative members of boykind are an emotionally crippled, forty-one-year-old academic who detests the very sight of you and a nine-year-old boy who tries to fart in your face, how the hell was I meant to know how to act around Smith?

"... where did he find her?"

"And, more to the point, where did she find that hat?"

I stiffened. There's nothing like having your choice of headgear dissed to interrupt a perfectly good pity party.

"I mean, can you say rude? Didn't say a word—just sat there with a face like a slapped arse. No surprise that she's a blood relative of Dr. Snark."

I had to stifle a giggle at that, hand clapped over my mouth, though really there was nothing funny about having to skulk in a toilet cubicle while two hipster girls tear you into little pieces.

"I don't know . . ." I had to strain my ears over the sound of a running tap but I gave it my all. ". . . seems too young for Smithy. He has the worst taste in girls."

There was a pause, and then they both said in unison, "Chloë!"

"And there was that girl in the first year . . . What's her name? The one with that lame tribal tattoo who dropped out, though everyone knows she had to have an abortion."

"Plus he's got a crush on Molly, which is never going to happen, and there were rumors . . ."

"God, where to begin?"

There was another silence while I sat there paralyzed with mortification that the boy that I may or may not quite fancy seemed to have a huge amount of relationship debris piled around him.

"He was a complete slut in the first term. I mean, well, let's just say I have intimate knowledge of that little mole. . . ."

"On his arse! Oh, yeah!"

"So you *did*, I always wondered."

"It was, like, this rite of passage thing. Y'know, blow your entire student loan on alcohol in a fortnight, not go to any lectures and shag Smith."

"So do you think he's shagging that sulky girl?"

"Getting pelvic with Dr. Snark's daughter? Really doesn't bear thinking about. Might cheer her up, though...."

"Maybe she'd even take her hat off and..."

I didn't get to hear the exciting details about what would happen once I'd taken my hat off because the door shut behind them. I folded my arms and contemplated the almost hole in the knee of my jeans and tried to get Smith out of my head. Eradicate all mental pictures of how he bit down on his squashy bottom lip with his pointy little eyetooth when he was thinking. Or how he made these extravagant gestures with his beautiful, elegant hands and when he touched me—I wondered what it would be like if he touched me in other places. Because really when you stood us side by side, I was way out of his league. I was pretty, kind of, supersmart and popular, and he was just a lanky student with annoying friends, a big nose, and really, really, really beautiful blue eyes.

Just the thought of him and all the secret things he'd done to other girls under the covers made my head ache. Like, it should be this really complicated Venn diagram and Smith would be this huge circle in the midst of all these other overlapping circles. And my circle would be tiny, unable to be seen by the naked eye, floating untethered at the corner of the page.

I stumbled back into the club. No way was I going back to Smith and his coterie of hard-faced hangers-on, all speculating about how far he'd got with me. Instead, I liberated a pint of beer that was sitting on the ledge in front of me and pushed my way through the crowd to an isolated corner on the other side of the dance floor.

The beer was flat and warm, but I chugged it down regardless because it would take me to someplace else. It was a blur after that. Everything hazy around the edges, as I sneaked glasses off tables and drank the contents. Beer, wine, vodka and cranberry juice, even neat whiskey, and it mostly tasted foul. But I liked how it made me feel. As if I was insignificant and nothing mattered, but also as if I could rule the world and everyone would bow down before me.

I danced, which had never happened outside the four walls of my bedroom. And when I couldn't find Dot or the others, I talked to the people hanging out by the speaker stacks—well, actually I babbled away about utter rubbish. It just seemed enough that I could force words out because my teeth had gone numb and my lips had suddenly turned to rubber. It was like water glancing off oilskin, nothing stuck. Even when I went skidding on a wet patch and toppled over, I simply lay on the floor and looked at all those legs stepping around me and the pretty lights until this girl I'd never met hauled me up.

"You're so cool," she kept saying as I swayed along to The Kills, with my arms spread wide for balance. "We should totally hang out more, just the two of us. What do you think?"

I smiled at her and patted her arm. "I think I'm going to be sick," I said calmly.

"Okay, see you later," she trilled as I tripped away. "Remember that you're beautiful!"

I'd had this vague notion that a toilet would be a good puke venue, but my feet carried me through the club and out a side door so I could take in big gulps of salt-tinged air and decide, yes—still going to be sick.

There was this little courtyard around the back, secluded enough that I could bend over and wait for the muscles in my alimentary canal to go into spasms. Didn't get an A in Biology GCSE for nothing.

I gripped my knees and coughed a couple of times and just as I felt a hand at the small of my back, all those drinks decided to put in a repeat performance.

A whoosh of jet-propelled ickiness sprung forth from my mouth and the whole time I was dimly aware of this hand rubbing my back soothingly. Finally, my stomach seemed to right itself, and I straightened up so I could look Smith in the eye. I was also pleased to note that I'd kept my hat on.

"Are you okay?" he asked in this concerned voice as I took a generous step back from the little puddle I'd just made.

I wiped my hand over my mouth and it came away red from my lipstick. Oh yes, my joy was now complete.

"Isabel, are you all right? Do you want me to get you some water?" he asked again.

"I'm fine," I gasped, and then found myself doubling over again. "Well, if fine means that I'm going to be sick again in about two minutes."

"You must be overheated," he remarked, and then before I could stop him, he pulled my hat off and ran his fingers through my hair, holding it back from my face. "Might as well get it all out."

"Thank you for that welcome piece of advice," I said sourly, which was a perfect match for the bile that rose up and had me retching pitifully.

Finally I was done. Or I thought I was done. I pressed my hand to my forehead and wished that Smith would just piss off.

"Are you all right?" he asked yet again. It was getting as annoying as his fingers still winding around my sweaty strands of hair.

I snatched my hat out of his hands. "Go away," I ordered, and pointed to the club doors. "Leave me alone."

"Why are you always so rude?" There was absolutely no accusation, just this flat tonality that made me stare at him in amazement.

And I guess that I was still drunk despite voiding the contents of my stomach, because I told him the truth. For once. "I'm shy," I confessed quietly so he had to bend his head to catch the words. "I'm really shy, and it makes everything come out like that because it's hard talking to people." I thought about it for another second. "And also I'm just . . . yeah, I'm *nasty*. I'm not very nice. I'm an utter bitch, if you must know."

"Don't say stuff like that," he practically begged me, but I turned away. "I'm really trying here, Isabel."

"Nobody asked you to. I'm sure you can find yourself an easier conquest if you just want a shag," I spat at him as I started walking back down the alley.

"I don't just want that . . . well, I want that, yeah. And I think you're cute, but I want to get to know you, too."

"I'll save you the trouble," I hissed, turning around so quickly I almost toppled over, and his hand shot out to grab hold of my arm. "There's nothing to know, don't you get that? You'll get to know me and then you'll wonder why you bothered. I'm not anything that you think I am. You're not going to break down my defenses and find this sweet, gooey soft center."

His face was in shadow, but I could still see the way those lips flattened out into a tight line. "Maybe you're frightened that if someone manages to break down your defenses, then they'll find that you do have that soft center. That you're not as badass as you think you are."

"Yeah, whatever. Thanks for that insightful analysis, Mr. Freud."

"Well, see you around, then."

I couldn't even muster a grunt in reply, just stomped toward the door that led back into the club, ripping off my corsage en route because it was soggy with sick.

7

I couldn't find the others anywhere. Normally I'd have been incandescent with rage at the mere thought of them blowing me off, but I was too busy having these really scathing conversations with Smith in my head.

"Do you think she's going to come?" I heard someone who sounded a lot like Dot say as I staggered up the stairs that led to the balcony. "Should we call her?"

"Oh, God, do we have to?" Nancy really needed stamping on hard. "Anyway, her mobile isn't working because she's had all her pocket money taken away by her evil papa and aren't I just the most pathetic little moppet in the world? Forget about Is, let's go into the chill-out area and chat up those guys."

For one second I contemplated going after them and giving Nancy my own special brand of hell. But my heart wasn't really in it. So I slumped against the wall (which wasn't doing a great job of holding me up), running my tongue over my furry teeth. It would be far more sensible to find a bathroom so I could brush my teeth and repair my makeup (which couldn't have survived the puking intact).

With a furtive look over my shoulder, in case the Trio of Evil were lurking, I scurried down the stairs and tried to think tactically. God, that really made my head hurt. Then I remembered that last time I'd come here I'd got off with this boy in a disused kitchen behind the top bar. I sidled through a likely-looking door and miracle of miracles! There was a sink so I could get the puke taste out of my mouth.

I took a cautious step forward and then stopped when I saw Smith sitting on a worktop with his head in his hands. He looked up as I shut the door and scowled at me.

"Piss off."

I held up my hands so he could see that I wasn't carrying weapons. "I need to clean my teeth, and then I'll leave you alone to wallow in misery or whatever it is you're doing."

He folded his arms and made a harrumphing noise as I hunted through my bag for my toothbrush. I like to clean my teeth after lunch; it's no big deal but the way Smith was boggling his eyes at me, you'd have thought I'd just pulled out a crack pipe.

I happily squeezed a huge blob of Colgate onto the brush, aware that Smith was watching my every move like he'd never seen a demonstration of dental hygiene before. I pointedly ignored him as I got to work. I counted to sixty in my head as I did my bottom row of teeth and then started on the top. Now there was a quizzical expression on his face as he watched my reflection in the mirror above the sink. Now, it's not like I'm a total neat freak but when it comes to my teeth, I can be a little . . . *precious.*

"You've got to be kidding," he muttered, his features shifting into complete disbelief as I squeezed out more toothpaste and repeated the whole procedure. My mouth was full of minty fresh foam so I couldn't snarl back at him, but when I finally finished spitting and rinsing, I glared at him.

"Take a picture, it lasts longer," I snapped, which had to be one of the weakest comebacks ever.

Smith smiled faintly. "Excuse me, are you, like, ten?"

I splashed cold water on my face to remove my makeup because there was no other option but to start again with a blank canvas. "So, you've gone from thinking I'm quite cute and wanting to get to know me better to what? Getting over me in, like, five minutes?"

He stretched out his legs. "Believe me, I was never under you."

"Huh?" I looked up from slapping on tinted moisturizer like it was going out of fashion. "What's that meant to mean?"

"You said that I was over you, which implied that I'd been under you first." He paused as if he were giving the matter serious consideration. "I'm sure I'd have remembered if I had been."

If I hadn't been doing precision work with the silvery green powder and my pocket mirror, I'd have rolled my eyes. "Do they teach you all that fancy semantic crap at University? That's really going to help you become a worthwhile member of society."

His shoulders slumped a bit, but then he tilted his chin and watched my attempts at beautification with interest. "You looked prettier without all that on your face."

"Whatever. So why are you sitting up here being all mopey. I mean, what have *you* really got to be depressed about?" Because it seemed to me he had it all, apart from manageable hair and a small but perfectly formed nose.

He was thoughtful. "I don't really need a reason. I have maudlin tendencies."

"It's probably because of all that whiny boy-rock that you listen to. You need to start getting into disco. A bit of Gloria Gaynor and you'd soon be feeling all kinds of perky."

Smith made this funny snorting noise. "Was that a joke?"

"Yeah, you wish." I looked better. I wasn't going to be approached by any model scouts, but I looked a little less like a walk-in to the nearest plague hospital. And it might have been because I didn't have any deep desire to go downstairs, and it might have been because I genuinely wanted to know, but I asked him again. "Really, why are you sitting in a deserted kitchen, looking like you're about to slit your wrists?"

Smith sat up and hauled his legs over the edge of the work-top, leaving his feet dangling forlornly as he rubbed a hand through his hair. "I'm not. Not thinking suicidal thoughts, anyway. I'm just having an off day, you know?"

"Yeah, I know," I said quietly, and there was something resigned enough in my voice to make him look up, startled.

"Girls like you don't have off days," he said. "You're pretty and you can have anything or anyone that you want."

I opened my mouth to spit out a furious protest, but he held his hand out.

"Shut the hell up, Isabel," he growled. "You're all, 'oh, no one understands me. My bitchdom is such a burden' but you have it easy. God, you have it so easy."

There should have been another furious protest bursting and I could see the words "you patronizing bastard" scrolling across my cerebral cortex in fancy type. But I wanted to be that girl. The girl he thought I was. Who had nothing else to angst about but how her hair looked and why her friends didn't understand her.

And Smith? Did he not just tell me to shut the hell up? No

one would ever dare say that to me. Well, not if they still wanted to have kneecaps come Monday morning. He was watching me from under his lashes with a wary smile, like he knew that I was mentally weighing up whether I should slug him or not. I decided not.

"Maybe I do have it easy. Maybe I have all sorts of dreadful secrets that you don't know anything about." I smiled in a manner I knew to be extremely annoying when he snorted in disbelief. Then I padded over to lean against the bench, right next to his bony ankles in their red woolly socks. "Everyone has secrets, *Atticus*. You should know that."

That snapped him out of his mopey mood pretty damn quickly. "I told you not to call me that."

"So what's bugging you?" I knew it was me. I was what was bugging him, when I'd made it abundantly clear that he wasn't going to be getting a guided tour of my lady parts. "C'mon, you can tell me. It's not like we know the same people or, like, even each other. Call it your reward for holding my hair back while I puked."

"You don't really want to know," he protested with just the barest hint of a pout—way to make it obvious that he was pining for the touch of my lily-white hands.

"Sure I do." I prodded his leg with my finger. "Spill."

God, talk about milking it for all it was worth. He nibbled on his bottom lip for a little while, brows furrowed with indecision, before he sighed. "It's a girl. It's always a girl, isn't it?"

I resisted the urge to gloat. I'd had a few boys tell me that I was a prick-tease because I never went past second base. But I'd never had a boy utterly desolate because I'd given him the brush-off.

"She doesn't even know I exist," he continued morosely. "And I have to listen to her talk about all these other guys who aren't half as devoted as I am. I mean, they don't care about her, not really. They just want to have sex with her. They've never sat up all night and checked her source notes for an essay that she has to hand in the next morning, and they don't know that she's all bad-tempered and hissy first thing in the . . ."

It was dawning on me at, like, the speed of light that actually I wasn't the cause of Smith's existential crisis. I was just the girl who'd walked in during the middle of it. All that scamming on to me when he was pining for some uptight student skank? What fucking ever!

"Lame, you're so lame," I hissed, banging my elbow into his knee and not even bothering to make it look like an accident.

Smith's head jerked up, but I was already striding toward the door, as he swore under his breath. I distinctly heard the word "bitch."

"You're totally *pathetic*," was my pithy, parting shot as I shouldered the door open.

I charged down the stairs like the hounds of hell were snapping at my ankles. I couldn't remember the last time I'd felt so angry. Smith'd had me convinced that he was different, but he was strictly regulation-issue. Talking of which, I started to hunt around for the others. I found Dot loitering by the cigarette machine so she could gaze adoringly at this bunch of guys who were shotgunning cans of Special Brew. Really, you couldn't leave her alone for a minute.

"This completely sucks," I shouted over the strains of Franz Ferdinand. "Come on, let's go."

She didn't look particularly pleased to see me. In fact, she had the audacity to scrunch up her face like she was in severe pain. "Do we have to?" she whined, gesturing at one of the boys who was jerking around spastically to avoid the foaming fountain of beer that was spurting in all directions. "I think he likes me."

I glanced at the object of her affections, who was okay if you liked Neanderthals. "He's revolting," I said witheringly, folding my arms and giving her the full benefit of my disgust at her dubious taste. "We're going to have to get your eyes tested."

Dot did her chin wobble, which she always pulls out on these occasions. "He's kinda cute," she said doubtfully. "Sort of."

"Yeah, if every other boy in the world suddenly dropped down dead. And it's not like he's going to fancy you," I snapped. Dot added in a lip tremble that wasn't faked, and I felt the teensiest, tiniest pang of guilt. "I'm just looking out for you," I protested, but she was already brushing past me.

"I'm going to find Ella and Nancy," she called over her shoulder, and I got the message loud and clear that she didn't want me to come with her.

After trailing through the club a couple of times with a "don't even think about talking to me" look on my face to fend off the attentions of any sweaty-handed lads, I found myself on the edges of the dance floor again. I leaned against the wall and watched everyone else having a really good time. Though maybe they were just faking it and that smiling and gyrating to The Faint was all show, and even that pretty blonde girl in the silver top would go home and pig out on ice cream because she used food as an emotional crutch and she couldn't connect with anybody. Jesus, I needed to lighten up or ship out.

But when I tried to smooth out my frown, because surely it

couldn't be permanent, I caught sight of Smith sprawled on a sofa, all of him slumped, like keeping any bit of his body upright was too much effort. I wasn't buying what he was selling for one second—he thought that if he sat there long enough, looking as if he'd been told that he had a week to live, some naïve, little airhead would feel sorry for him. Or if that didn't work, he'd pretend to be drunk because that had worked so well for him in the past.

He was awfully good at looking tortured, though. His fingers tapped nervously against his knee and he was gazing forlornly off . . . I followed his eye line and caught sight of two girls huddled by the DJ booth. They were crouched in the shadows so it was hard to see what they looked like. But I could see Smith and all the longing on his face so clearly—he wanted someone who didn't want him back.

My feet started walking over to him, like they were acting independently from my brain. My brain still thought he was a treacherous skank who shouldn't hit on girls when his heart wasn't in it. But my feet were off message and intent on planting me right in front of him.

He flicked his eyes upward. "Go away," he shouted over the harsh beats of Bloc Party.

"I want to talk to you," I said, because now my mouth was getting in on the act. "It's important."

"You thought of a few more really hurtful accusations to fling at me?" he sneered, trying to angle his body away from me so I was talking to one bony shoulder.

Well. it felt bony underneath my hand because I was touching him now, leaning down so I wouldn't have to shout, and up close he was strangely beautiful. All of him quivering in misery.

"Don't be sad," I pleaded, and I rubbed my thumb against the corner of his mouth as if I could smudge away the pain. "Come with me."

His hand was warm in mine, and he let me haul him up from the sofa. "You need to start watching these mixed signals of yours," he grumbled, but he was following me out of the room, and as we got caught in the doorway, all of a sudden he was leading and I was winding my fingers through his and there were a thousand tiny electric shocks running through me.

Smith led me up the stairs to the street and even the sudden blast of cold air couldn't sober me up. Because I was still drunk. I must have been drunk. That was the only explanation for why my hands were all over him, stroking his face and tangling in his messy hair.

I wasn't the only one, though—he lowered his head to make it easier for me, and his arms snaked around my waist and they didn't slide to my arse, but stayed there, holding me, hugging me, and it felt amazing. It felt even better when I wrapped my arms around his neck so not even the fierce breeze that was tugging at my hair could come between us.

"What's going on with you?" he asked me gently, and his arms tightened around me. "Can't you just pick a personality and stick with it?"

I didn't answer because I had my face burrowed in the crook of his neck, which was toasty and soft and my new favorite place in the world. When I kissed him there, he giggled, then tried to turn it into a manly cough. But really there was nothing to say because all my mouth wanted to do was kiss him, and it turned out his mouth was totally down with that, too.

When he kissed me, it felt like he meant it. His lips . . . it's hard to describe this stuff, too intimate. But it was strange how his mouth moving on mine could make me feel hot and cold and light and dark. His arms cradled me to him: one hand stroking my hip, the other cupping the back of my head were the only thing stopping me from floating away.

"Do you want to come back to mine?" he whispered in the wafer-thin gap between our mouths when we remembered that we had to breathe.

His hands were in places that there had never been hands before, not without someone getting slapped around the face, so I knew he wasn't talking about a coffee before he walked me home.

If there'd been some sci-fi movie device and the street had started shimmering around us in a slo-mo special effect so the next thing I knew we were in his bedroom, there wouldn't have been much I could do about it. But the street wasn't doing anything much and Smith was looking at me expectantly.

"Back to yours?" I repeated breathlessly. "Could be tricky. Maybe you should kiss me again."

"Maybe I should," he agreed with this quirky smile that I wanted to lick off his face—and that led to more kissing and swooning and, hmmm, hair stroking.

"Oh! My! God! What is that and why the hell is she snogging him?"

Nancy's piercing shriek killed the mood as effectively as a bucket of cold water. I unpeeled my lips and turned my head to see Nancy, Ella, and Dot, arms folded, faces incredulous, and Smith was *still* sucking on an incredibly sensitive patch of skin behind my left ear.

I squirmed away from him. "Get off me," I muttered furi-

ously, and there was no nice way to do it. If there had been, I'd
have much rather played it that way.

"It's him," Nancy declared in a stage whisper. "It's that freak
show from the party the other week."

I was too busy slapping Smith's hands away to answer at first.
"Tell them to piss off," he said softly, hands around my wrists so
his thumbs could press against my thundering pulse. There was
this second when our eyes collided, and I tried to tell him I was
sorry. That what I was about to say was just for their benefit.

"Jesus, will you stop mauling me!" I announced dramatically,
wrenching myself out of his embrace. I turned to the others,
feigned a coughing fit, and then made my eyes go really big.
"I'm like, *so* drunk, please tell me I did not just suck serious face
with him?"

8

"I mean, can you say fugly?"

If the streets hadn't been almost deserted, and if she hadn't just bought me a bag of chips, I'd have pushed Nancy into the path of an oncoming car. It would have been the most justifiable homicide in the history of justifiable homicides.

"I know," Ella chimed in. "I was about to tell him that Seth Cohen wanted his DNA back, but he stormed off before I could get a chance. Funny that." I could feel the stinging heat of their sly little glances as I trudged along ahead of them with Dot.

"Just ignore them," she warned me quietly. "They want to get a reaction out of you. Don't give them one."

And since when did Dot think she could give me advice? But I was too busy racking my brains to come up with some devastating retorts that would whip Nancy and Ella back into line to start in on her. "What were they doing when you found them?" I muttered out of the side of my mouth.

"Ella was getting off with that acne-fied guy she gets off with when she can't find anyone else, and Nancy was peeing in a broken toilet with no door," Dot recalled with a fair amount of malice. Didn't know she had it in her. We shared a conspiratorial smirk.

"How far down her throat was his tongue and you could totally dust her tits for fingerprints 'cause—"

I whirled around and pointed a finger at Ella, which stopped her in mid-flow. "What?" she asked belligerently.

"Nothing. Well, it's just . . . I think you're breaking out," I said innocently, squinting at her flawless complexion. "Maybe all of Gary's suppurating sores have finally become contagious. You really need to find someone else who'll snog you."

Ella's hands were already scrambling over her face as Nancy turned to look at her. "Ewww! And what's suppurating mean?"

"It means to produce a discharge of pus," I explained patiently before I gave her the swift once over. "Urgh! What are those weird stains on your legs?" All four of us turned to look at Nancy's white jeans. I could have pointed out that when your arse is the size of a mountain, white jeans are not your friend, but it would have been too easy. No finesse to it. "It kinda looks like . . . no, it's too gross, but have you wet yourself?"

Now it was Ella's turn to "Ewwww!" as Nancy cast a horrified look downward. "No! It's just . . . It's the streetlights, they make everything look yellow-y."

"Whatever you say, sweetie." With all signs of rebellion firmly squashed, I could enjoy the rest of my chips in peace.

It had been a long and strange night, but it wasn't until I was curled up in my bed next to Dot, with a very subdued Nancy and Ella on the floor beside us, that I realized how bone-weary I was.

I could feel my eyelids drooping before Dot even switched the light off. There wasn't even time to tell Nancy that she was snoring, even though she wasn't, before I fell asleep.

We were on a plane, which was strange because the only time I can remember flying was the year we lived in America when Dad was teaching at Amherst College. Usually we'd load up the car and have to spend two sticky days driving to fricking Umbria to be bored godholy.

But we were on a plane. Mum and I were on a plane, and I was small enough that my feet didn't touch the ground, and I was wearing this pink flowery dress from when I was little.

She was holding my hand tightly, the weight of her wedding ring digging into me, but I didn't want to tell her that she was hurting me, otherwise she'd let go.

"You have to be brave, Bella," she said soothingly. "Have to get used to flying. Here, have some peanuts."

Then this little bag of nuts suddenly materialized on my lap and we both sat there and looked at it. She unpeeled her fingers from my tight grasp so she could pick up the nuts and rustle them enticingly.

"Go on," she urged me. "Open them."

It took ages to tear into the bag, my sweaty hands fumbling with the plastic, and when I finally tore them open, there weren't nuts inside but these dried-up insects that suddenly swelled into life and started climbing out of the packet.

I turned to Mum and—oh, God, not again!—I couldn't scream or speak or even whisper. She peered over at the rapidly multiplying cockroaches and spiders and insects bursting out of the bag and crawling all over me. Furry feet skittering up my arms.

"Oh, Belle, now what have you done?" She sighed wearily. "It's no use pulling those faces. It's not you they're after."

And she was right because I was just the climbing frame they were using to get to her. I tried to brush them off her, I really did. But my hands hung limply by my side, and I tried to call for help, attract the attention of a stewardess, but no one would look at me.

"It's all right," she said, sitting there calmly, even though there were tiny rivulets of blood streaming from her face and her neck and her arms as the insects bit at her. "Worse things happen at sea, don't they? Or should that be worse things happen in the air? I told you not to open the bag but you never listen."

I could feel her blood dripping onto me as she suddenly lurched to one side....

"Is! Jesus! Wake up!"

There was this strangled yelping noise and as I opened my eyes, I realized it was coming from me.

"Nance, get her a glass of water. Is, are you all right?" Dot touched a hand to my face. "You're really hot."

I struggled upright and balled my hands into little fists so nobody would see them shaking. "Just had a bad dream. I'm fine," I said in this scratchy voice.

Ella was hovering by the bed, which looked like it had been caught in a hurricane: duvet on the floor, pillows scrunched up. "We thought you were having some kind of fit," she reported gleefully. "Is there, like, epilepsy in your family?"

There were icy fingers clutched around my heart and squeezing it so tight that it was forced to beat in this frantic rhythm. "No. I had too much to drink," I snapped, and I hated that it came out all quavery. "Made me have a nightmare, that's all. Sorry about the bed, Dot," I added, and she sat down next to me and shrugged.

"It's okay, worse things happen at sea. God, now you've gone really pale. Shall I go and wake your dad up?"

I closed my eyes in the hope that when I opened them, Dot and Ella would have disappeared. No such luck. "Really, I'm okay."

Nancy padded back in with a glass of water. Knowing her, she'd probably spat in it. "There you are," she said without a shred of sympathy. "I'm never going to get back to sleep after that."

"Yeah, can you say drama queen?" Ella snickered and I knew what she was thinking: that with my hair all sticking up, face drained as I tried not to drop the glass, I wasn't anyone special. Wasn't someone you had to respect.

I placed the glass on the nightstand and got to my feet so I could help Dot straighten up the bedclothes.

"I mean, it's not really normal, Is, this whole *Exorcist* routine. Maybe you should see someone," Nancy suggested with saccharine sweetness as she snuggled down on the nest she'd made out of sofa cushions and blankets. "You might be going mad. Delayed reaction and shit. I've read something about it."

"Yeah, like post-traumatic stress syndrome," Ella piped up. "Would probably explain why your cute boy radar has got seriously malfunctioned because, y'know, you've gone insane."

"Well, I might be going insane but you've always been retarded," I snapped, practically hurling myself back under the covers. "And if you've all finished diagnosing my mental condition maybe we could get some sleep."

The three of them were snoring happily within minutes of turning off the light, and I had to lie there on my back, limbs rigid, counting the shadows on the ceiling because I was too scared to go back to sleep.

Thankfully, Nancy had to piss off at the crack of dawn because she goes to this lame drama group on Saturday mornings in the vain belief that she has star quality. And that meant that Ella slunk off behind her because without Nancy there, she'd have to take some serious shit from me for the big can of whupass she tried to open last night.

It wasn't until Dot and I were finally alone that I could let out the breath I'd been holding.

"I thought they'd never go," she said feelingly, turning and giving me a tired smile. "I know we're all friends and stuff, but sometimes I really don't like them."

"They're a pair of evil little trolls," I admitted with a wry twist of my lips. "But you know what they say. Keep your friends close . . ."

"And your enemies closer," Dot finished for me and because it was her and we'd been friends for ages, I let her put her arm around me and we shuffled toward the kitchen so we could eat our body weight in toast and scrambled eggs.

We sat there in a silence that didn't have claws for once. Just me and Dot hanging without the gang, like we used to when life was simpler and we were eight and there were Barbie dolls and Jammie Dodgers and we really thought that if you were nice to people they'd be nice right back to you. Then we grew up and got over it.

That's why I let Dot come along for the ride. Even though she's really built for better than being one of my evil henchmen.

She knows me, the real me, no matter how deep I've buried her. Which is another reason why we're still friends. She's got far too much on me to ever let her kick it freestyle.

She looked up and gave me a smile. "Just like old times, isn't it?"

"I guess. Wanna braid my hair after this?"

"So, okay, I want to know what's going on with you," she said calmly, ignoring my feeble attempt at humor. "It's like Isabel has left the building. No, it's more than that. Even when you're here, you're not here. You know what I mean?"

"Not really," I replied, and gingerly speared a little heap of egg with my fork.

"Is," she tried again, this time with a lowered voice for added dramatic emphasis. "I know that you've got stuff going on, but I'm here for you."

"I'm fine," I said. "Really, I'm fine. Just lighten up, will you? Jesus, you'd think someone had died the way you keep going on."

A mottled flush swept over her face. "That's so not funny, Is. It's kinda harsh, actually."

And then she glared at me because I wasn't fitting into any of the acceptable patterns of behavior she'd read about in the manual on *How to Deal with the Recently Bereaved* that she'd obviously been consulting.

"What do you want me to say?" I asked her and I was completely serious. "Would you like me to walk around weeping and wringing my hands and getting all snotty? 'Cause I could have a go, if that would make you feel any better."

"I don't know," she wailed helplessly. "It's just, like, you're not you."

"Well, who the hell else would I be?" I shrugged and I could see that she was struggling, forehead pitted with effort and oh no, her eyes were filling up. "Dot, I'm fine. I just want things to be like they were, and I want people to treat me like they normally do, okay?"

Dot gave me a tiny nod and pushed her chair into the table so sunlight sliced across her face from the big picture windows, and I could see how all her freckles had joined up over the summer. She had the exact same tremulous look as the time we got caught shoplifting nail varnish from Boots and I tried to pretend that it had been all her idea.

"I guess . . . this is hard for me," she admitted, resting her chin on her hand. "Like, I don't know. I thought yeah, you'd be crying all the time and wearing lots of black."

We both looked down at my ratty blue V-neck jumper and waited for it to materialize into a T-shirt that said, "My mum's died. Stop me and ask me how." "I was working on this whole sackcloth and ashes thing but it really chafes." I grinned, reaching across the table to squeeze her hand. "Can we please talk about something else now?"

Dot smiled gratefully. "Well, Ethan Parker actually acknowledged my existence yesterday and not much else. My mum's on at me about choosing a university already and you know what she's like . . ."

She clapped her hand over her mouth; her eyes two perfect circles of horror because I couldn't possibly know what mothers were like as I didn't have one.

"Still on your case about going to Cambridge so she can tell everyone that you take after her side of the family?"

"Yeah, yeah!" Dot nodded frantically, her voice far too shrill.

"Like, spending three years with a bunch of snotty, posh kids is going to be a rewarding experience. She's the original Desperate Housewife."

"Well, at least she hasn't learned everything she knows about life from a fusty novel written about a hundred and fifty years ago by some emotionally crippled Victorian guy." Even I was surprised at how venomous I sounded. Dot nodded again so she could show me how big she was with the empathy. And the really annoying thing? It was working.

Dot and I stood up at the same time and before it could even register, she was gathering me up in her little skinny girl arms and trying to hug me. "I'm sorry. I'm so sorry," she kept saying.

I knew she was and I knew that she meant it, but I didn't know what to do with her sorry. I struggled away from her and scurried down the hall to grab her bag.

"Is, I'm here for you any time," Dot said, getting to the front door before I could and making it evident that she didn't have plans to exit in a timely fashion.

"I know," I said, reaching past her to close my fingers around the door handle. "Thanks."

"Don't mention it." She stepped aside and I wrenched open the door and shoved her through it.

"If you tell anyone about this, I swear I'll make you sorry," I hissed so vehemently that Dot took a step back and almost collided with the lavender bush.

And finally she stopped being there for me and that wounded, worried look was back in her eyes. "O-kaay," she said hesitantly. "So, um, okay. I'll call you."

"No, I'll call you. If I need you." I let the words hang around for a while so she'd get the message that my likelihood of needing her was highly unlikely. Then I gave her the fakest smile I had in my repertoire. "Hey, this was great. We really should do it again sometime."

9

I never cry. Like, ever. I don't write bad poetry. And I certainly don't phone up this carefully hand-picked selection of confidantes and whine about what a bad joke my life is. I deal with whatever's bugging me and messing my shit up by getting down on my hands and knees with a bottle of Flash and a scrubbing brush.

So after I'd got rid of Dot but the gut-gnawing after-effects of her little chat wouldn't budge, I cleaned the kitchen and the bathroom. I even did Felix's bedroom, which had several new species of amoeba festering in the collection of mugs and plates under his bed. My bedroom was already a shiny paean to hygiene, but the lounge and the dining room took me the rest of the afternoon.

The only two places I avoided were their ... *his* bedroom and the study. Even if we'd been grooving along in perfect father/daughter harmony (oh, my aching sides!), I'd have avoided all those piles of paper, which apparently are in some kind of order that's only understandable if you have a degree in astrophysics. And then there are the books. Big books, little books. Crisp new books, static clinging to their pages. Old, yellowing books that smell of dust and damp. Books in his study, books in the box room, books in every room of the house, and when I come across them, I just stack them up neatly and carry on with my one-woman mission to annihilate every speck of dust that gets in my way.

He and Felix had gone out. They'd left me a garbled message on the answerphone about art-supply shops and possibly a trip to the museum, but the washing machine chose that moment to go into its spin cycle, which reverberated around my pounding head, and it wasn't like they'd have wanted me along, anyway. Two's company, three's a crowd and all that.

They came back laden with shopping and plans to rent some DVDs, just as I was tweaking the last cushion into place.

I unplugged the vacuum and looked up to see Dad staring in bemusement at the kitchen, which was now a gleaming advertisement to the benefits of Mr. Muscle.

"You make a mess and I'll make you wish you were never born," I told Felix as I relieved him of the bags he was holding. "I'll put this stuff away before you muck the cupboards up."

"You cleaned *inside* the cupboards?" Felix giggled, whacking me on the arse as I reached up to the top shelf. "You need to get out more, Is."

I ignored him and started unpacking tins and bottles, arranging them to my system. Yeah, I had a system. Not alphabetical because even I haven't reached that level of anal control freakery, but more by genre.

There was a cough behind me and I realized that he was still there, standing and watching me as I happily shuffled the tinned tomatoes to the side of the spaghetti hoops.

"Isabel, could you stop that for a second, please?"

I nudged the last tin into place, took a deep breath, and turned around with my face a perfect blank.

He gestured with his hand to encapsulate the total spick and spannery of the kitchen. "You've done a wonderful job." He sounded like I'd dragged the admission out of him with a pair of rusty pliers. "Though I recall, your moth— Should I be alarmed by this obsession with tidying?"

"No, I'm not . . ." I protested, and then folded my arms so my hands would stop fluttering about. "I just like things to be neat, orderly."

"Do you remember the time you were being bullied by that awful creature—what was her name? Jasmine, Rose, something flowery . . ."

"Daisy? In middle school." I shuddered at the thought of the ten-stone ten-year-old who'd made me cry every day for six weeks.

"We didn't even know there was a problem, but you came home every day and insisted on laying the table with a ruler to measure the exact distance between each knife and fork." He paused and gave me a considered look.

Which I returned with knobs on. No way was I about to go into overshare mode about—well, any of it, really.

"Anyone else would be pleased to have a daughter who's not a total slob," I pointed out. "This house would look like the inside of a trash can if I didn't keep on top of it."

He nodded his head in acknowledgment of my kick-ass housekeeping skills. "I've been talking to Felix about the thorny topic of pocket money, or allowance as I understand it's to be called. It seems that you received money straight into your bank account in return for certain chores?"

"I got thirty quid a week for cleaning and doing the laundry and picking Felix up after school and—" I narrowed my eyes to see if he'd buy it and then continued— "and a hundred quid a month clothing and sundry allowance."

"A hundred pounds seems a little excessive," he murmured, switching on the kettle. "Define sundries."

"Tampons, sanitary napkins," I began, and smirked when I saw his pained expression. "Shoe repairs, books for school if there aren't enough to go around, stuff for my face so I don't break out . . ."

He nodded his head. Sucker! "That seems reasonable, if you give me your bank details, I'll set up the direct debit. I haven't had a chance to do anything more than close the accounts."

He pressed his hand over his forehead as if he could rub out the frown lines, which seemed to be a permanent fixture—and it was so strange that we could be having this conversation and not mention her by name.

"Cool," I said. "Thanks."

"And please don't keep stealing money from my wallet," he added softly.

I didn't bother to deny it. I was too busy concentrating on the chilly feel of the goose bumps rising up on my arms, but I tilted my chin so I could look him in the eye.

"I won't."

"Good." He sighed heavily. "This coldness between us . . . I don't like it, Isabel, I don't like it at all."

"I know." My voice was this tiny squeak.

And just like that, in a split second, in the blink of an eye, in the time it takes to draw breath and not even have a chance to let it out again, he straightened up and went from soft to hard.

"I promised Felix that I'd spend some time with him this evening watching DVDs and ordering some takeout." He curled his lip like Felix was going to force him to eat dirt. "If you think you can be pleasant company, you're welcome to join us."

I could tell that he thought he was offering me, like, this huge olive branch. Maybe even a whole bloody olive tree. But an evening spent watching *Shrek* (Felix *always* wants to watch *Shrek*) and pretending that I wasn't gritting my teeth and digging my nails into my palms hard enough to draw blood because it was all bullshit and lies, wasn't worth a hundred quid a month for clothing and sundries.

"I have stuff to do."

"Very well."

I was just settling down for an evening of hardcore skulking in my room, which involved lying like a starfish in the middle of the floor and listening to Smith's Mope Rock Playlist Number Five when Felix barged in and threw the cordless phone at me.

"For you," he said. "And we're ordering Chinese, do you want some?"

"You're such a little suckass." I suddenly remembered that we needed to have a conversation about presenting a united front. "But thanks for the whole allowance thing."

"Hey, it wasn't my idea to give you money!" Felix protested, put out by the very thought that he might have done me a good turn. "I told Dad that you didn't deserve any."

"Whatever, monkey boy. Get me some fortune cookies and a . . . oh, egg rolls and some Kung Pao chicken," I told him, picking up the phone. "Okay, you can piss off now!"

He slammed the door with great force as I said a cautious hello.

"Isabel. You still have my iPod."

I closed my eyes and sank back down on the floor. He sounded like the dictionary definition of "I hate your guts."

"Yeah, I know." I waited for him to tell me how to get it back to him, but apparently I wasn't going to get anything from him but a frosty shoulder. "Well, I can't tonight because I have a thing."

"Oh yeah, you and your things," he drawled. "You and your little brother—it was your little brother, wasn't it?—and some Chinese. Sounds enthralling."

"How much did you hear?" I demanded, scrolling back to my slanging match with Felix to see if I'd said anything which might indicate that I was a sixteen-year-old compulsive liar.

"Fortune cookies. Egg rolls. Kung Pao chicken. Something about an allowance and that even being a blood relation is little protection against your infamous nastiness. Do you snub him publicly, too?"

I decided to ignore his last dig. "No one asked you to eavesdrop."

"I kinda couldn't help it." He exhaled heavily. "Look, I need to get my iPod back. I can't do tonight, anyway, so shall I come around and pick it up tomorrow?"

Come around *where*? "No!" I hissed. "I'll meet you somewhere."

"Where do you live?" he asked.

"You're not coming around here," I repeated furiously, already seeing the horrific scene unfolding in front of my eyes.

Dad acting as if Smith was some grubby-pawed potential rapist and then letting slip my real age within, like, ten seconds.

"Isabel, look, the hissy fit is a nice change of pace, but I was just trying to find out if you live near me," he said with teeth-gritted exasperation, which made me feel like a complete drama queen. "Like, do you live out in Hove or something?"

"I live near Seven Dials. Montpelier Villas," I admitted somewhat unwillingly. Our nabe was pretty posh. In fact, we lived on the swankiest street in Brighton. "And you?"

"Kemp Town, George Street, behind Safeway. So do you want to come around here tomorrow afternoon? Just to swap iPods . . ."

"Well, why else would I come around?"

He made an impatient "pffffting" sound. "It's number seventy-three. Come around about two-thirtyish."

"Fine, whatever," I said, like I didn't care one way or another.

"Fine. Maybe you'll be in a better mood," he snapped.

"Don't count on it," I said, but he'd already hung up and I was talking to dead air.

10

It was a beautiful afternoon. There was still a faint hint of summer in the air, even though it was late September, and I decided to walk along the seafront to Kemp Town, dodging day-trippers and strollers with every step I took. I scowled at every single one of them, but I had my sunglasses on so it was all wasted.

There's this little stone-walled spit by the pier that I like to stand on and watch the water, but it was knee-deep in fat-faced hordes down from London for the day. Besides, it's best when there's rain and wind and the sea comes lashing up at you. I bought a bag of fresh doughnuts from the stall at the pier entrance with the last of the money I stole from Dad and crossed over the road, listening to Broken Social Scene's "Anthems for a Seventeen-Year-Old Girl" one last time. I was going to miss Smith's iPod—there was some really good stuff on it and I hadn't worked out how to transfer it on to my computer.

Not like I could ask him to do it because that would really ruin my mean girl rep, I thought as I stood on his doorstep and tried to will my fingers to ring the bell. After a few moments they obliged, and then I had to stand there, quaking in my flip-flops while a pair of feet thundered down the stairs followed by swearing that was so fluent and graphic even I was shocked.

The door opened and this pretty girl with a MRS. SETH COHEN T-shirt and an aggravated expression gave me a quizzical look. "Yeah?"

I was planning on taking my sunglasses off but thought better of it. She was really cute and I wasn't having a good hair or a good anything day. "Is Smith in?"

She nodded and then stepped aside. "Come in and mind the bike. I just banged my hip on it." She laughed. "Hence the bad language."

There was something really familiar about her. Like I knew her from somewhere, but maybe she'd been at the club the other night.

I followed her up the stairs and into the living room. "Wait here and I'll see if he's up," she said. "I'm Molly, by the way."

"Isabel," I murmured, perching gingerly on the edge of a chair. Molly? So this was the paragon of perfection that Smith was hopelessly crushing on. She flicked her honey-blonde hair (which in no way was natural) back from her elfin face and, yup, she was definitely crush-worthy. Molly seemed to be waiting for me to say something else. I pulled the iPod out of my pocket. "I need to give this back to him. So, like, maybe you could do that and get mine?" I asked hopefully, but she was already out the door.

"I'll just go and get him," she called over her shoulder.

I looked cautiously around the room. Everything I'd heard about student accommodation was true. It was a complete hovel. There were magazines and newspapers obscuring the carpet. Dirty cups and saucers, most of them doubling up as ashtrays, littered every surface, and I shuffled my buttocks further along the seat to minimize contact. Just sitting there made my skin crawl.

"Sorry, it's a bit of a mess in here," Molly said as she came back into the room. "We keep having people around and they keep making a mess and we keep not clearing it up. It's a never-ending cycle of untidiness."

I smiled weakly and racked my brains for something to say to her. "It's really not that bad," I lied. "You could shove most of it into a bin bag and it would look better."

Hi, I'm Isabel and housework is my passion.

"Yeah, we could," she agreed, nudging a stack of magazines with her socked foot. "Anyway, Smith says you can go up if you like. Do you want some tea or something?"

There was no way I was drinking out of any mug that lived in this flat. Not without getting dysentery or Legionnaires' disease or something. "Oh no, that's okay. I'm fine."

I stood up and tried not to look clueless. "So, where am I going?"

"Up the stairs, last door you come to." Molly was still poking at the debris on the floor. "He's in a foul mood. He's got a bitch of a hangover," she added cheerfully.

I was really careful going up the stairs so that I didn't have to touch the banister or the walls, which were probably coated in years' worth of dirt. Yeah, they looked freshly painted, but bacteria lurks everywhere.

There was music leaking out from under Smith's door as I tapped on it lightly. No reply. It wasn't until I hammered on it with both fists that I heard a grunt and pushed the door open.

All I could see was him. Not just because the sun was streaming in through the windows and backlighting him in this golden glow that made his eyes bluer than normal and cast this little halo around him, but because his room was tiny. There was a double bed, a ton of CDs scattered over the floor, and a complicated stereo system perched on a milk crate.

"It's you," he said, in a way that suggested that he wasn't exactly pleased to see me. But for once, my hackles weren't rising. I'd never been on my own in a boy's room (Felix's didn't count), especially not one where the bed was the dominant feature. I was so far away from anything approaching a comfort zone.

In the end I lifted a limp hand in his direction. "Hey."

Smith took a step toward me so I could get the full benefit of his bloodshot eyes, stubbly chin, and damp hair; he must have just come out of the shower.

"You got my iPod, then?" he asked tersely, and I pulled it out of the back pocket of my jeans.

"It's fully charged." I wedged the bag of doughnuts under my arm and prayed that I didn't get grease stains on my Topshop wrap top. Then I yanked out my headphones and handed him the iPod.

He held it up to the light and scrutinized it as if he couldn't quite believe that it was still intact. "I thought about flushing it down the loo but I had a change of heart," I said, and he showed me all his teeth in something that didn't even remotely resemble a smile.

"That's big of you. Stay here, I'll get yours."

He walked across the room, or took about three steps toward what I thought was just a really big *Lost in Translation* poster but was actually a door. I peered over his shoulder as he disappeared into a narrow strip of a room, with a long desk taking up one wall and cupboards along the rest of it.

Smith was fiddling around with a computer and then turned to me with a frown. "I'm just taking some stuff off yours but it's not quite finished," he said. "Do you mind waiting?"

"I could come back," I heard myself say when I realized I had to get out of there before the silence killed me. "Like in an hour maybe?"

"No . . . hang on . . ." he mumbled, fiddling with his keyboard. "You can come in here if you like."

Anything was better than being rooted to the spot, so I squeezed through the narrow doorway and crept up behind him so I could watch him, whizzing through my playlists on iTunes.

"I tried to do that," I blurted out. "Transfer some stuff across, I mean, but I couldn't work out how to do it."

He stiffened as I leaned closer, like I was about to jump his sorry bones, then said in a much friendlier voice: "You need to download this program off the Internet. I'll show you. Here, you can sit down and I'll crouch."

We spent the next hour ripping songs off his iPod onto mine and bickering happily about music. I even let him eat the rest of the doughnuts because he hadn't had any breakfast or lunch.

"And oh, can I have The Hormones' songs, too, please?"

Smith grinned and started uploading them. "Do you like them, then?"

"They're okay. Well, they were, they kinda suck now. I liked them better when Mol— Shit! Oh, my God, it's *her*." My hands flew up to cover my flaming cheeks. "I'm so lame."

He nudged me with his arm. "You didn't recognize her? Well, I guess she looks different now."

I shook my head. "She seemed familiar, but I thought she was at the club and, anyway, she used to have pink hair."

"Well, if you hadn't been such charmless company, I'd have introduced you," Smith said, propping his arm on my leg. "Her and Jane are in this new band called Duckie."

"Don't say anything else," I begged him. "I need time to process this information."

He gave me about thirty seconds. "Are you done processing?"

"Okay, you're trying to tell me that Molly Montgomery, ex-lead singer of The Hormones, is now living in a grimy student flat in Brighton . . ."

"That's because she's a student, Isabel. It's what we do, we live in student flats, we go to lectures. And in Molly's case, get sued by her former record company for walking out on her contract."

"Ouch." I winced.

He lowered his voice conspiratorially. "Really sore point. Never bring up The Hormones, lawyers, or ex-boyfriends called Dean who've just landed their first film role."

I nodded gravely. "Right, I'll remember that." Then I flash-backed to the conversation I'd overheard. "So is she your girl-friend, then?"

"Hardly." The look he gave me was pretty intense, and I don't think it was my imagination that he seemed to be less resting his arm on my leg than stroking my knee. "We're just friends. C'mon, we should leave this doing its thing—I'm getting a cramp."

He got up and stretched, which made all his muscles shift, T-shirt riding up to show a faint trickle of hair on his belly. I looked down at the frayed hem of my jeans because I just knew he was smiling at me. One of those smiles that made me want to touch the corners of his mouth.

"Do you want some tea?"

I shook my head and wriggled off the stool.

"Now, look, you've gone all quiet again," he teased, and laughed when I pouted at him.

"I haven't."

"Yeah, you have. Come back into the other room."

There was nowhere to sit except the bed, but I didn't mind because Smith flung himself down on the mattress and started telling me about how he went to the first ever Hormones gig at some girl's sixteenth birthday party after he met Jane and Molly in a garage. I sat cross-legged next to him and listened, not to the story (even though it was pretty engrossing), but to the quiet pride in his voice when he talked about Molly and what she'd been through. She might not have been his girlfriend but there was something there that was about more than just being mates. Something like a major case of unrequited love.

"So we kinda became friends during what she calls her blue period, which means she wore a lot of black and stayed in bed most of the time," he finished, and rolled over onto his side.

"Well, I guess it must have been tough for her." I couldn't stop myself. "So has she got a boyfriend?"

Smith's eyes were closed, but they snapped open then. "No. I think there's some DJ guy she fancies," he said neutrally, so I couldn't tell what he thought about that. "So have you?"

"Have I what?"

"Have you got a boyfriend, then?" he asked me really casually.

"As if!" The very concept of me having a boyfriend was so freaky that I started giggling.

"Oh, now I'm getting smiley Isabel," Smith drawled, and his hand was back on my knee, and the warm weight of it was comforting, like it was anchoring me so I couldn't float away. "And what do you do when you're not being shy or mean? You on your gap year?"

Lies get so complicated. You tell one lie. And it makes you tell another lie. And another one. And another one. Until you've got this big tangle of them that you can't even begin to start unraveling.

"Yeah," I said. "Maybe if I get a job, I'll go traveling."

"S'weird." He frowned. "August birthday, right?"

"August 8, 1987," I said emphatically, like there could not be even a smidgen of a doubt.

"Well, shouldn't you still be doing your A-levels, if you've only just turned eighteen?"

I imagined loose pages of a calendar fluttering in the wind, like they do in old films when they want to show that a big-ass amount of time has gone by. Then all the pages disappear, until all that's left is a big sheet of paper with huge red letters that say, "She lied about her age. She's sixteen!"

"No . . . no," I stammered. "You got it wrong. See, I'm the youngest in my class. I *was* the youngest in my class. 'Cause the end of July is the cut-off point, right? If I'd been born nine days earlier, I'd have been in the year below." As explanations went, it was far too garbled to be believable, but Smith was nodding in all the right places.

"Do you think you'll go to University?"

"I'm not sure. I'm kinda over the whole academic thing already, with my dad and all," I mused, pleased we were back on safer ground. "I'd like to do something artistic, but I really suck at it."

Smith propped himself up on his elbows. His hair had dried into this mess of curls and sticky-up bits, the ends tinged with bleach, and I wanted to touch them to see if they were as soft as they looked. "So, what do you want to do?"

I'd told him so many lies already. I couldn't even begin to remember just how many, so for once he deserved an honest answer.

"What do I want to do?" I echoed. "I want to kiss you."

He didn't say anything, just lay there with his eyes closed again and I knew I'd blown it. That he didn't want me to kiss him after what had happened the last time. Or I'd short-circuited his brain with too many mixed messages. Then he opened one eye and smiled at me.

"Go on, then," he said with just a hint of challenge.

I crawled up the bed, focusing on his slightly pursed lips like I was climbing up the freaking beanstalk and they were the pot of gold. He was smiling so it made it that much easier to rest a hand on either side of his head and kiss the upturned corners of his mouth.

I kissed him so many times—just tiny little presses of my mouth against his. I didn't really have a clue what I was doing but I didn't care because those hundreds of kisses made my lips tingle. My fingers stroked the arch of his eyebrows and the bridge of his nose and even the plump, tender flesh of his earlobes. I mean, who ever really thinks about earlobes? But I couldn't keep away from his, gently pinching them between thumb and forefinger, and all the time I was kissing him.

Could have stayed like that forever; the sun beating down on us, warming his skin and turning it the color of toffee. But nothing is forever and my gentle assault made him groan right into my mouth and his hand cupped the back of my head as he rolled me over so he could show me how it was done.

And suddenly I got what the big deal was about kissing. How someone could suck on your bottom lip and make you come completely undone. That someone stroking the hair back from your face could make you swoon and someone sliding his hands underneath your top could make you feel wanted for the first time in your life.

"Is this all right?" he whispered in my ear as he traced figures of eight over my skin, and I nodded.

He kept asking me that over and over again as we dragged the covers over us and our clothes fluttered away like feathers on the breeze. Except it wasn't as poetic as that, it was more real. And I couldn't explain what I was doing in fancy phrases and metaphors. Just that it felt good and the way he looked at me and touched me; like I was precious, like he cared about me, made the decision for me.

Because he just wouldn't stop asking me if all the delicious things he was doing were all right. And "yes" was the only word I could force out. It wasn't until he stopped holding me so he could reach the nightstand and I heard the rip and crinkle of the foil wrapper that I really understood what I was committing to.

But there wasn't time to analyze the whys and wherefores of losing my virginity in the middle of a chalk-bright Sunday afternoon on bedclothes that smelled of fabric softener and cigarettes. I had to lose it sometime, right?

"Is this okay?" he breathed against my neck.

I tried to say yes, but I'd forgotten to form words because I was living in this new reality of the shocking feeling of skin against my skin. Of hands touching me in new places. Of legs pressing against and parting mine.

"You've done this before?"

I went crimson from my toes right up to my hairline. And I knew that for a fact as I was in the perfect position: naked in someone else's bed, to be able to witness my swift and thorough reddening.

"Yes! I've done it loads of times." My voice had never sounded so squeaky and I'd never sounded more like a big, fat slut.

We both frowned, and Smith gave me a very prim look considering he was lying on top of me. "Okay, um, good to know."

I thumped him on the arm. "I haven't done it loads of times," I whispered, 'cause it seemed like it should be a whispered conversation. "I'm not, like, the biggest ho in Skank Town. Just, y'know, I'm not a virgin." My voice dipped down so quietly on the last word, that I wasn't even sure if he'd heard me.

"Virgins are overrated, anyway." He smiled down at me, and I think he meant to reassure me that my supposed lack of virginity was meant to be a good thing, but that quirk of his lips was verging on predatory and now I was meant to act like some porn queen who knew what she was doing, so I pulled him down so he could kiss me.

It didn't really hurt that much. It was like the burn in your throat when you drink a really cold can of Diet Coke too quickly or your mouth gets sore from eating a big bag of salt and vinegar crisps.

And a little bit of discomfort was easy to deal with. I was way too busy trying to coordinate the "my God, I'm having sex" freak-out fest with the part of my brain that was trying to instruct my body on how to behave during the having of the sex.

I wasn't really sure what to do with any of my stuff. In films, women seem to have their knees up around their ears, but I just couldn't begin to figure out how to get my legs hoisted that high and nearly poked Smith's eyes out with one of my toes.

"Sorry!" I mumbled, and really, the whole thing was just so ridiculous. Sex was ridiculous. It made Smith's face shift into new and unusual shapes. And his fingers danced across my skin so lightly that it was one touch away from being a tickle, and I had to bite my lip really hard to stop myself from giggling.

I always thought that when I had sex it would unlock this great mystery, but really, not so much. It was just this strange tangling of limbs and body parts that were nothing like the pictures I'd seen. I much preferred what happened post-sex, which was snuggling into the crook of Smith's arm and listening to Rilo Kiley while we shared a cigarette. It was intimate in a way that all that thrusting and grinding wasn't.

I guess we were having a companionable silence until he had to go and ruin it.

"So . . . how was it?"

I squinted up at him. "How was what?"

He brushed a stray strand of hair behind my ear and let his hand linger against my cheek. "Was it okay? Did you enjoy it? Do you think you'll wanna hook up with me again?"

"Well, that's too many questions for one sitting," I pointed out, and he went from holding me to not holding me with three feet of wrinkled sheet between us. I stretched out a hand so I was touching him again, his skin like warm plasticine as I stroked it. "C'mon, what do you want me to say? I just came around to get my iPod back and now you're being all emotional and weird."

"We just had sex, Isabel," he said, like I might need some

reminding. "That tends to make things all emotional and weird."
He rolled over so he was facing me, and he looked all rumpled
and little boy lost, which really didn't help. "Are you having second thoughts?"

I was having second thoughts. I was having third thoughts.
Can you have millionth thoughts? If you could, I was having
them, too. "I d-d-don't do this. I don't just jump into bed with
people," I stuttered. "So, like, if I've broken some post-shag code,
I'm sorry but . . ."

"What do you usually talk about after you've had sex then?"
he asked, and his voice was as tart as a bag of acid drops.

I sat up, pulling my knees to my chest and making sure the
duvet was clutched tight to me. "I don't know." I closed my eyes
because I could fake it so well when we were having sex and all
I had to do was wrap my arms around him to make him cry out,
but now he was looking at me like I kicked cute little puppies
for fun. Again. I missed the feeling of my head resting on his
chest already, listening to the thrum of his heart get steadier and
steadier. But mostly I wanted him to stop glaring at me. "I don't
know," I repeated. "Actually I've never talked about anything
after I've had sex because I've never had sex before."

His face collapsed in on itself, which was interesting. All the
features that usually sat in happy harmony together slipped off-
kilter so his eyes bugged out and his mouth hung open. I didn't
like seeing him like that and, God, I just couldn't do this.

"I have to go now, anyway," I muttered, and the one way to
tear my eyes off his stricken face was to crawl under the covers
so I could retrieve my clothes. My jeans and top and, Jesus, my
knickers and bra were scrunched at the bottom of the bed, and

I had to contort myself into a pretzel to pull them on while I protected my not-so-maidenly modesty with the quilt.

Smith was saying something, but my bra strap was giving me all kinds of grief. Finally all my clothes were on and I could scramble out of bed with my dignity in tattered shreds all over the floor, along with my flip-flops, which had disappeared into some other dimension.

"You should have told me," he said in this dull, flat voice as he lay dull and flat on his back, smoking a cigarette.

"It was no biggie," I said, and the effort to make my voice sound light and casual nearly killed me. "Had to get rid of it sometime and you were . . . well, y'know, it didn't suck."

That came out so wrong, and Smith gave a little snicker before he remembered that I'd lied to him and had my way with him under false pretenses and he was the injured party.

"It was your first time," he said throatily, and I wondered when the violins were going to start playing. "It should have been special and you should have told me so I could have . . ."

I clapped my hands over my ears. "So you could have what? Been *gentle* with me? Actually, I don't want to know. Look, it was fine. And I shouldn't have lied to you, I get that, but will you stop going on about it?"

"Oh, God, you're fucking impossible!"

"Yeah, you're not the first person who's mentioned that," I said, and then ducked from sight so I could grope under his bed for my flip-flops. I almost chinned him when I emerged because he was leaning over so he could grab hold of my shoulders before I could wriggle away. Didn't stop me from trying, though.

"Get off me," I hissed, resisting the urge to melt under the strong grip of his hands, his thumbs kneading little circles into all those lumps and bumps of tension that were a permanent fixture. "I need to go."

"Come here," he said gruffly, and he hauled me back onto the bed so he could do that thing where he held me tight and I felt like I was safe.

11

It was dark when I woke up from the best sleep I'd had in months. I lay there for a second, disorientated by the way the glow of the streetlamps seemed to be slanting through the window at the wrong angle, and the weight resting comfortably around my waist. Slowly the pieces fitted together. I was in Smith's room, in his bed, with his arm wrapped around me.

I lurched forward and he clung tighter to me.

"What's the time?" My hoarse whisper sounded deafening.

"Shhh, it's late, go back to sleep," he rumbled into my ear, but I was wriggling in earnest now.

"Shit! I've got to go, he's gonna kill me."

Smith had mistaken me for his very own security blanket because as I was making a superhuman effort to hurl myself out of bed, he was intent on draping me over him.

"Look, you might just as well stay till it gets light," he murmured sleepily.

"I really have to go. I mean is it ten P.M. late or, like, the wee small hours late?"

Smith held his hand in front of his face and squinted at his watch. "It's just past three."

The sound that came out of my mouth was inhuman. Somewhere between a wail and a shriek. "How could I . . . we . . . this is all your fault!" I dug him in the ribs with my elbow. "Let go!"

He let go and I was off the bed and out the door like a streak of girl-shaped lightning. Not that it was much help. I could smash the record for the four-minute mile and I'd still be home hours after my curfew because I'd had sex. With Smith! And if it wasn't for the fact that I had aches in places that I really didn't want to think about it, I was almost prepared to pretend that it hadn't happened.

"Isabel, hold up!"

If anything, I put on an extra spurt of speed, but all that smoking had obviously had a disastrous effect on my ability to sprint because as my hands fumbled with the door, Smith touched my shoulder.

"It's dark, I'll walk with you."

"You don't have to be nice to me because, y'know, you . . . You deflowered me. Took my maidenhood and all that shit."

He flicked the latch and pulled the door open. "I know I don't, but I want to make sure you get home in one piece."

"Well, that's a total moot point because when I do get home the only excuse that he's going to accept is if I'm actually missing a limb."

Smith glanced back at the shadowy length of the hall. "I could go and get the bread knife. Might be able to hack off your pinkie finger."

"Ewwww! And stop being cute."

"I can't help it, I am cute," he pouted, and I couldn't help but giggle because it was all so normal. Well, not the whole shagging and violating all curfew laws thing, but standing on a boy's doorstep and flirting with him.

And as soon as I thought that, my mouth stopped working. Because I wasn't a normal girl. I was this stupid, fucked-up girl who was in a world of trouble.

"So, come on if you're coming," I said gruffly, and I stepped out into this torrential downpour that was practically Noah and the Ark-esque.

"Maybe I should go and get an umbrella."

I turned around so I could give him a soggy glare. "There isn't time. And there's no point in both of us getting waterlogged so . . ."

I didn't get a chance to finish my sentence because Smith took hold of my hand and then I had no choice but to run because he was tugging me so hard that dislocating my shoulder was a definite possibility.

I think he thought that it was really romantic—running along the seafront while the rain and the wind whipped in our faces. But it wasn't. There's nothing, absolutely nothing, romantic or charming or cool about racing on rain-slicked pavements in flip-flops that squelch on impact, then nearly falling flat on your face when one of them tries to break free.

We got as far as the pier before we had to stop because I was about to go into cardiac arrest. Then we did the whole Scouts' thing of ten paces walking and ten paces running, but it was all pretty academic. Because, as we slowed to a crawl to navigate the steep slope of Montpelier Villas and my house came into view, I could see all the lights blazing, which meant that I was going to get the all singing, all dancing welcoming committee. And the welcoming committee had probably sunk a couple of bottles of red wine while he was waiting for me.

"Shit, shit, shit," I moaned. "I'm going to get thrown to the freaking lions."

I didn't think Smith had heard me over the Force Ten gale, but he squeezed my hand. And if we weren't both cold and soaking wet, it might even have counted as a comforting gesture.

"I could come in with you," he shouted in my ear. "Talk to your dad . . ."

"Yeah, and what would you say? Sorry, Isabel is home so late, but we were busy shagging on my crusty sheets and then we fell asleep," I suggested. "I don't think that's going to help."

"You should remind him that you're eighteen—y'know, a proper, legal grown-up."

I nodded gravely and made a mental note to do that two years from now when the argument might actually carry some weight. The meaningful good-bye part of the conversation was rapidly approaching, but the shivering, soaking, drowned-ratness of it all was really killing the mood.

Smith was fumbling in the pocket of his jeans, the sodden material making him swear until he finally hit paydirt and pulled out my iPod with a proud smile as if he'd hunted it down, killed it, and dragged it home all by himself. "So if I give this back to you, then I'm thinking that I won't have any excuse to call you."

I held out my hand and watched the raindrops bounce off my palm. "You can call me if you want," I said, as if I wasn't bothered one way or another. "I should give you my mobile number 'cause I've got it topped up now."

I looked down at my wet jeans and top and Smith patted down his clothes as if he expected to find a handy pad and pen.

"It doesn't matter . . ." I started to say but he tucked his hand into the waistband of my jeans and pulled me into this sodden embrace, kissing me hard to make up for the rain lashing down and robbing us of the taste and feel of the kisses we'd had earlier.

Smith had really good arms: they held me up and held me close and were almost enough to make me forget the unwavering glare of the lights, but out of the corner of my eye I was sure I saw the curtains twitch, and I gently disentangled myself from the good arms and the good lips.

"I really, really, really have to go," I reminded him.

He ran a finger down my cheek. "I know. But I'll see you again, yeah?"

It was too late and too near my imminent ass-whupping to start wondering if this meant that he was my boyfriend or if he just thought that I was an easy lay. "Yeah, I guess." And because I never knew what to say, I turned to go, then thought better of it. "Thank you."

Smith didn't ask me what for and I don't think I'd have been able to tell him. He just gave me a not-quite kiss and murmured against my mouth, "You're welcome."

I watched him bound down the hill, picking up speed until he was this fast-moving blob in the darkness, but I was just delaying the inevitable. My guts felt as if they'd shifted down around my ankles as I lifted the latch on the gate and slunk down the path. I hadn't even got my key into the lock with the barest minimum of noise before the door swung open and I fell into the porch.

My hair was sticking to my face in tangled whorls, plastered over my mouth, and I shook my head so I could look up at the blank mask my father was wearing. There was this little tic banging away in his cheek. When I was little I used to try and chase it with podgy fingers and he'd laugh and tell me I was tickling him. Sometimes when I remember stuff like that, I think that I dreamed it or it happened to another Isabel who looks like me and has all the same memories but who's not me.

He kept one hand on the open door so I had to sidle past him, flinching away so my arm didn't brush his. That wasn't the only reason. He'd never, ever hit me, but there was always a first time.

The door closed behind me with a resolute click, and I shuffled around so he could shoot me down with another of those hydrochloric acid stares as I dripped a small puddle over the parquet flooring.

I opened and shut my mouth a few times, but getting actual words to come out wasn't working. Then he made this "talk to the hand" gesture and snarled, "Don't say a bloody word, Isabel!"

I never did what I was told. "I went around to a friend's house and I fell asleep. Don't know why you're getting so bent out of—"

"And would this be the same friend who was mauling you outside the house?" he asked me pleasantly.

Talk about leading questions. "It was just a friend." I knew he was expecting an apology or an explanation or some defensive bluster because he folded his arms and leaned back against the door. But my bones ached, even my hair hurt, so I just inched toward the stairs. "You didn't need to wait up for me."

"No, I suppose I didn't. But I wanted to be awake in case the police phoned to say that they'd found you dead in a ditch."

"Sorry to disappoint you but I'm still in one piece." I concentrated on the difficult task of lifting my feet up and down. Jesus, I could *feel* his eyes boring into my back and coming out the other side. "I'll try harder next time, if you like."

I heard him suck in a breath and was mentally preparing myself for a blistering stream of invective, but he just sighed, long and loud. "Oh, just go to bed, Isabel. I'll deal with you in the morning."

His threats amounted to shit. They always do. He couldn't ground me because then I'd be hanging around the house and sharing his oxygen. And he couldn't stop my allowance because then he'd have to wallow in general squalor and filth. Couldn't take away my TV privileges, either, because he'd have to come into my room and dismantle the TV and the video and the DVD player and his brain would leak out of his ears.

Halfway through the lecture from hell—as I perched uncomfortably on one of the kitchen stools while he towered above me—his voice becoming more clipped with each word, he did ponder on taking away my Internet access. But as he can't even log on to his e-mail without referring to a detailed flowchart of instructions, I knew my days of illegally downloading songs were far from over.

The lack of suitable punishment really got to him until his lips were so thinned I didn't think he'd be able to talk out of them anymore. He still managed to interrogate me to within an inch of my young life.

"Where were you?"

"Who was that boy?"

"How long have you known him?"

"What on earth were you thinking about when you decided

to come home so late? Were you even thinking at all? Do you ever consider anyone besides yourself?"

It was like he'd entered a competition to see how many questions he could fire at me in half an hour. I didn't bother to reply, that would have just distracted him from the sound of his own voice.

"You're not to see him again, of course," he decreed, pacing a well-trodden path from the sink to the pantry. "I absolutely forbid it. And you're not to have any of your other friends around here, either. I won't have hordes of adolescents traipsing in at all hours."

He paused to see the effect of that little bombshell, but, as I don't like any of my friends that much, I figured I'd be able to deal. I looked down at my hands neatly folded in my lap and hoped my bent head signaled how completely I didn't care.

"Yes, well, let that be a lesson to you," he finished with this note of satisfaction like he'd finally been able to make me see the error of my wicked, wicked ways.

Then he stomped back to the study and nothing had changed except that on the other side of town there was someone who might actually give a toss about me.

12

Smith never called, though. As I floated through the next week, I learned to live with this sick feeling of expectation every time the phone didn't ring. Why would he ring when he'd already had the toy surprise?

My new favorite thing in the world was to obsess over how I should have played him. If I'd been funnier, or smarter, or hadn't dropped my knickers so quickly, he'd be calling and *begging* to take me out. I was going slowly mad as I had all these conversations with a lovesick Smith in my head. The only thing that made me come up for air was when the school exploded. Not literally, because that would have been very cool and I'd have had more time at home to dwell on my stellar skankiness; it was more of a metaphorical explosion. One of the inner clique of Year Ten was found in the science block loos throwing up her lunch, so we had to have a special assembly about eating disorders and self-cutting and other fun things.

It all fell on deaf ears. Because my school is stuffed full of overachieving girls who try to outdo one another with extra homework assignments, like it's going to impress some stuffy old academic at their Oxbridge interview because they stay up till 2 A.M. every night writing essays on the causes and effects of the Hundred Years War. Occasionally, one of the parents would kick off at a PTA meeting about the school's impossibly high standards and we'd have to troop off to see Ms. Richie "just call me Hazel," the guidance counselor, who'd trot out some well-meaning platitudes about a healthy life/work balance, and it would all blow over.

But not this time. *The Argus* got wind of little Saskia puking up her spaghetti marinara and ran with the headline BULIMIA EPIDEMIC HITS TOP GIRLS' SCHOOL on the front page. A meeting was held, questions were raised, parents were concerned. Bothered.

And Smith *still* hadn't called. It was all I could think about as I sat with Nancy in the canteen at our usual table. I tried to avoid alone time with Nancy on account of pretty much hating her guts, but Ella and Dot had some science project to finish, so here we were.

I pushed a twirl of pasta around my plate, trying to avoid the congealing cheese sauce as Nancy cast dark looks at the Year Ten bulimics who were all not eating their chicken salad, hold the dressing.

"It's all their fault," she said savagely. "Last night . . . God, last night, they came in from the meeting and it was all, like, are you depressed? You're looking pale, do you have an eating disorder? Did your dad go?"

I glanced up from my farfalle Alfredo, or whatever it had been in a previous life. "He had some reception to go to at the University. 'Sides, he never goes to school meetings because he despises Mrs. Greenwood ever since she took Classics off the syllabus."

Nancy snorted dismissively. "Whatever. Your dad is so weird."

"'Studying Euripides, Sophocles, et al, is essential to any well-rounded course of education,'" I parroted. "'Platonic theory is the tenet of every civilized society.'"

"You need to come with subtitles. But anyway, this meeting turned into a huge shitstorm and Hazel's been sacked and they've got some new tree-hugger coming in."

I shoved my plate away and leaned my elbows on the table. "Why do you care?"

"Letters are being sent, we've all got to have a one-on-one with the new guidance counselor, and there's this big ruckus that it will go down on our permanent record so it can and will be used against us on our University applications."

"That's crap," I said, rolling my eyes. "It's like this whole data protection thingy—and they can't force you to see a counselor if you don't want to."

"Yeah, they can, unless you have a note from your parents," Nancy insisted, giving me a wicked grin. "Heads are gonna roll, Is. Bet the new counselor can't wait to get her hot little hands on you, you poor, motherless thing, you."

I stuck my tongue out at her. "Piss off. No way am I going to a guidance counselor. One upside to having a freak as a father."

"We'll see," Nancy said slyly, and then gave an exasperated groan as I pulled out my phone and looked at the screen to see if it had rung in the three minutes since I'd last checked, even though it had been silent and Smith didn't have my number, anyway.

"You expecting a call?"

I shoved the phone back in my pocket. "No," I said shortly. "We should probably get to French. Did you even understand any of the homework?"

"Don't change the subject. It's that boy, isn't it? The drunk one with the squishy face from the party."

It was on the tip of my tongue to defend Smith and his decidedly non-squishy face, but I've known Nancy long enough not to get dragged under. "Him?" I asked, wrinkling my nose like the very thought filled me with abject disgust. "Hardly. Just checking it was switched on."

"If you say so," she hissed. "Not like you'd *want* to see that fugly creep again anyway, would you?"

Nancy is such an evil troll—it's been a long and illustrious career. Before I let her and Ella hang with me and Dot, they'd been cast out of every clique in school with their double-crossing, backstabbing tricks. I know Nancy doesn't think I should be the boss of her and really, I preferred it when lunch meant that Dot and I could just tune out everyone for one sweet hour. I don't see what the big deal is about social interaction.

"Oh, come on, Is. Move that fat arse of yours or we'll be late for French," Nancy snapped, jumping to her feet and looking at her watch pointedly.

God, I *loathe* her.

Felix had his after-school fencing club because poking people with a pointy stick is such a healthy hobby for a nine-year-old with violent tendencies. But it meant I'd have the house to myself so I could *69 to my heart's content and telepathically will the phone to ring, even though it wouldn't because Smith was a beautiful loser who obviously wanted nothing else to do with the skeevy girl who'd had sex with him as if it was a free gift that came with the loan of an iPod.

But what do you know? The little red light on the answer-phone was bleeping merrily away as if it had all sorts of secrets it couldn't wait to share. I didn't even take off my jacket before jabbing at the "play" button.

"Hey, this is a message for . . ."

"Isabel! I've had a very odd letter from your school."

". . . Isabel. Um, it's Smith here. Hi. How have you been . . . ?"

Now I was stabbing at the "off" button frantically before Smith could go into details of . . . it really didn't bear thinking about.

I whirled around to face Dad's horrified expression. "I take it that was your friend from the other night," he said sourly. "I made it perfectly clear that you weren't to have any contact with him."

"You said that I wasn't to see him, so it wasn't like I could go around there and tell him never to call me again," I snapped, and ha! Try and wriggle out of that watertight logic.

"I don't want people calling at all hours of the day and night," he fussed. "It's why you have a mobile. Not that you're going to stay in touch with him."

"Why? Have we turned Amish? Am I not allowed to have friends who are boys all of a sudden?"

He frowned and rubbed the bridge of his nose in exactly the same way that he does when he's grading a particularly imbecilic dissertation. "You're not allowed to have friends of either sex who think it's a wonderful idea to keep you out until three in the morning."

"I fell asleep!"

"So you keep saying in that extremely querulous tone. It's getting very tiresome." He waved a piece of paper at me. "Could we move on to something new, or do you have a few more phone messages from irresponsible young men to listen to?"

I gave the phone a longing look. "Okay," I said unwillingly. "My, that's an interesting letter in your hand, and from the school you say?"

"A little less sarcasm, please." I guess he was worried that I was infringing on his copyright. "It appears that 'there's grave cause for concern about certain elements among the student body who have been exhibiting symptoms of stress and depression.' Anything you'd like to tell me, Isabel?"

He almost looked disappointed that I wasn't speaking in tongues, frothing at the mouth, and displaying other symptoms of stress and depression.

"No," I barked, my hands clenching into fists, which I hid behind my back. "You know what the place is like. Everyone's like, 'Ooh, I'm so depressed because I'm not allowed another Louis Vuitton bag, which is like only big enough to hold a lipstick, and I'm going to write really shit poetry and post it on the Web.'"

I was so on a roll. I hadn't even realized how much I hated my school and all the tragic little girls who went there until I opened my mouth and all this vitriol came pouring out.

"And they have half a salad for lunch because they think it's really glamorous to have an eating disorder, and they pretend to carve boys' names into their arms with their compasses during geometry so they have these barely-there scratches, and then they go on and on about self-cutting like it's a worthwhile pastime . . ."

To say that Dad looked astonished would have been an understatement on the same level as saying that Renée Zellweger is the most annoying woman alive. His body was statue still, like I'd shocked him into immobility, apart from his left eyebrow, which was stuck somewhere up around his forehead. BUT I STILL COULDN'T SHUT UP!

"... such a bunch of drama junkies," I spluttered, wiping my eyes furiously when I felt them start to fill up, then staring him down once I was defiantly tear-free. "If something bad happened, something really terrible came along and tore them into tiny pieces then they'd ... they'd know that depressed—it's just this word invented by other people that doesn't even come halfway to describing how you actually feel."

Immediately, I wanted to gather up everything I'd just said and stuff it back into my mouth. But once you've said stuff, you can't unsay it. Your words are out there, aren't they? Buzzing around in the quiet of the room so you can hear them echoing back at you, and all he could do was just stand there, and I had this horrible feeling that the anguished expression on his face was because he agreed with everything I'd said.

Then he straightened out the creased piece of paper that he'd crumpled into a little ball and looked at it again. "They have a new guidance counselor," he said tonelessly, and I waited for him to go into his own rant about self-indulgent, middle-class parents treating therapy as another designer accessory. It didn't happen. "I'm booking you an appointment as soon as possible."

There was a lot of door slamming after that. Plus swearing. The swearing was my contribution to the discussion about how I wasn't going to see any counselor. Period. Full stop. End of discussion. Fuck you, you patronizing bastard.

He shouted. No, he roared, his face an angry red contortion of open mouth and narrowed eyes. Then he smashed a glass down so heavily on the draining board that it shattered and he cut his hand, and I was glad. I was also glad that he couldn't do the cool, sarcastic thing anymore. That he wasn't superior to the rest of us. He was just as messed up.

The only thing that stopped The Biggest Row We've Ever Had Since the Day of the Funeral™ was Felix leaning on the doorbell. Which was my cue to storm upstairs and slam my bedroom door so hard that the coat hook fell off.

I stayed up there for hours, occasionally putting my ear to the door to see if the coast was clear enough to slink downstairs and get to the answerphone. I wouldn't have put it past Dad to erase the message in a fit of pique.

But eventually, I had to emerge because my bloody allowance was contingent on feeding other people. While the grill was heating up, and I'd made sure that Dad was sulking in his study and, no doubt, getting me measured up for a straitjacket, I marched into the lounge with pen and paper and played back the message to the accompaniment of Felix trying to work my very last nerve.

"Oh, our little girl's becoming a woman," he taunted as we both listened to Smith's garbled explanation for his phone silence, which seemed to involve a trip home to pick up some mystery object.

"Shut up, or I'll spit on your lamb cutlets," I snarled, while I tried to scribble down the number, pausing the machine to swipe ineffectually at Felix's hand, which was ghosting toward my arm in a Chinese burnlike motion. "And stop trying to attack me. Jesus! What is wrong with you?"

"'Ooh, Smith, I love you, I want to have your babies,'" Felix crooned in a high-pitched falsetto that didn't sound anything like me.

I really wanted to listen to the message again and again, especially the bit at the end where Smith gave this throaty chuckle and said, "So, I really hope you're going to give me a call even if you're being monosyllabic 'cause, well, I'd like to see you again," but it was impossible because Felix had this shit-eating grin on his smug little face and was making kissing noises.

After dinner, which was eaten in stony silence, and ten minutes of cajoling and threats to get Felix to load the dishwasher, I was finally free to curl up on my bed and tap in the number, which seemed to have taken forever to get.

Smith answered the phone on the first ring with a sleepy, "Hey?"

"It's Isabel."

I could hear a rustling noise like he was sitting up, and then his voice, more alert, and maybe I was imagining that he sounded pleased to hear from me. "Oh, hey! Hey. How are you?"

"I'm okay. Got your message—well, obviously, I got your message, otherwise I wouldn't have been able to call you." I smacked myself on the forehead for pointing out the painfully obvious.

"And now I've got your number so we shouldn't have any more communication problems," he said smoothly. "You missed me, then?"

I wasn't expecting that, and it seemed to violate some kind of relationship etiquette, like we weren't in a place to miss each other yet.

"I guess," I ventured after a moment. "So . . . you went home?"

"Yeah, had to go back to Southport and pick up, well, something. It's a surprise."

"What kind of a surprise?" He sniggered softly and I rushed on. "Don't you dare say that if you told me, it wouldn't be a surprise anymore. That's so predictable."

"Well, it wouldn't! And it's the kind of surprise that's more show than tell," he said.

My mind flashed on all sorts of possibilities, most of them with at least a 15 certificate. "I hate surprises. They usually turn out to be the bad kind."

"Oh, this is the good kind, I promise," he purred in a way that did nothing to revise my earlier opinion.

I made a skeptical little grunting noise, which was deeply unattractive, and I heard him shift again.

"It's nothing scary. And I can put you out of your misery . . . let's see, what are you doing tomorrow?"

Being dragged into school by my overbearing father to see a guidance counselor, which had been the last threat hissed at me before I was uncharacteristically saved by Felix.

"Tomorrow's kinda difficult. Maybe the day after, Saturday?" And that seemed like I was being really pushy. It was the weekend and he probably had a ton of exciting things to do with his rock 'n' roll friends instead of hanging out with me.

"Saturday's good," he said immediately. "We can make a day of it, and I'll have you back home before you turn into a pumpkin. Did you get a major bollocking the other night?"

"I'm still dealing with the fallout," I muttered.

"I'm sorry. Way to get off on the wrong foot with your dad."

And there he went again, acting like, I don't know, he was my boyfriend or something. "All you have to do is breathe around him and you get off on the wrong foot with my dad. It's a whole thing—we don't get on." There was nothing else to say. I traced a pattern on the quilt with my finger. "So . . . Saturday? Shall I come around to you?"

Smith gave another laugh. "Anything to avoid your dad! See you at eleven?"

I could feel my mouth curving into a smile. It felt strange and unusual. "Eleven, cool."

"Good," he said abruptly. "Look I have to go so I'll see you then."

And before I could tie myself up in knots worrying about whether I should say good-bye and who was going to hang up first, there was a gentle click and he was gone.

13

I don't think there are many things more humiliating than being frog-marched down the school corridor by your father who likes to really rack up the torment by barking at the top of his voice, "Stop dawdling Isabel, I don't have all day," and giving me a not at all gentle shove at the precise moment that we passed a gaggle of Year Thirteens, who—judging by their titters—were going to have my shame broadcast around the school before the first bell.

I was formulating a cunning plan to lead him around to the back of the art block and hit him over the head with an easel when we bumped into Mrs. Greenwood, who exchanged icy greetings with dad. If they'd been two dogs they'd have been straining at their leads and trying to bite each other.

"Isabel seems to be experiencing some difficulty in finding the guidance counselor's office," he gritted out. "We must have been up and down this particular corridor at least three times."

Mrs. Greenwood patted me on the shoulder and bared her teeth in what she fancied was a comforting smile. "I'm sure Isabel's looking forward to her first session." She gave a braying laugh. "I wish I had the luxury of sitting down and talking about myself for an hour."

Dad and I shared a rare and beautiful moment of bonding as we stared at each other in disbelief. "Indeed," he said heavily, and then he froze her on the spot with his iciest look, until she gave an uncomfortable wriggle.

"It's just a little further down and the last door on your left," she said at last. "Mrs. Benson is very experienced. I'm sure she and Isabel will get on wonderfully." And on that note of hope in the face of overwhelming odds, she all but scurried off. Sometimes having my father around can be *helpful*.

"I can take it from here," I assured him, trying to hurry off, but his long legs caught up with me in no time.

"I'll just see you to the door," he insisted. "And introduce myself to Mrs. Benson. She really did seem very nice on the phone," he added, as if that made the slightest bit of difference.

Mrs. Benson wasn't very nice. She was every cliché of a guidance counselor rolled into one. She opened the door after Dad's peremptory knock and I was confronted with the poster girl for tie-dye. Or the poster middle-aged woman for tie-dye. She was wearing these revolting dung-colored trousers and a shirt that looked like an explosion in a paint factory. The ensemble was accessorized with these hokey wooden beads that people in the Third World got paid about five acorns an hour to make for overprivileged women who think they're all down with fair trade. Did I mention the hair? It was the exact same shade of orange as this old ginger cat we used to have. It had looked much better on the cat.

She stared at me for a while and I was sure she was trying to psych me out with all the eye contact, so I just raised my chin and held her gaze until she suddenly held out her arms to me and said breathlessly, "Isabel, welcome. Please call me Claire."

That's what I hate about these people. Like I was going to let her hug me.

Now he'd delivered me in one piece, Dad couldn't get out of there fast enough. He gave me another fierce poke in the direction of Claire's outstretched arms. "Off you go," he said without a shred of sympathy, even though I'd caught the way he'd shuddered when he'd clocked her hippy hangover ensemble. "I'm sure you're going to have a very . . . useful chat." And he was gone in a whirl of charcoal wool.

I sidestepped Claire. "Would you like a cup of tea?" she asked me in this carefully modulated voice, as if I was going to get skittish from any high-pitched noises.

I shook my head. I wasn't going to make this easy for her. She was getting paid to do this, I wasn't.

"I have some lovely homemade black currant cordial if you'd prefer," she said brightly, and beamed at me. "And some oatmeal and raisin cookies."

I shook my head again. Even though there hadn't been time for breakfast and I was so hungry that I would have eaten the rattan furniture, given half the chance.

I had to sit in this chair opposite her. There was a low table between us, with a box of tissues perched on it because all these people ever want to do is to see you cry. I think they must be on commission from Kleenex or something.

In the end, she had to do all the talking while I just sat there and stared at the Klimt print behind her.

"I can see from your school records that you're a very bright girl," she said, shuffling all the colored bits of paper that were my school career. "There was even some discussion of condensing your A-levels into one year last term, but your parents were concerned about you being so much younger than the rest of the class. How did you feel about that?"

I shrugged because when in doubt, shrug. And I tried to drown out the memory of all the screaming rows from last year about how pushing me up to the next class would just make me even more bratty.

Claire gave a polite little cough to let me know that she didn't appreciate my glassy-eyed trip down memory lane, and I fixed my gaze back on her horrible ankh pendant.

"Gifted children can find it very difficult to connect with people their own age," she continued, pausing like she expected me to get all riled up when she called me a child. "I notice that you don't participate in any extracurricular activities, though Mr. Wells says you're an excellent writer. Have you thought about joining the school paper?"

I shook my head because it seemed rude not to, but restrained myself from telling her that the school paper was run by a bunch of journalist wannabes who thought that exciting editorials about whether low-carb options should be available in the canteen would get them an internship on *Vogue*.

But all this interest in my ginormous brain was just softening me up. Trying to break down my defenses so that she could start in on all the juicy stuff.

"I talked to your father last night, Isabel. He's very worried about you. Everyone is. I can't imagine how you must feel, losing your mother so suddenly. Having her taken away at a time in your life when you need her so much. I know there's been a lot of anger," she said at last. "A lot of anger and loss and pain. You're hurting, aren't you, Isabel?"

She was starting to really piss me off. But shouting and

screaming and saying "fuck" a lot doesn't really get your point across. Sometimes silence is the most violent option to choose. It makes people uncomfortable, which is, like, my superpower or something.

But only a direct hit from a weapon of mass destruction would have paused Claire's yapping for a nanosecond. "There's no right or wrong way to grieve," she told me, like I hadn't heard that a thousand times from well-meaning relatives and the stupid books they'd thrust at me. "Sometimes you want to shut down emotionally because the things you're feeling are overwhelming."

She finally shut up and decided to try and do the mind-meld thing by staring into my eyes. I'm sure she thought she was being perceptive and that she was looking deep into my soul, but I was actually counting down from one thousand, backward.

"Do you want to tell me how you felt when your mother died?"

"No." Her eyes opened wide, and I realized I'd said it out loud. "No," I repeated. "I don't want to tell you anything. I'm not anorexic. I don't cut myself. I'm not suffering from post-traumatic stress syndrome. I'm a straight-A student. That's it. That's all you need to know, because I'm not coming back. And even if Mrs. Greenwood and my dad tie me to this chair every Friday morning, they can't force me to open my mouth and make me talk to you, so I suggest you tell them that and spare us all the bother."

And I stood up, calmly hitched my bag over my shoulder, and walked out while she bleated about how we still had twenty minutes left.

14

I could smell the damp earth of autumn just starting to creep in as I strolled over to Kemp Town. The sun wasn't really warming anything and there was a stiff breeze, which made me glad that I'd invested in a pair of red woolly tights, which went perfectly with her black dress. Was it creepy to walk around in a dead person's clothes? And would it be weird if I had sex with Smith again and he unbuttoned my dress, which used to belong to my dead mother?

And just as his name popped into my head, my phone started to ring as I turned the corner into Edward Street.

"I'm only five minutes late," I said by way of a greeting. "I didn't have a thing to wear, you can fill in the rest yourself."

"And good morning to you, too," he said silkily. "How far away are you? You sound out of breath."

"Hill," I explained shortly. "I'm just getting to the bottom of your street."

And there he was, phone to his ear and waving to me. I stretched out my fingers to show willing and switched off my phone. It was far too much like a dumb rom-com cliché to walk toward him while we were talking on our phones. Didn't run into his arms, either, I just sent a silent prayer to whichever genius had invented sunglasses and took what felt like forever to get to his side.

"Hey," I muttered, but the sound never left my mouth because his lips were on mine and then gone before I had time to register the baby brush of his kiss.

He looked different—twitchy and springy, like Felix when he's had too much sugar, but that wasn't it.

"You've cut all your hair off!" I gasped, reaching up my hand to scrub at the dark brown fuzz. It was soft but bristly at the same time, and he bent his head as I rubbed my fingers down toward the back of his neck and then snatched them away because . . . well, it was like tickling a dog behind his ears. Any second now, his foot would start thumping against the pavement in ecstasy.

Smith gave me an arch look. "I wouldn't have had you down for public displays of affection."

Once again I'd never been gladder of the masking effects of sunglasses, though it was a pity they didn't cover my entire face. "I wasn't being affectionate. I just wanted to . . . did you know you have this bony bit at the back of your skull? It looks majorly weird."

"Ah, there's the Isabel I know and love." Smith grinned and it was taut as cheese wire, just so I didn't get the wrong impression about him mentioning the L word.

"So your new hairdo, is that the big surprise?"

He shook his shorn head and stepped to the left with a grandiose sweep of his arm, which he couldn't quite get away with. He'd been blocking my view of the most dilapidated excuse for a car I'd ever seen.

It had been a mustard color in a previous life, but now it was hard to see where the rust ended and the car began. I checked to see if it actually had wheels because there was a good chance it was mounted on bricks. In fact, there was a good chance it would get towed away before the end of the weekend.

"It's cool," I said brightly. My enthusiasm was as rusty as the hood. "It's really cool. Really, really cool."

"You think it's lame," he said flatly, as if what I thought was suddenly his new criteria for whether stuff was good or not.

"I don't! I like it. It's very quirky." I pounced on the word triumphantly. "And the leopard skin steering-wheel cover is a nice ironic touch. It is ironic, I hope?"

"A hundred percent ironic," Smith assured me gravely. "And a hundred percent roadworthy."

I must have looked pretty doubtful because he gave me another reproachful look. "I'd already decided that if you were more or less pleasant, I'd take you out for a drive," Smith said, fishing the keys out of his pocket and dangling them from one finger.

"And have I been?" I loved the way he totally called me on my bullshit. Didn't try and understand me; I just was, and he let me know it.

"Kinda fifty-fifty," he decided, unlocking the passenger door and holding it open so I could gingerly climb in.

I watched Smith walk around, pausing to stroke the hood in this caress-y way that would have got his face slapped if the car had suddenly turned into a girl. I shifted onto one buttock to avoid the spring that was digging into me and tried to take little breaths so I didn't get asphyxiated by the smell of mildew.

"For God's sake, do you have to be so rough with it?" Smith yelped when he finally got in to find me wrestling with one of the door levers, which I fervently hoped would open one of the windows.

He leaned over me so I could smell the pine-fresh, clean boyness of him, which was far more pleasing to my olfactory nerves. His arm brushed against my breasts and I could feel my face turn red as I stuck my head out of the now open window.

"So, where do you want to go?" he asked me, turning the key in the ignition—and what do you know? It actually started first time.

"Surprise me again," I said, leaning back in the seat and inhaling great whiffs of fresh air.

We drove along the coast road in silence. I liked watching him drive. Liked watching the muscles in his arm flex as he shifted the gear. Liked the little put-put sound of the car climbing up the cliffs. I even liked hearing Smith mutter and swear under his breath about the ineptitude of every driver on the road who wasn't him.

We'd been going for about an hour and I was lulled into this almost doze, when I recognized the smooth grass lawns and the splendidly maintained, brilliantly white rain shelters along the Promenade.

"Eastbourne?" I spluttered.

"Eastbourne," he echoed with a decisive nod of his head, a smile ghosting across his face.

"This is where old people come to die." As far as the eye could see were blue rinses and walkers, blazers, and thermos flasks as hordes of septuagenarians slowly ambled along. Then something else occurred to me. "What's the collective noun for old people, anyway? A flock of geriatrics? They probably can't flock too well, what with the arthritis. A pride of geriatrics?

Probably more like it, all banging on about how they fought in the war and . . ."

Smith laughed. And it was a proper laugh, not his usual snide chuckle. "There's always something going on in there, isn't there?" He took his hand off the wheel so he could tap a finger against my temple, stroking the tiny dent in the bone where Felix had thrown a cricket bat at me during his most infamous snit.

I sighed because he didn't know the half of it. He didn't even know, like, the tenth of it. "Oh, hey! Mini golf! I love mini golf!"

And I'd crossed the line where I couldn't or didn't want to be cool anymore. Not for that afternoon, anyway.

So we sat on a bench and looked out to sea and talked to Ida and George, who were visiting from Nantwich and celebrating their golden wedding anniversary. I even let Smith feed me chips so soaked in salt and vinegar that they made my mouth sting, then let him kiss it better before I totally kicked his arse at mini golf. I even did my victory dance with the put. Or a modified version of it that mainly involved holding it high above my head and slowly twirling around, while shouting at him: "No! I'm not just the winner. I'm the outright winner, *say it!*"

He refused, shaking his head and brandishing his golf club at me. "God, I've created a monster. I'm never playing anything competitive with you again. I bet you're even worse at Scrabble. You're one of those really annoying people who puts down like, three tiles and makes four different words and never opens up the board?" he teased, swinging my hand before wrapping his arm around my shoulder as we walked back to the car.

"Pretty much, and you don't even want to begin to know what I'm like when it comes to Monopoly."

"I'm making a mental note to hide all board games from you."

I shivered slightly because of the breeze coming off the sea. Or maybe it was because this flirty banter was just tripping from my mouth and it made me feel like I was walking around naked. That would be naked and completely exposed, if you really wanted to work the metaphor.

"You're cold," he stated, linking his fingers through mine. "Actually, I'm upgrading that to frozen. You should have said something."

"I'm fine." And I was. It's funny but I'm cold a lot now. I looked it up on the Internet, and it's another amusing by-product of my fun lack of sleep, along with a faint feeling of nausea most of the time.

"Is that fine as in 'I'm really trying not to make a fuss because I've been on my best behavior all day and I don't want to jinx it?' Or are you going all monosyllabic because you've used up your entire word quota for the week?"

I gave him a significant look from under my lashes, which he met without flinching.

"Okay, I'm getting chilly," I conceded, and I had a sudden brain blip as an image flashed up of me curled around him, under the funky-smelling covers of his bed. Then I wouldn't be tired or cold.

"See, that wasn't so difficult," Smith said approvingly. "You're really coming along nicely."

"Don't fucking talk about me like I'm some pet project you've got on the go, like growing watercress or . . . I don't know, studying the life cycle of a stickleback."

As he unlocked my door I noticed that a seagull had, well,

relieved itself on the roof, but I didn't have the heart to tell Smith because he was talking. Saying words about me that if it had been anyone else, I'd have taken their head clean off their neck.

"Don't you get it yet, Isabel? You *are* my pet project," he said without a shred of humor, hands on either side of my shoulders as I leaned against the car and found myself unable to look away from his intense, blue stare. "You can be as pissy and bitchy and unpleasant as you want, but it doesn't matter. I'm so onto you."

"Onto me?" I croaked and didn't that turn of phrase conjure up all sorts of intriguing thoughts?

"Yeah. Your whole push me/pull me routine is really textbook," he drawled. "You think that if you're mean, I'll just run true to type and tell you to fuck off. And then you can feel all validated and have no excuse to actually, y'know, interact and have human emotions because you're so sure that every other person in the world is a useless, uncaring bastard and you have proof."

"I don't think that," I began angrily. "It's just people are . . ."

"Shut up," he said sweetly, kissing me slowly to take the bite out of his words. "Even you can't keep up the bitch goddess act forever, this afternoon being a case in point," he murmured against my lips, before pushing me gently into the car.

And it wasn't true, what he said. Not really. It wasn't that I was testing anyone. I didn't need to, because I'd already given up on people as a lost cause. They all let you down in the end, whether they meant to or not. Even Smith would in the end. But right now, he was rummaging on the backseat for a rug, which he tucked around me.

"Shall we go back to my place so I can take your clothes off?" he asked conversationally.

I forced myself to stay calm and serene. "Sounds like a plan," I said in a steady voice.

As soon as we got inside the door, he was tugging me up the stairs, even though a sharp voice called from the living room, "Smith! Aren't you going to introduce us to your little friend?"

I had a vague impression of a mop of white-blonde hair and a mocking smile, but I was still in a state of forward motion as Smith snapped out, "Piss off, Jane."

He rolled his eyes at me as he pulled me across the landing. "You can meet her some other time. Though there could be a copyright issue on the whole bitch thing."

"It's not very nice to call me a bitch when you want to"—I took a deep breath— "have sex with me."

"What do you want me to call you? Darling? Sweetheart? Cutie?" he purred, yanking me into his room and kicking the door shut.

"You could call me Isabel," I suggested dryly, and he pressed me up against the wall and murmured my name before he kissed me.

And then I didn't have to think about anything anymore. It was all feeling. So I just became this creature made up entirely of all these separate sensations: the scrape of Smith's teeth dragging against my bottom lip, his warm hands on my cold skin, the edge of the bed hitting the back of my knees as he danced me across the room, and then the curious, clumsy grace of *it*. Of how it turns you inside out and back to front so you say things that you think you'd never ever say and your body twists into shapes that shouldn't be possible and your eyes are screwed tight shut . . .

"Hey, hey, Isabel," he said to me in a voice that was impossibly tender. "C'mon, open your eyes."

I peeled my eyelids back and stared blearily up at him, his face going fuzzy around the edges as he leaned forward and kissed me, sweetly, softly like I wasn't a girl who'd just done what I did but as if I was someone he walked home from school every day and never let him get past first base.

And I was learning fast that what you said in these moments didn't count and couldn't be thrown back at you later on. "Hold me," I pleaded, and he was already holding me but he wriggled one hand free so he could brush the hair back from my face, and it was too much effort to keep my eyes open.

He said things, too. Things I'm sure he'd never admit to under the toughest interrogation, and I drifted off to sleep with his voice in my ear, soothing, cooing, so loving . . .

When I woke up he was still holding me, dotting kisses along my neck. I lay there for a minute or two, wondering why I wasn't freaking about being butt naked in bed with someone equally naked pressed against me.

"I know you're awake," he rumbled in my ear. "You make these weird little whuffly noises when you're asleep."

"I do not," I said automatically, and carefully stretched out my legs, which had been tangled with his. "What time is it?"

"Don't worry, it's not even eight."

I sighed a little because really, it was so nice and I could have just gone back to sleep and stayed there till morning, apart from the fact that I really needed to pee and my throat was parched.

"Don't have to be back till eleven, maybe twelve," I mused. "It *is* Saturday night."

"Wish you could stay," he said, tracing a line down my spine, and I squirmed away because it tickled, then rolled onto my back, dragging the covers up and clamping them under my arms. "I might . . . I guess I could phone home and see if it would be okay." I hesitated because he might have just said it to be polite.

But Smith was nodding his head and I missed his rumpled, pillow-tossed hair already. "It's not like you'd have to say what you were really up to."

"On one condition, though." I smiled and his eyebrows were already shooting up in expectation of whatever he thought I was going to say. Not like he was even close. "Make me a cup of tea. Milk and two sugars, please."

The second he was out of the door, after pulling on his jeans and grumbling about how I was taking him for granted, I shot out of bed, grabbed something T-shirty from the floor, and hauled it on before I dashed into the hall and prayed that the bathroom was the first door I tried.

I peed for England and then, because I'm stupid and sixteen and not anywhere near blasé, I had the quickest shower humanly possible.

By the time Smith shouldered open the door with two steaming mugs in his hand, I was perched on the bed, still slightly damp and about to lie through my teeth.

"Hey, it's me," I said when Dad answered the phone. "How are you?" Then I winced because way to act suspicious. I never asked how he was.

"I'm fine, Isabel," he said crisply to let me know that he was already on to me. "And how are you?"

"I'm okay."

Smith set a mug down on the nightstand next to me and hovered awkwardly. I made fluttery gestures with my hand to let him know it was all right and realized that Dad wasn't saying anything.

Usually I make him speak first, just for the small amount of satisfaction it brings me, but it didn't seem appropriate when I was about to infringe on at least ten of his rules.

"So, anyway, I'm at Dot's and I was thinking about staying the night." Not a question, just putting the facts, or the kind of facts, out there and seeing what he did with them.

"Really?" I heard the clink of a glass in the background and then his voice clearer than before. "You want to sleep over?"

"Yeah. At Dot's, because we've just got some DVDs out and we were going to phone for pizza and it's getting late . . ."

"Forgive me but I find it extremely curious that you're expressing such a fervent desire to have a *slumber* party." His voice curdled on the last two words.

"Sleepover," I corrected him politely.

"And will there be boys at this DVD-watching, crashing-out fest?"

"*What?* No!" I held the phone away from my ear and shook it. Then I lowered my voice. "Felix stays over at his friends' all the time and you don't give him the third degree about whether they're going to pool their pocket money for a stripper."

"You're hiring a stripper?" he spluttered. "Well, then I insist that you come home immediately."

"Oh, my God . . ." I started, and then stopped because there were no words.

"I'm joking, Isabel," he said, and he sounded like he used to. "I am capable of doing that sometimes."

Smith turned around and grinned at me, holding up a Broken Social Scene CD and waiting for my nod of approval.

"Well, I'll be home by lunchtime. There's some shepherd's pie in the fridge, just take the tin foil off and heat the oven on five for about twenty minutes, and then it should take about . . ."

"I'm quite capable of heating up some dinner," he said in that same jovial voice. "Have a good time. Please don't get drunk or smoke or take drugs or do anything foolish. Not until you're at least thirty."

It was far too late for that, and I shifted uncomfortably on the bed that I'd had sex on and wished that he wasn't being so fucking nice when I had never deserved it less.

" 'Kay. Well, I'll see you, then. Remember to turn the oven off and leave the dish to soak, otherwise . . ."

"Get off the bloody phone and go and watch your DVDs. Good night, Belle," he added before he hung up, and it was a slip of the tongue, just an echo of the way we'd been and what he'd used to call me that made me sit there, clutching the phone and feeling like this utterly worthless scrap of humanity.

"You okay?" Smith asked as "Capture the Flag" started to play.

I picked up my tea and pasted on my Sunday best smile. "Peachy."

He crouched down in front of me. "So your mum's not around, then?"

I didn't think he was prying . . . much. It was just a natural conclusion to draw from my side of the phone call. "I can't talk about it," I said in a tiny voice.

"But . . ."

"I can't," I repeated and I ran the flat of my hand over the knobbly ridge of bone at the back of his skull because he was the one thing in my life that had nothing to do with her and I wanted to keep it that way. "And thanks for the tea."

"Way to change the subject," he muttered under his breath, but when he lifted his head, his smile glittered. "So I've got you for a whole sixteen and a half hours?"

"Yeah. Wanna play some Scrabble?"

"The others have gone to this bar, do you wanna meet up with them?" he asked, twisting around to snatch his cigarettes up so he couldn't see the face I just pulled. Molly was all right. In fact, Molly was a source of endless fascination to me, but Jane seemed like she was a bitch from way back.

"We could stay in," I said, pulling his T-shirt down over the large expanse of thigh I was showing.

"We should go out," Smith argued. "It will be fun."

And I was about to argue about just how much fun it wouldn't be when he bent his head and kissed my knee as if it was the most natural thing in the world.

It was almost as if Smith has sprinkled me with some of his own supply of hipster dust, so when we strode into Alicats, not one person questioned my right to be there, even though I hadn't had time to do anything more transformational than slick on some lip gloss and smooth down the sticky-out bits of hair that were starting to be the bane of my freaking life.

And because Smith had paid for everything during our Eastbourne adventure (and that was an oxymoron if ever there was one), I brandished a tenner at him. "I'll pay for the drinks if you go to the bar and get them."

He closed my fist around the note. "I'll get them. You're not working."

"Neither are you," I pointed out, standing on tiptoe so he

could hear me and shoving the money back at him. "Vodka and Diet Coke, please."

"I'm not planning on holding your head while you puke, just so you know," Smith said sternly as he led me through the sweaty crowd to the bar.

"Well, I'm not planning on puking, so that works out really well."

We were still arguing about just how many drinks it took for me to reach my cut-off point when I saw we were heading for the dingiest corner of the bar and it was déjà ewww all over again . . . because Smith's friends? Not the most user-friendly gang in town. Then Smith slid his arm around my waist and one of the girls looked up and smiled.

"Isabel! I'll budge up and you can sit here," Molly said, scooching over and patting the seat invitingly. "Don't worry, Smith, most of your secrets are safe with me. Well, apart from the time you tried to snog my cat for a bet."

I smirked at him. "Very smooth."

"Go and sit down," he said, pushing me in her direction. "I just want to say hello to someone. Molly's sweet, she'll look after you."

And Molly was sweet, or else she just really knew how to fake it as she gave me a fleeting hug and pulled me down next to her, nudging the girl on her other side who was smooching the face off the guy whose lap she was on.

"Jane," she shouted. "This is Isabel. Smith's Isabel."

Jane's head shot up and she pinned me with the deadliest stare I'd seen in at least a week. "Ah, Smith's Isabel," she said knowingly. "And not any of the other Isabels we know. Hey, kid."

"Hey," I said back because she was far too intimidating to call on the whole "kid" thing. I poked at the ice cubes in my drink with the end of my straw, but when I decided to chance looking up she was still eyeing me.

"So just how old are you, anyway?" she asked belligerently. "'Cause I didn't realize that our Smith had taken to loitering around the nursery school gates."

"I'm eighteen," I bit out, fumbling for my cigarettes to give me something to do with my hands and because if I was smoking, I was sophisticated and cool. Obviously. Or else, puffing my way to emphysema in the mistaken belief that I appeared to be sophisticated and cool. It was a judgment call.

"Jane's being tested for Tourette's syndrome," Molly said soothingly. "It's the only explanation we can find as to why she never thinks before she opens her mouth."

"Oh, whatever, Moll," Jane snapped. "And if she's eighteen then I'm the fricking queen of England."

"Give us another kiss, Your Majesty," said the guy she was sitting on, and she wriggled happily and flung her arm around his neck. He was seriously not ex-rock star boyfriend material. If you were being kind you'd call him homely. If you weren't being kind you'd call him a ginger minger. Then I realized his piggy little eyes were gazing adoringly at her as she ruffled his hair and matched his besotted look with one of her own.

I sat there and smoked my cigarettes while Jane and Molly bickered good-naturedly about whether Seth Cohen had any right to be emo if his parents were so damn rich. It was the kind of easy friendship I'd always dreamed about having if I didn't have only two settings, which were either silent and/or vicious.

Jane was the most beautiful person I'd ever seen in real life.

Model gorgeous. Film-star sexy. It was almost too overwhelming to look at her perfectly symmetrical features; a bee-stung kiss of a mouth, limpid green eyes, the delicate curve of her eyebrows, the sweep of her cheekbones, all topped off with a tiny smudge of nose.

But it was Molly who my eyes kept sliding back to. Not just because she was pretty in this quirky, mischievous way but because she was never still as she laughed and twirled her straw around quick fingers, knees bumping against the edge of the table in time to Ladytron. *"They only want you when you're seventeen, when you're twenty-one, you're no fun,"* she sang, and then laughed at me. "Story of my life, this song." I guess she had charisma or something. Like, when she went to the loo, shoving her way through the clumps of people, it was almost as if she was giving off some kind of chemical or pheromone because people turned to look at her as she brushed past them.

Smith was still someplace else. I craned my neck and saw him talking to a couple of guys over by the entrance. He was jiggling about in time to the music even though he really couldn't dance for shit.

And it was easy to get more and more mopey as I sat there surrounded by people who were so adept at just being themselves, while I had to make such a hash of it.

"Jeez, Isabel, you look like you're about to slit your wrists," Molly said as she climbed over my legs so she could sit back down. "I got you another drink."

"Thanks." I gave her a crooked smile and then sat there, racking my brain for something witty and interesting to say to her that didn't involve lawsuits or ex-boyfriends or . . .

"Do you think the DJ's cute?" she suddenly piped up, and

then pinched my arm as I swiveled my head in the direction of his booth. "Don't look!"

I'd got a glimpse of what seemed to be a standard issue hipster with mop-top hair. "He's okay, I guess."

"He always plays The Hormones. Well, original Hormones." She sniffed. "Do you think that means something deep and significant about his feelings toward me?"

Just how much had she had to drink, anyway? "Well, maybe, or else he just really liked The Hormones when you were still with them."

Molly gurgled with mirth. "I should so get over myself. It's all about me!" She gave me a sly little nudge. "I'm gonna get that printed on a T-shirt."

"Actually it's all about *me*," I countered, because it was, and Molly laughed so hard that she sprayed a very unamused Jane with a mouthful of vodka and cranberry.

"You wanna know the worst piece of advice I ever got?" Molly asked me, once she'd finished snorting. She was pressed up against me, her hot breath hitting the side of my face. I nodded, and she gave me a secretive smile. "The worst advice handed down to me by someone who should have known better was, just be yourself. Like, I could be anything else, huh?"

She glared at me and then shook her head like I wasn't the person she wanted to be glaring at. "Sorry," she muttered, running a hand through her hair. "Vodka makes me maudlin, and then I start remembering all the reasons why my life is so shit sometimes."

I wanted to say something incredibly insightful and empathetic but, as usual, I couldn't think of a single thing. "Vodka . . ." I echoed, staring at my own glass.

"I envy you," she continued. "You haven't had time to fuck things up too badly, and you and Smith are just getting together and that whole start of a relationship is so giddy and you're just, like, completely into that person and everything they say is meaningful or pant-wettingly funny and you feel like you're the only two people in the world and . . ." She tailed off and hugged herself as if she really wanted someone to do it for her. "God, I really miss that."

"It's not like that . . ." I started to say, because what she was describing sounded claustrophobic enough to press down hard on my ribs and choke me, but Smith was winding his way toward us, looking first at me and then at Molly as if we'd had nothing better to do than talk about him the whole time that he was gone. Which, not even.

There was this whole to and fro when he got back of too many people and not enough seats, and I found myself perched on his lap. Molly smirked knowingly, as if she'd just discovered how to split the atom, when Smith wound his arms around me and absentmindedly kissed the back of my neck.

He was always touching me after that. He talked to Molly and Jane and Jane's not very pretty boyfriend, and I tried to listen but mostly I just felt his hands, so very warm, settling on the violin curve of my waist and raising a host of goose bumps as they traced a path along my arms.

Then on the way home, fingers clasped together, lagging behind the others because it was hard to walk fast with my head on his shoulder and that rock-steady arm around me.

By the time we got back to their place, it already smelled of tea and toast, and Smith finally had to let me go so he could eat four pieces with peanut butter and raspberry jam. His teeth crunched into it and I could have snatched it straight out of his mouth I was so hungry, but their kitchen was a cesspool of filth and I'd have probably gone down with one of about a thousand deadly diseases that can happen when soap and water are alien concepts. Just as well they lived in a second-floor flat because otherwise they'd be the party house for a colony of cockroaches.

I lasted say, ooooh, about five seconds before I gingerly opened the cupboard under the sink with my thumb and fore-finger and pulled out a crusted bottle of dishwashing liquid.

"You don't have to do that, Isabel," Smith said through a mouthful of toast as I let the hot water run until it was scalding.

"Yeah, I really do." I sighed feelingly, and I didn't care that the two coolest girls I'd ever met plus an assorted group of people in ironic logo tees and cords were staring at the weird girl doing what looked like a year's worth of washing up, and that was just a conservative estimate.

"She's such a freak," Jane stage-whispered and I heard a slap and an 'Ow!' before Molly stage-whispered back, "Ssssh! She's doing the dishes, just shut up before she changes her mind."

They didn't have pan scourers or a scrubbing brush or a pair of rubber gloves so I was slightly handicapped, but after I'd done the washing up, it seemed kinda silly not to wash down the worktops or wipe the toast crumbs off the table, and by the time I'd finished, it looked better. It was no Flash commercial, but it was clean enough that I could shove two pieces of bread under the grill and not worry about my stomach lining being eaten by unfriendly bacteria.

"I guess I scared everyone off with my mad housekeeping skills," I said to Smith, who was still sitting with his legs outstretched so he didn't get footprints on the newly washed floor.

"Wouldn't say scared." He smiled. "And I think Jane and Molly want to adopt you if you promise to do the washing up every day."

I smiled back. So typical of me that I couldn't make friends by being really good at doing Paris Hilton impersonations or sharing a passion for Bright Eyes. No, I had to do the dishes for them.

"Hey, turn that frown upside down," Smith said, patting his thighs, and if I liked sleeping with him curled around me, I was starting to like sitting on his lap, too. I leaned back against his chest and let him rub little concentric circles on my nape with his thumb.

"I could do your living room next time," I murmured, half to myself. "Before you get rats. Do you, like, ever throw anything away?"

"Housework would ruin my dangerous mystique," he protested, and I snorted inelegantly before I had to get up and rescue my toast, which was just one second away from burning.

The flat was silent as we crept upstairs, holding hands and our shadows on the wall loomed large and long so I couldn't recognize myself. But in Smith's room with the red lightbulb in his bedside lamp turning everything pink, there was nothing to be frightened about.

15

I had eight hours of bone-melting, soft as lace sleep. It was as simple as putting my head on the pillow, dragging Smith's arm around my waist and closing my eyes.

I didn't suddenly get shocked awake by bad dreams that made the sweat drip off me, either. Instead the world came gently into focus, shapes and colors becoming sharper and brighter as I realized that the insistent beeping noise was my mobile phone.

Smith groaned, turned over, and huddled into the duvet as I groped on the floor for my bag and pulled out my furiously shrieking, vibrating phone.

Dot's name was flashing on the screen and my finger hovered over the "off" button until Smith groaned again. "Just answer the bloody thing."

I held it up to my ear cautiously.

"Dot, hi." My perky, "no, you really didn't wake me up" voice needed some work. "Why are you calling me so early?"

"I have to go to church in a minute," she spat, because her parents were freaky religious types who expected her to save her virginity for her wedding night. Double whatever. "I'm in such a state. I need your Art History notes, so I'm going to come over now."

It was a bad dream. Just had to be. Because I was sitting bolt upright in bed, waiting for the sweat to pop out any minute. "No! You can't. No. Can you borrow someone else's?"

Cue sorrowful snuffles and even without the puppy-dog eyes that usually went with them, I was squirming under the covers. "I can't," she whined. "Nancy and Ella are, like, terminally stupid and they're not doing Art History. You're it, Is. Please! You're meant to be my friend, and if I don't get those notes I can't do my essay. So I'll be around in ten minutes."

There was no reasoning with Dot when she was getting hysterical. "You can't," I whimpered, trying to think of an excuse that would stop her turning up on my doorstep when Smith snuck his head out from under the quilt.

"Do you have to talk so loud?" he demanded plaintively. "This is meant to be the day of rest."

"Ssssh, go back to sleep," I soothed, trying to drop my voice so low that Dot couldn't hear.

"Who's that? Is that Felix? Didn't sound like him." I could hear the cogs, or maybe that should have been *cog*, slowly whirring. "I know why you don't want me to come around! You're not there. Oh, my God, where are you and who are you with?"

"Where else would I be?" I hedged, trying desperately to play for enough time to get dressed, run back to my house, and be there to give her my Art History notes. There was never a handy temporal fold around when you need one.

"You always get pissy when anyone else tries to answer a question with another question," Dot said waspishly. Religion always puts her in a fiendishly bad mood. "Boy, am I glad that I didn't ring your house first . . ." She tailed off meaningfully, and she must have grown a pair since Friday when I'd made her cry by relentlessly mocking her new shoes.

"I'm not there," I prevaricated, looking around the room for some divine inspiration and meeting Smith's sleep-befuddled gaze instead.

"Tell whoever it is to piss off," he suggested helpfully. "I'm still aiming to have a lie in."

There was an outraged gasp from the phone. "You're with a boy!" she deduced with the logic that had put her in the top twenty percentile of her class. "I don't believe it! You spent the night with A BOY! Who is he?"

"No one," I said automatically. "It's just the TV."

"Yeah, right," she practically crowed. I could hear her mother shouting in the background. They were probably late for their weekly spot of God-bothering. "I have to go. I'm going to come around after church and then you're going to tell me everything."

"But . . ."

"*Everything*," she repeated in a distinctly unDot-like way. "I can't believe you, Is. Always the quiet ones."

And on that clichéd note, she rang off.

"Shit!" I threw my phone across the room and flung back the covers in preparation for banging my head repeatedly against the same spot of wall, except there was a hand holding tight to my arm. "Get off me!"

"Come back to bed," Smith said in his most cajoling voice, trying to brush my hair away from my cheek so he could kiss me, but I gripped the side of the mattress with one hand and attempted to work myself free.

"I've got to go now," I bit out, because he was not appreciating that I was on a Code Red. "My friend, who's turned into a gloating bitch overnight, is coming around to my house and I have to be there."

"Hmmm," he mumbled into my neck, still trying to make with the smoochies—and I didn't want to do it, but desperate times call for desperate measures and all that, so I pinched him really hard on his upper arm. Hard enough that he yelped like a girl and immediately let me go so he could rub the red mark and do the reproachful, "you really hurt me" thing with his eyes, while I scooped up my clothes.

"Sorry," I said, crouching down so I didn't flash him with any bits of girl flesh because everything was different in the morning when we were both sober, and daylight made the shadows go away.

"This hot and cold thing is getting really boring," he said flatly, and I yanked my T-shirt over my head so I didn't have to look at the disappointment on his face.

"It's not a thing, it just is," I said through a mouthful of cotton. "It's not you. I just have stuff going on and I need to go home and sort it out." That sounded better. Like, the kind of thing that an eighteen-year-old girl would say. Get me! With my sort-outable stuff.

Smith reached for his cigarettes and sat there, propped up by the pillows, looking totally unamused at my endearing attempts to locate my phone.

"It skidded under the crates when you threw it." He sighed. "I hate this. I feel like Paul Varjak in *Breakfast at Tiffany's*."

"Huh? What the hell are you talking about?" I lay flat on the floor, swatting my hand through a mound of dust bunnies to get to the phone. "Are you too good to plug in a vacuum cleaner?"

"It always ends up the same way," he elaborated. "You scrambling to get out the door as fast as possible and I'm left feeling like a mug. Like, I'm just convenient."

"You're not convenient," I said, then realized how it sounded. Though it was true in a way. He was one of the most inconvenient people I'd ever met. I managed to get a fingertip on my phone and concentrated on prying it free.

"Here, let me. I've got longer arms than you," Smith said behind me, and I shifted over so he could pull out my phone with an ease that was really, really irritating. "Not gonna give it back, though, till you at least give me a kiss," he drawled.

I bussed my lips against his for a count of three and rolled my eyes when he tried to slip me some tongue because we were kinda in the middle of an argument, and he knew I had my sort-outable stuff going on, so it was just inappropriate.

"Thank you," I said snottily, snatching the phone from him, but it was too cold to just leave him kneeling there on the floor when things were getting scratchy and I wanted to come back. Wanted him to want me to come back. I kissed him again and I think it worked.

"I'll call you and you can come around and start on the living room," he said when he saw me to the front door.

"Make sure you get some proper cleaning fluids and bleach," I reminded him. "Bleach is good."

"Isabel, I was joking." He laughed, even though household hygiene is not something I can ever laugh about.

I spent the whole morning hanging in the hall, waiting for Dot and her usual two rings on the doorbell. There was no way I could risk her bumping into Dad and having an illuminating little chat about the sleepover that never was.

He'd even acted pleased to see me when I got home, though that might have been because I had a hankering for toasted bacon sandwiches and made him one, too, as I craned my neck and kept the front door in my line of sight.

But even I had bodily functions and, of course I was in the downstairs loo when she arrived. Still zipping up my jeans, I hobbled toward the hall, but I was far too late.

"Hello, Dr. Clarke," I could hear Dot chirping. "Jeans! I didn't know you had anything but suits."

She was such a little suck-up at times.

"Thank you, yes, Dot. On weekends I've been known to experiment with other forms of clothing," he replied, which would usually be the cue for awkward silence as Dot tried to figure out whether he was joking or being deeply sarcastic. But she was too het up about the Art History notes for it to even register.

"There you are!" she said as I hurried toward them, like she'd been waiting for hours. She was wearing a pale blue twinset and a tweedy skirt designed not to offend the eyes of the Lord, who obviously hadn't seen the bum-skimming dress she was wearing the other night.

"Let's go upstairs and I'll get those notes for you," I muttered, dragging her stairwards.

Dot nodded eagerly. "We've got so much to talk about!"

"But you only saw each other a few hours ago." Dad chuckled, shaking his head in bemusement and all but vibrating with joy at the way I appeared to be exhibiting the normal tendencies of an adolescent girl. Dot's head swiveled around and I watched her slowly and succinctly get a clue, her eyes opening wide and then closing slowly as all the facts slotted themselves into the right order.

"You know Isabel, it's hard to shut her up when she starts talking." Dot grinned, and I could feel her hand tight against my shoulder, see the malice behind her smile, and I never knew she could look like that. Nancy and Ella, yeah, but not Dot.

"Stairs, now," I growled, and I knew it looked like I couldn't wait to drag her to my inner sanctum so we could settle down for a long girly gossip. But, really? I just wanted her as far away from him as possible.

Which was just as well because we were barely out of earshot before she started.

"So, spill," she ordered bluntly, throwing herself down on my bed with total lack of regard for my clean quilt and her dirty shoes. "Who is he?"

I pulled out my computer chair and plunked myself down. "No one you know."

Dot rested her head on my pillow, which made me grit my teeth and make a mental note to wash it when she finally left and please, God, let it be soon. "Oh, c'mon, Is, I promise I won't tell anyone! Where did you meet him?"

"It's the guy from the party," I admitted unwillingly, because she was going to get it out of me sooner or later and, at least, sooner meant it would be over quicker. Like yanking off a plaster in superfast time so it hurt for a second and then the pain was just a distant memory.

"I knew it!" she said triumphantly. "So how long have you been shagging him, then?"

"It's not like that," I snapped, because she made it sound so dirty and cold. When it should have been private. It *was* private; it was between me and Smith, just like all the things we said to each other in the dark. "I bumped into him a couple of days after the party and we swapped iPods and started hanging out. And last night, I popped around and I ended up crashing at his place. No shagging, no big mystery, no big deal, okay?"

"Oh, please," she snorted. "You were in bed with him this morning."

"I was on the sofa," I insisted doggedly. "We fell asleep on the sofa."

"Yeah, right, and your dad was all sunny smiles this morning after you stayed out all night. I don't think so! He thought you were staying around at my place while that geek ravaged your tender young flesh." She gloated, and held up her hands dramatically. "Now, there's an image that's going to be permanently etched in my mind."

I jiggled around in the chair for a bit. "He's not a geek," I said finally.

"Looks like a geek. Talks like a geek."

"He's said about three words to you ever!" I protested. "It's hardly enough to base an opinion on."

"What*ever*. I'm not leaving until you tell me all the gory details." She settled back on the bed and peered around curiously before her hand crept out to the drawer of my nightstand.

"Don't open that!"

"Is that where you keep your stash of condoms for when you're having sex with geeky boys?" Dot's hand closed around the drawer knob and I was off the bed in a flash, slamming it shut so hard that she squealed as I caught her fingers.

"How fucking dare you?" I was right in her face, so close I

could see the mascara clinging to her eyelashes. "Who the hell do you think you are? You just come in here and start trying to trample over my life . . ."

"Is, Is. God, I'm sorry," she wheezed, giving my arms these jerky little pats to calm me down. "I was joking. Please, chill."

I slumped down heavily on the bed next to her. "What is wrong with you? Why are you being like this?"

Dot finally had the good manners to look sheepish. It didn't last long, though, before she gave a tiny, couldn't-care-less shrug. "What? Like, you and Nancy have the monopoly on hurting people's feelings? I've tried being nice and that didn't get me very far, did it?" She took a deep breath like she'd suddenly had a great epiphany. "Do you ever wish that we weren't like we were? That we'd never started it? I don't even remember how it all happened."

"Neither do I," I said, but that wasn't exactly true. It was the very first day of the first term at Brighton Girls' when I'd made myself a solemn vow that I was done with being bullied and tormented and letting anyone walk all over me.

"So sometimes, maybe I need to take my inner bitch out for a walk," Dot muttered, staring at her nails.

"You don't. You really, really don't," I told her, stretching my legs out in front of me. "It doesn't solve your problems, just makes them more complicated."

I expected Dot to make some dismissive remark and call me a loser, because she seemed to have been taking lessons from Nancy and Ella, but she leaned over and touched my leg. "It sounds lonely."

"Being alone and being lonely are two different things," I

pointed out. "Y'know, I used to be happy being quiet, but no one would let me get on with it."

"Well, you've managed to hook a foxy boy somehow, so it can't be too bad," Dot said carefully.

"You just said he was a geek!"

"Well, he's a foxy geek or a geeky fox, whatever." She patted the bed invitingly. "So, what do you talk to him about?"

I gave up after that. Instead I sat cross-legged on my bed and I told Dot about how Smith made me feel like I wasn't just some awkward loner, but an enigma that he wanted to unravel. And how I liked it when he unraveled me. Liked how he looked at me and smiled at me and held my hand. Liked how he didn't want me to hide my oddness but to wear it like a shield.

But what I didn't tell her was all the stuff that she was dying to hear. That the first time we'd had sex, it hurt for a second. Like, stubbing my toe. And that I'd never get used to being naked in front of him. Or, well, anyone. Didn't tell her about all the lies I'd told him, either, and that there was no hope that it was going to last or be meaningful because I'd built our whole relationship on this precarious web of deceit.

"And he thinks I'm a complete bitch, too," I finished. "Because that's the only thing I know how to be, but he never lets me get away it. Not for one second. He's all, like, 'You're being nasty, stop it right now,' and the really weird thing is that usually I do. Like, he's my Kryptonite or something . . ."

There was this dreamy tone to my voice and I knew that it sounded as if I was madly, hopelessly, irredeemably in love with him, but I somehow couldn't shut up.

16

Dot finally left, after a lazy day of homework, eating our body weight in chocolate, and curling up on my bed to watch *Eternal Sunshine of the Spotless Mind* again. She swore that what had happened in Smith's room would stay in Smith's room, but I knew how easily she caved in under pressure. 'Sides, Monday morning meant a brand-new week, which meant a brand-new power struggle.

"Snogged any geeks lately?" was Nancy's cheery greeting as I strolled into the common room, and Dot, who was perched on the arm of her chair, became engrossed in the rickrack around the hem of her skirt and wouldn't look me in the eye.

"Not lately, no," I said blandly, heart pounding, but then Nancy started a convoluted story about some girl from her drama group and someone who played football with her brother and nothing had changed.

Except everything had changed because just after lunch, I got a text from Smith: "When can we hook up again?"

I looked up to see the Trio of Evil, power-walking down the corridor *Mean Girls* style, and settled for a cryptic, "Patience,

Grasshopper, patience." It sounded far more alluring than the sad truth—that I wasn't allowed out on school nights under pain of death.

"You're surgically attached to your phone today," Dot said, linking her arm through mine so she could haul me off.

"He just texted me," I hissed once we were sitting on the stairs that led up to the Domestic Science kitchens. I couldn't hold it in any longer, despite all the stern lectures I'd given myself about trusting no one, not even Dot. "Do you think he's really into me?"

I'd officially turned into one of those sappy girls who had no topic of conversation other than a boy. It didn't help that Smith and I were now having text sex, like, all the time. Man, he could be really rude without using any vowels. Not that I showed Dot his hundred and sixty character eulogy to my "bttm," but the way I went on about Smith, you'd have thought that he was the main reason why the sun rose up every morning and the earth rotated and there were stars in the sky.

Dot took it in very good humor. She listened dutifully, every afternoon, eyes wide and head nodding gravely as I glossed over that day's text messages and speculated on how I could string him along until the weekend. But all she really wanted to know was about the sex, because obviously the scant details I'd already provided weren't enough.

"What did it feel like? Did it hurt? Did he say weird stuff while you were doing it? Did you have an orgasm?"

It was like I'd become the Oracle of doing it. She followed me home so she could keep throwing these X-rated questions at me out of the side of her mouth. Felix was lurking, and every now and again, his eyes would go really wide and he'd squeak, "Ewwwww!" He sounded uncannily like Summer from *The OC*, which freaked me out.

I could just imagine the great delight he'd take in asking Dad what a condom or a multiple orgasm was, too. There was only one person in my life who didn't make my skin itch with irritation and that was Smith. He made my skin itch in an entirely different way.

"Is! I just asked you if you got completely naked," Dot hissed at me frantically, and I blinked at her in horror.

"Oh, God, just stop going on about it." I shoved my Art History textbook at her. "I thought you wanted to look something up in this."

After she'd gone and after I'd all but written her essay on Cubism for her, I didn't feel good. Wasn't that how you were meant to feel when you and a friend had exchanged some deep, meaningful bonding? I felt horrible and grubby, like she'd rooted through my knicker drawer. Letting people into your life really and truly sucked. Not for the first time, I wished that I could be homeschooled, if the homeschooling was done by someone who wasn't my father.

But it wasn't quite that simple, and when I got home from school the next day—so grouchy that I nearly punched Felix when he burped in my ear—I realized that the irritable, "just lost my keys" feeling was because I was missing Smith.

I wanted to tell him about how the Kit Kat I'd eaten at lunch had turned out to be solid chocolate and no wafer. And the A-minus I'd got on my French literature test. I wanted to tell him all the boring shit that had happened to me during the day and I couldn't. Or maybe I could.

"I was just talking about you," he said when I rang him. "How are you?"

"I'm fine," I squeaked. "What were you saying about me?"

"I was musing out loud about your plans for next weekend," he said, and I could hear him breathing heavily, footsteps, and then a door shutting. "That's better. So, yeah, what are you doing next Saturday?"

I lay back on my bed and closed my eyes so his voice sounded even huskier. "I don't know. Painting my nails. Washing my hair. I might even go really wild and rearrange my sock drawer."

"Well, what if I said you were already pretty enough to skip your thrilling beauty routine and go out with me instead?" he purred.

"I'd say that you were being really cheesy." I giggled.

"No, I'm flirting with you; you're meant to flirt back."

I racked my brains for something flirty to say that didn't contain the phrase "big boy" anywhere near it and came up blank. So, I changed the habits of a lifetime and told the truth. "I missed you today," I blurted out. "Does that count as flirting?"

"Oh, that's much better than flirting," he assured me, and there was a click and then a long slow breath and I knew he'd just lit a cigarette. "And I missed you, too. Wish you were coming over."

At 9:47 P.M., on a school night? Never going to happen. "I wish I was, too." I was overdosing on the warm fuzzies, and I needed to stop that right now. "'Cause then I could make a start on cleaning your lounge."

"God, that's romantic. I did go out and buy some bleach, though. Just for you. I got the expensive kind that smells of meadow flowers."

"Toilets should always smell of meadow flowers. So what's happening next Saturday?" I asked him, and then I got bolder than ever. "You want to hang out?"

"Of course I do. But, see, Duckie have got a gig in London and then there's going to be a party..."

"Oh..."

"Don't 'oh' me in that hurt little voice. Do you wanna come? There's room in the van, and I think we're going to sleep on someone's floor and then drive back the next day. You'll have to promise to leave your evil alter ego at home."

"I don't have an evil alter ego," I hissed. "I have layers."

"And some of your layers are more evil than others," Smith teased. "I really want you to come."

"It sounds cool. Can I let you know?"

"By tomorrow? 'Cause there's a hot competition for places in the back of the van. Isabel?"

He sounded so serious that I could feel the pitter-patter of impending doom. "What?"

"This time can you promise not to pick your usual fight with me before you flounce off?"

"I don't flounce," I protested, squirming from the unfairness of his accusation. "Actually, I have a hissy fit, storm out, and then regret it when I'm five meters down the road."

"That's good to know. I'll make a mental note not to get offended next time."

"I never mean to offend you. It just kinda happens. Like, every time I open my mouth without thinking first."

"You really open up on the phone. Maybe we should just talk on our mobiles when I finally get to see you." Smith chuckled, and I had to bite back the crushing retort that was nicely coming to the boil.

"Oh, whatevs," I muttered, then cast a sorrowful look at the pile of books and papers on the bed. "Got to go now. I have stuff to do."

"Ah, the infamous stuff. I have this theory that you're an international spy, which would explain why you're mysteriously unavailable."

"You've been watching too much *Alias*, Smith."

"Admit it. You're on a secret mission to recover some shiny little gizmo from a lab in Uzbekistan that could destroy the world with its evil death rays."

I could hear my dad yelling at me from the hall about dinner or possibly a Martian invasion. It was hard to tell.

"Going now, sad boy," I told Smith, but he was still knee-deep in international master-spy land.

"And all the labs you break into are attached to dodgy nightclubs for some strange reason so you have to dress up in these really outlandish costumes and . . ."

"My God, you really need to get out more. I have to go, things to do, worlds to save from shiny little gizmos," I said, like it was no big deal.

"I knew it!" he exclaimed excitedly. "How many wigs have you got?"

"Okay, going now . . ."

"Have you got a gun and a lipstick that doubles up as a . . ."

And I was in such a good mood as I went to investigate Dad's plaintive cries that when I passed Felix on the stairs, I couldn't stop myself from ruffling his hair in a manner that could have been misinterpreted as affectionate.

Our little care and share sessions had really gone to Dot's head. In return for an alibi so I could go cavorting off to London in the back of a Transit van, she wanted me to write two unspecified essays for her at a time of her choosing, lend her my *Lost* boxed set, and imposed a moratorium on wearing Felix's Sea Scouts T-shirt to school ever again. She never did understand irony.

"As if! Whatever happened to just doing someone a favor?" I asked her incredulously when she actually had the nerve to come around to my house for the DVDs.

"Supply and demand. You want something from me, then I'm going to want something back," she insisted. "That's what you always say when it's my turn to need some help. I thought that was how it works."

I stood my ground, and with some well-timed vitriol about the spot on her forehead and how it must be visible from Mars, I sent Dot scuttling away without my beloved boxed set in her eager little hands. She was getting ideas way above her station, and that needed my attention before they got completely out of hand.

Then I felt my phone vibrate and my brain fell right out of my head. "R U on a secret mission right now? Will your spymaster let you out to play on Saturday? Smith x."

And there I was, getting all bent out of shape about Dot and her ludicrous attempts at blackmail, when I should have been saving my emotional resources for dealing with my father.

"Is it okay if I spend the weekend at Dot's?" I asked him as I served up his favorite dinner of lemon chicken with wild rice and asparagus.

"I suppose so," he said, his nose twitching as I held the plate in front of him. "You two seem to be getting on very well."

"We have a lot in common," I said sweetly, pouring the chicken and lemon stock I'd made onto his rice. "She's so very loyal."

"I find your other friends a little acerbic for my tastes," he commented, eyes tracking every movement of the plate. "But Dot seems nice. Hmm, this looks delicious!"

"So, I'm going to go straight to her place after school on Friday and then I'll see you Sunday night," I ventured, amazed by my own audacity. I'd carved another day with Smith out of thin air. "And I'll call you and you've got my mobile number so . . ."

"Stop fussing, Isabel. I'm sure Felix and I can manage without you for forty-eight hours. Just make sure you find some time to do your homework."

I had to stuff a whole asparagus spear into my mouth sideways to mask my triumphant smirk.

17

If my bag hadn't been so heavy, I think I'd have run all the way to Smith's student hovel. As it was, I walked at a brisk pace and felt drunk with freedom. Like, for forty-eight hours I could escape all the crap that usually pulled me down and be the new, improved version of Isabel that I liked much better than the current one.

There'd be kisses. Lots of kisses, all sticky-sweet and smoky. And we'd curl up under his covers so I could let him cuddle me and whisper stories in my ear and, if he really begged, I'd even cuddle him back.

But oh, the best-laid plans of mice and Isabel were not to be, because when Smith opened the door he had doom and gloom writ large.

"Um, surprise!" I tilted my face for at least a peck on the cheek, which I didn't get as he stood aside to let me in.

"I thought I wasn't seeing you until tomorrow. I've got this essay to write," he whined, and he sounded just like Felix when he doesn't want to go to bed. "On Nietzsche. Why am I doing a degree in philosophy?"

"Well, it's not exactly going to lead to steady employment, is it?" I chirped gaily, following him up the stairs. "Not many vacancies for fully qualified philosophers." I needed to start building up my tact muscles; Smith's brow was so furrowed it had to be causing him immense pain.

"It seemed like a good idea at the time," he mumbled, nudging open the door of his room. "But I've got to get this sodding essay done tonight so I can have the weekend off."

"Oh, I've already . . ." I stopped. I wasn't supposed to have done all my homework in my lunch hour and fortuitously placed study break because I was a lady of leisure and not someone who was still doing the book-learning thing.

"Already what . . . ?" Smith muttered. He was staring disconsolately at an open book, which was littered with annotations and scrawled notes in the margins. If my dad could see it, he'd have had Smith publicly flogged for cruelty to the printed word.

"Um, I've already . . . er, planned to make you dinner," I exclaimed hurriedly. "I'll make you dinner and you can do your essay while delicious cooking smells waft up from the kitchen. What do you fancy?"

"You cook? Food?"

I was *this* close to slapping him upside his fuzzy head. "Of course, food! I'm going to cook some for you as soon as you tell me what you'd like to eat."

"I'm not fussed," Smith mumbled, giving me a face full of sulk. "Anything. And can you close the door behind you?"

Half an hour later, I was back from Safeway and chopping up some mushrooms so I could add them to the rat poison I had sautéing gently with the onions and garlic. Technically, it was chicken, but it would have totally served him right if it had been rat poison.

I should have known that when I get all anticipatory and excited about something it's doomed to royally suck. Smith hadn't even deigned to look a teeny bit pleased to see me, but as I chopped and sautéed and stirred, the familiar rituals calmed me down, soothed my inner pain, and I was even able to hum a few bars of the really lame Geri Halliwell song that was on the radio.

"Well, well, if it isn't Miss Jailbait herself. You allowed near a stove unattended, kid?"

I carefully put down the wooden spoon and turned around to see Jane standing in the doorway.

"Oh, it's you," I said icily. If Smith and Molly weren't around, then there was no reason in the world why I should be polite to her.

"Guess so," she agreed. "You're really domesticated. You might want to watch that—it's prematurely aging."

"Did you want something or did you plan to just stand there and try to piss me off?" I picked up the spoon and gave the chicken cacciatore a quick stir, so I'd have something to do with my hands that didn't involve throttling her.

She glided further into the kitchen, getting right into my space as she peered at the stove top. "Hmm, is there enough for me? If I eat any more ramen, I'm going to get scurvy."

My little halfhearted daydream of having a romantic candlelit dinner on the sofa was instantly destroyed as I pictured Jane sitting between the two of us, shoveling food into her gob as she kept up a running commentary on how young I looked.

"I don't know how hungry Smith is," I prevaricated, pushing a piece of chicken around with the spoon. "There might be some left."

"Am I ruining your little plans for a cozy dinner *à deux*?" She smirked and then straightened up, the patronizing smile replaced with something more dark and resolute. "It's okay, I'm just pushing your buttons, sweetie. But you and I need to have a little talk."

Was there ever a sentence more likely to make your heart sink toward the floor? "What on earth have we got to talk about?" I snapped, slamming the spoon down on the counter so I could put my hands on my hips and glare at her.

"There you go," Jane cooed. "I knew you couldn't keep up that goody two-shoes act forever."

"It's *not* an act . . ."

"Yeah, yeah, whatever," she breezed with an airy wave of her hand. "So I know you're lying about your age and it makes me wonder what else you're lying about. I've seen you and your friends out . . ."

"And what?" I snarled so ferociously that Jane raised her eyebrows and took a step back. "What have you seen? Us walking around with our dates of birth tattooed on our foreheads?"

"I've seen you," she repeated doggedly. "Your little girl gang gives off some deeply screwed-up vibes, and I'm not having you pulling any shit on Smith. He's my friend. I look out for my friends, so think of this as a warning. You step on him, then I'm gonna step right on you twice as hard and for ten times as long."

She was really scary. Like, the original Japanese version of *The Ring* scary, but when it came to being bullied I could always give as good as I got.

I held up a hand to my heart. "Oooh, I'm quaking in my boots here. Not. When I want your opinion I'll ask for it. Now, was there anything else you wanted or have you fulfilled your bitch quota for the day?"

Jane was distinctly underwhelmed by my scariest voice. "I mean it—you do anything to hurt him and I'll make you wish you'd never been born."

"Do I look bothered?" I could tell she was itching to slap me. "Smith's a big boy, he can take care of himself. Not like he's been getting all riled up about your totally wild accusations, is it?"

"That's because I haven't said anything to him." Jane paused for effect "Yet. But if you don't behave like a good little girl, then I will."

And she wasn't to know that I was used to this threat and counterthreat. Attack and defense. Sometimes I think I invented it. Certainly I knew enough not to show the slightest sign of weakness. "And if you start sticking your gigantic nose in where it's not wanted and coming between me and Smith, then well, it's hard to think up a really credible threat, what with you having been in rehab and stuff . . ." I tailed off meaningfully. "Now that I think about it, you do seem a little unhinged. I hope you're not using again 'cause that would be . . ."

"Oh, God, you're good," Jane said, and then to my utter surprise, she started laughing. "Wow! All credit to you, sweetie, you come out fighting, don't you?"

"Damn straight," I growled, and she patted my arm condescendingly as I flinched away from her.

"I'll be watching you," she caroled in a singsong voice, wagging her finger at me.

"Why do you have to be such a cow?" I hissed. "Smith likes me, Molly likes me, why can't you just leave me alone?"

Jane shrugged. "There's just something about you that really gets under my skin," she admitted. "And Molly? Love her to bits, but she's a terrible judge of character."

"No, I'm not," said an indignant voice, and we both whirled around to see Molly standing there, with Smith looming behind her. I could feel my heart suddenly start banging away as if I'd just run a marathon. How much had they heard?

"I am a fantastic judge of character," Molly insisted, folding her arms across her chest. "Most of the time. And we're going to be late for rehearsal and something smells like it's burning."

"Shit!" I turned back to the stove where dinner was just about to stick irretrievably to the bottom of the pan. I quickly added some more water and chucked in a good handful of herbs and then stirred the mixture like I'd never stirred anything before. And if my face was bright red that was just because I was standing too near to an open flame.

"Right, we're off, then," I heard Molly say after a three-minute diatribe on how ace she was at judging people's characters unless they were "lanky wankers who play guitar and think with their dicks." "See you, Isabel."

I grunted something that sounded vaguely like good-bye but didn't turn around until I heard them thundering down the stairs. Smith was leaning against the kitchen table, rattling his keys on one finger.

"Did you get your essay done?" I asked brightly, like I was being tested for my Brownies homemaker badge.

Smith nodded his head morosely. "Yeah, and it blows. I might have to take another look at it after dinner." He gestured in the direction of the cooker. "Smells good."

"I just need to make the pasta and it's done." I opened what looked like the cutlery drawer. "It's a novel idea, but you could actually wash your knives and forks before you put them away."

"Do you want something to drink? I'm going to the off-license."

When he came back with two bottles of wine and I'd laid the kitchen table and dished him up probably the first home-cooked meal he'd had since he'd been, like, home he just sat there, pushing the food around with his fork and not saying anything.

And I was practically mirroring his fork-pushing and the not-saying-anything because it was obvious he'd heard every thrilling exchange of my catfight with Jane. He was working up to asking questions that were going to ruin the rest of the weekend. Though from where I was sitting on a slightly wobbly chair, the weekend looked like it had pretty much been ruined already.

"Sorry," he said at last, shoving his untouched plate away. "I'm going to take another crack at the essay. I think there's some theory brewing in my head that I want to get down."

"Oh . . . okay. Um, do you want . . . I could go, if you like," I heard myself say. He could hardly bring himself to look at me. Might as well swap the awkward silence here for the awkward silence at home.

"No, Isabel. God, no." Smith leaned across the table so he could cup my chin. "Just give me two hours and then you'll have my undivided attention for the rest of the night, I swear."

"I didn't mean it like that," I protested as he pressed his thumb against my quivering bottom lip for a fraction of a second.

"It's just, well, I thought I'd see you tomorrow. I didn't realize that you were planning to crash here tonight as well," he said at last, and if he hadn't still been holding my chin I'd have banged my head against the table. Repeatedly. I thought he'd be pleased that we'd get to spend more time together, and instead he was acting like I was the pushiest girl in southeast England. Point of fact, I *was* the pushiest girl in southeast England.

I must have looked like a puppy with a sore paw because he gave me an anxious look and opened his mouth to make me feel a million times worse. I clamped my hand over his mouth, gently, so I didn't cut off his air supply.

"No, it's fine. I can go. Really. No trauma," I assured him, aiming for perky and ending up somewhere around petulant.

Smith jerked his head back from my sweaty palm. "Is, *Is*," he said gently, brushing the back of his hand along my hot cheek. "I'm really glad you're here and I'm just annoyed that I spent all day faffing about when I should have been working. It's not you, okay?"

It not being about me was another dent to my ego, but I managed to muster up a smile and let him disappear to do battle with the forces of philosophy. I restored the kitchen back to a far better state than I'd found it and then claimed the carpet in the lounge for Britain. Underneath all that cigarette ash and newspapers, it turned out to be a rather bilious green color. I hauled out two bin bags full of debris, vacuumed, polished, and, at one point, got down on my hands and knees to scrub at the skirting before I decided that Smith's two hours were up. Anyway, I was completely out of dusters.

Smith was lying on the bed, blowing smoke rings up at the ceiling when I poked my head around the door. I could see the computer screen glowing in his little study as I inched toward him.

"I might just as well give up now," he announced suddenly. "Just drop out and spare everyone the inevitable."

"What are you talking about?" I asked him with a lot less exasperation than I'd show anyone else.

"I'm stupid," he sighed. "I don't know my Heidegger from my Derrida. It's like that episode of *The Simpsons* where Bart gets an F, but with lots of dead Frenchmen in it."

My entire life has been punctuated by students having these kinds of crises—usually when they were due to hand in an essay that was already three weeks late. We'd had so many dinners ruined because Dad was on the phone talking some brainiac down from the ledge because he couldn't get a handle on James Joyce's *Ulysses*. Usually Dad just barked at them to pull themselves together, but if they were his little protégés, he'd do much the same as I was doing now. I got Smith to read through his essay and let him figure out the problem for himself. Though I sincerely hoped that Dad didn't do it with as much head stroking.

By the time Smith had finished typing up his conclusion while I looked up words in the thesaurus for him, the downward droop of his features had been replaced by a look of utter adoration.

"I bet this all seems really dumb to you." Smith shifted me on his lap so he could press controls. "You're a secret geek, aren't you?"

"There's, like, a formula to it. You just need to get into the rhythm and throw in a few really long words. Doesn't make me a geek, you know!" I huffed.

"I didn't mean it like that," Smith protested, pushing me off his lap so he could shuffle me over to the bed and pull me down on that. I was his personal lump of Play-Doh. "You're pretty cool, Is."

After the worst beginning to a weekend ever, I was starting to remember why I liked Smith so much. I rolled over onto my side so we were eyeball to eyeball, and I could see the minute green flecks amid the startling blue of his eyes. "I didn't have any friends until I started senior school," I confessed, because there were some things I could still be honest about. "I was really quiet and smaller than everyone else in my class, and I read loads of books and had the shit kicked out of me every day."

Smith pressed a kiss to my forehead. "What happened?"

"I got over it," I said flatly, running my hands under his T-shirt because I could. "And then I was really popular at senior school, but I wasn't really popular, I just had this whole power thing going for me. Like, in *Mean Girls*. I was the mean girl prototype."

"You're not as mean as you think you are," he said, tangling his legs with mine. "You're really, really not. I'd go so far as to say you were kinda sweet, if I didn't think you'd hit me."

"I'm not sweet," I growled. "In what alternate universe am I freaking sweet?"

"Well, maybe not sweet," he conceded, kissing the scowl off my face. "Somewhere between a sweet girl and a mean girl. Unless you're going to give me the mean girl manifesto again."

"Well, I'm kinda getting over that, too." And I wished I were. Wished there was a reset button on my life that I could press and have the last four years wiped away so I could start again.

"You're getting over a lot of things, Isabel," Smith said, and he smiled, even though I could tell his heart wasn't in it, which was probably why he rolled over so I was left looking at the back of his head.

"I'm not getting over you, though," I whispered, and I snuggled myself against the tense line of his back and curled my hand over his heart.

18

Being stuck in the back of a van and feeling every single pothole and bump on the highway jarring against my spine was an occurrence that I never wanted to repeat. Even if I had to walk back to Brighton.

Jane acting like, well, like she was in a really cool band who were going to London to play a gig, didn't improve matters. She commandeered the CD player with a mix she'd made of the worst songs to ever get to number one. Then throw in the official entourage, all wearing these stupid DIY "I'm with the band" T-shirts, talking about people I didn't know and places I'd never been, and Smith was, like, their vice chairman or something.

He'd been all sweetness and light when we woke up this morning. Didn't get snarky about the way I'd fallen asleep before we could have sex or that I drooled on his shoulder all night, but the minute his friends had entered the equation, I might just as well have not existed. He was so predictable sometimes.

I clung to the speaker I was sitting on for dear life as Jane's boyfriend kept changing lanes. If I said that I needed a wee, maybe I could hitch a lift back to Brighton at the first service station we came to.

"Why are you pouting?" Smith hissed at me from the other side of the van. I was forced to adjust my bottom lip as all eyes turned to me.

"I'm not pouting," I hissed back, trying to tamp down the screech in my voice. "I'm just thinking about stuff."

"We should have made you a T-shirt," the girl with the most perfect bob in the world suddenly said. "Sorry. But, oh, hey, badges! I've got badges."

"It's all right," I protested, because now everyone was rustling through their pockets and bags trying to rustle up some amazing crafty outfit for me to wear so I didn't feel left out, and Smith was shaking his head in disbelief.

Molly craned her neck from the front seat. "There's T-shirts in a box with the word *T-shirts* on it," she supplied helpfully. "They're pink. Really bring out the blue in your eyes, Is."

One of the boys was already crawling toward the back of the van and becoming an object of derision as he trod on people's legs. "Really, I'm living T-shirt-free these days," I insisted, but he was already thrusting a handful of pink cotton at me.

"'If they can do without you, Duckie, so can I.'" I read out the words that were scattered over the black-and-white print of Audrey Hepburn.

"It's from *My Fair Lady*," Smith explained. "Not that I'm an expert on musicals. It's the band's mission statement."

"Right . . ." I said doubtfully, but the girl with the most perfect bob in the world ever (I wished I could remember her name), was already squatting down next to me with a clutch of badges.

"We'll have you Duckie'd out in no time," she said. "Which ones do you like best?"

Ten minutes later, I was kinda proudly wearing the T-shirt over my own long-sleeved top in an Emo style, while Smith pinned badges on me that said things like, "I ♥ reading," "I am totally awesome," "Dinosaurs are the new robots," and "Born to do stuff."

There was one badge left, and he opened his palm so I could see it nestling there like a one-inch time bomb. "Real friends don't lie," it screamed at me.

"Where shall I put it?" he asked me casually, and I closed my hand over his.

"I'm all buttoned out now. You put it on." I pinned the badge onto his jacket collar and patted it. "There. Fit to have your picture taken."

Then he leaned so he could kiss the tip of my nose and squeeze my hand. "I'm so glad you're here," he whispered.

"Me too." I nodded. "I mean I'm glad I'm here and I'm glad you're here and . . . feel free to think of something that will stop me babbling any second now."

Smith gave me a wicked grin. "Okay, I can do that." He turned his head. "Isabel thinks that Death Cab are, and I quote, 'whiny mope rockers.'"

There was a chorus of disbelief and agonized expressions all around. I punched Smith on the shoulder, but then I wasn't on the outside looking in anymore, I was right there at the center, clutching Smith's hand and not minding when I got teased about my musical preferences all the way to London.

Being with the band was definitely overrated. It mostly involved dragging their amps on stage and being really quiet while they twiddled about with their guitars and did some weird techy shit with the levels. All I know is I had to listen to one song over and over again, even though it sounded the same every time.

Molly had a minor meltdown because she thought her guitar amp was hissing and then actually stamped her foot and quit the band when everyone else was all like, "What*ever*!"

"Maybe you should be more sympathetic," I advised Smith, who'd just jumped off the stage so he could have a sip from my bottle of water. "I think she's really upset."

Smith shrugged. "She quits the band once a week on average. It's just preshow nerves and the fact that she's a total drama queen."

We both looked at Molly who was wringing her hands and saying to the sound guy, "My God, why are you trying to stifle my creativity?" without any noticeable hint of irony.

"Yeah, you might have a point there," I agreed.

"Your diva crown is still very much intact, though," Smith assured me, patting the top of my head and once again I thrilled to the fact that if he'd been anyone else I'd have bitten his hand off; instead I just flashed my teeth at him.

"As long as we're clear about that."

"As crystal," he said solemnly, before tugging me off the crates I was perched on. "C'mon let's go and get something to eat."

The streets of Camden were thronged with tourists and weekend goths all intent on buying nasty silver jewelry, T-shirts with really unfunny slogans on them, and dope-smoking paraphernalia, which meant that Smith and I had to hold hands really tightly.

We managed not to fight at all. Even after it started drizzling in this relentless way, and I vetoed the first five cafés we found on hygiene grounds and refused to let Smith buy a crêpe from a stall because the man in charge of the hot plate looked like he didn't wash his hands after he peed.

Eventually we found a little Thai restaurant, bagged the last table, and sat huddled in the corner, bumping knees as we drank green tea and looked at the menu.

"I'm having Disco Duck," I announced decisively. "Mainly because it's called Disco Duck, or Ped Ron, as it's known in Thailand."

"I wanted that! God, can't believe you're bogarting the Disco Duck."

My eyes scanned down the menu. "Have the Weeping Tiger, if you want the whole comedy food experience, and I'm going to have the spinach with ginger and garlic. Unless my mouth feels like it's about to burst into flames, then there's really no point in having Thai."

"We'll share." Smith gave me a heavy-lidded look. "Then we'll both taste of garlic."

And it seemed like we'd reached that stage where even having shared stinky breath was romantic—and Smith was fumbling one-handed with his chopsticks so he could stroke my leg with his free hand. Everything was perfect until I had to chug back two glasses of water when the spinach set my mouth ablaze.

"You can't handle the hot, little girl," he admonished me, stroking my cheek as I stuck my tongue out and tried to see if it was blistered.

"Hey, I've been eating spicy food ever since I went on to solids," I said, taking little ladylike sips of the water he'd just poured me.

Smith raised an eyebrow skeptically. "That's pretty hard-core for a baby."

"Yeah, well, my mum didn't believe in fussy eating, so she made me eat whatever her and Dad were having. He says that I used to demand pickle on my egg soldiers as soon as I learned to talk."

"You never talk about your mum," Smith said, so casually that I knew he'd been dying to bring up the subject forever.

It was like having my body submerged in ice. Goose bumps popped out all over my arms, and I shifted my leg away from his stroking fingers. "There's nothing to talk about." I couldn't have made it plainer that the topic was closed with a DO NOT DISTURB sign pinned on the door for good measure.

"I get that, I really do," Smith said, but he obviously didn't because why was he still talking? "But if you did want to bring it up at some unspecified time in the future, then you know where I am."

Right then, all I wanted to do was to kick the chair out from under me and get far, far away from the understanding look in his eyes. I took a couple of deep breaths and forced myself to look. "'Kay," I mumbled. "That's good to know."

"Cool. Do you want to get some coffee or shall we head back?" Smith said, his hand back on my knee. And I could pretend that everything was all right in the world.

It wasn't until halfway through Duckie's set that I realized actually everything *was* all right in the world.

I'd been canoodling with Smith in a corner before the band came on, tasting limes and green tea on his tongue as he kissed me, before we got distracted by a surf-tastic version of *The OC* theme tune, which made us look up to see the girl with the most perfect bob in the world bearing down on us.

"Down the front!" she squealed by way of greeting, grabbing our hands and pulling us through the crowd in time to see Jane cartwheel on stage (show off, much?) and Molly place her Ruby Gloom lucky mascot on one of the speakers.

The lights dimmed as Molly started picking out a delicate tune on her guitar, then the drums came in and they were whooshing into one of the songs Smith had downloaded for me, all disco beats and "yeah, yeah, yeahs" on the chorus. Most times when I'd been to see a band (well, apart from the Spice Girls at Brighton Centre, which I've tried to write out of my personal history), I stood at the back and bitched about what people were wearing, but that wasn't going to be an option here.

Instead, I took the bottle of beer that one of Smith's friends passed to me and then sloshed most of the contents away as I jumped about and tried not to fall over when the crowd surged forward. It was so much fun!

Duckie didn't have a slow setting. Each song got faster and faster until it seemed like the entire audience were verging on mass hysteria. Molly stood there in the center of the stage, poised like she was the queen of everything, and I guess she was in a way. Like, she had all this power to make people happy because when she played her songs, she took them to a better place.

Then, between songs, she looked down into the mess below her, caught my eye, and waved. "This is our last song, 'Boy Meets Girl,' and it's for Isabel and Smith, who are causing havoc in the pit. . . ."

There was this sudden ungodly whooping noise, which was

Smith thundering toward me so he could pick me up and whirl me around until some guy who was much bigger and uglier than us threatened to punch him if we didn't stop.

"I've never had a song dedicated to me before," I shouted in Smith's ear once I'd managed to tug him away. "I feel very rock 'n' roll."

"Oh, I've had songs dedicated to me a hundred times," he proclaimed loftily, and looked so unutterably smug that I had to dig him in the ribs and make him dance with me again. It was all kinds of cute watching him shuffle just a few seconds behind the beat.

By the time Duckie went off stage, I was a sticky, sweaty mess of girl, made worse by Smith wrapping me up in these damp bear hugs every few steps we took. And there was nothing to do but give in to it and stop worrying about when I'd get to have a shower and if my hair looked like a fright wig. I didn't even panic when we went backstage because backstage was just a tiny room with a plastic barrel full of cold beer being drunk by the official entourage. 'Cept now I was one of them, which meant that everyone acted pleased to see me, and I even got a towel so I could wipe away the mascara that had slid down to my chin.

We helped the band pack up, then the night descended into a seamless blur of the top decks of buses, dark streets, and sitting around someone's front room with toast and tea and *Buffy* DVDs going in the background while each second of Duckie's performance got dissected. Apparently, this was what you do when you're in a band, though Jane nearly decked Sanjay, the drummer, for insisting she'd played the wrong bass line to "Teen Confidential."

"I have to pee," I whispered in Smith's ear, and struggled up from the depths of the armchair that we were sharing.

He gave me a proprietary pat on the bum, earning him my most withering glare, but he was talking to Molly who wanted to know if her guitar amp had been distorting.

It was rather lovely to have a bit of peace and quiet even if it was for only five minutes. I pulled a comb through my hair, but it was like throwing a glass of water on a raging fire. So I sat on the edge of the bath, brushing my teeth and, well, mooning over Smith.

My whole life had split in two: Smith and not Smith. I liked the Smith parts of it so much better. Already I was calculating how much of the weekend we had left and greedily clutching every hour to me as if it was precious. Was this what it was meant to feel like when you were really into someone? Was this what it felt like if you were *in love?*

And as soon as I thought it, I knew that it was true. I kinda loved him. Or, like, I was in love with him. Either state of being was just too freaky to contemplate. The dripping toothbrush stilled in midair as I tried to pull myself together. I was a heartless, ungrateful wench of a girl who promised everyone who came into contact with me a one-way ticket to pain and hurt. I didn't know how to love and I didn't deserve to be loved back.

The almost-drunk feeling that had been softening my edges, disappeared and the world snapped back into focus, everything sharp and spiky again, including me. Not the girl I'd been fooling myself I could be, but the one staring back at me in the mirror with a thin line where her lips used to be and shadows under her eyes.

"Is? Are you in there?" Smith gave a gentle tap on the door and panic rose up in my chest.

"I'll be out in a sec." My voice could have cut glass. "I'm only cleaning my teeth, you can come in if you like."

"You on the second rinse yet?" Smith asked me teasingly as soon as he opened the door, catching my eye in the mirror and giving the Isabel he saw there a tender look.

Luckily I had a mouthful of Colgate so all I could do was nod vaguely and scrub my teeth with renewed vigor.

"So, everyone's about to crash out," Smith continued, picking up one of the rubber ducks that were sailing across the windowsill. "I managed to bag us the box-room. I think we'll both fit in there if we hold our breath."

I spat out an unseemly amount of froth and delicately wiped my mouth. "That's fine."

"Hey, what happened to you in the five minutes that you've been in here?" Smith pulled me around so he got the full benefit of my stroppy face.

"Nothing happened, though I'm sobering up and it feels horrible. And I feel horrible," I blurted out. "I'm like something out of *Lord of the Flies* or I'm one of those animals that eat their young or something."

"Are you sure you're sobering up?"

"Yes, no, I don't know." I put my hand to my forehead. "Why do I have to think so much all the time?"

Smith smoothed his thumbs into the hollows under my eyes. "Please don't be sad. C'mon, give me a smile," he begged, and I obediently pulled up the corners of my mouth.

"I'd give that effort three out of ten," he said softly. "Four if I was being really generous." He took hold of my hand and turned it over so he could press a kiss into my palm. And I don't know where he'd learned these moves, but he must have been the teenage girl version of a horse whisperer because I could feel myself calming down, my heart stopped trying to escape from my chest, and I rested my head against his shoulder.

"Can we go to bed now?"

He didn't let go of my hand as we inched down the hall and into a box-room that violated the Trades Description Act. It was more like a cupboard with a single bed in it. I lay down and let Smith peel off my clothes like he was unwrapping a present. Then he stretched out next to me so I could run my hands over his skin again and again, tracing patterns over his back, writing poetry with my fingertips down his arms; all the words I was longing to say. Then Smith was kissing me hungrily as if he hadn't kissed me for months, not minutes, and maybe making love was the same as being in love.

19

Monday morning sent me crashing back to reality with a thud and a really shaky dismount. Even getting home last night, after spending the day entwined around Smith, hadn't lessened my freakish good mood.

I'd sailed into the lounge—where Dad and Felix were making final adjustments to that stupid diorama—and given them a dreamy smile when they'd asked me if I'd had a nice weekend.

"It was totally awesome," I'd enthused with a killer-watt smile that made my face ache. "I love spending time with Dot. She's so caring and funny and . . ."

"Are you going to make dinner?" Felix had asked hopefully. "We had sausages last night and Dad burned them."

"They weren't burned, they were chargrilled," Dad had insisted, giving me a curious look because I was still grinning inanely like I'd got all six numbers on the lottery during a rollover week. "Are you up to cooking, or should I order pizza against my better judgment?"

But I'd cooked a Thai curry so I could get a complete sense memory of kissing Smith's fiery mouth and even played

Scrabble and let Felix win. Which I don't normally do because losing is character building.

I'd got a full eight hours' sleep and sailed into school still wreathed in sunny smiles, and at first, I thought I'd just imagined the nudges and whispers that trailed in my wake like a little dust cloud. Or else they didn't recognize the new, deliriously happy Isabel and thought I was some new kid with a dodgy haircut.

By the time the lunch bell rang, my good mood was long gone and I was forced to admit that, once again, I was fueling the school's vicious-rumors industry single-handed. I lined up with the others to have some kind of vegetable gunk slopped onto my plate and racked my brains for anything particularly heinous that I'd done lately. There didn't seem to be anything. I've been keeping my hood up and my head down.

"Hey, have you noticed how everyone's acting weird around me?" I ventured as we sat down at our usual table so I had a bird's-eye view of the smirk of every girl in the canteen as she looked in my direction.

And surely I wasn't being paranoid, because Nancy and Ella, worthless bitches that they were, had just exchanged a look of unbridled glee.

"You're just imagining things," Dot assured me, glancing around the room. "I can't see anyone acting weird. Well, no more than usual."

I caught the eye of a frizzy-haired little witch from the year below and gave her the evil eye right back until I'd made her blush and spill yogurt down her top through sheer force of will. "They're all looking at me," I hissed, leaning forward. "Has someone been saying something about me?"

And ha! Ella was staring at her plate and blushing, but before I could totally call her on it, Nancy snorted. "Jeez, could you be any more paranoid? FYI, it's not always all about you, Is."

"I know that," I replied with all the dignity I could muster, which actually wasn't that much. "I'm just saying . . ."

"Could we get through one lunchtime without a bickering match?" Dot asked wearily, like her application for sainthood was already in the post.

Ella wriggled in her chair with a sly little smile. "Yeah, we do argue a lot for four girls who are meant to be best friends. Maybe we should do something bond-y."

I was about to remind them that I wasn't allowed out on school nights in case my A-minus average suddenly plummeted all the way to a B-plus, but Dot and Nancy were squealing like doing "something bond-y" was the best idea ever.

"Yeah! We should do something really old skool like hang out at the park, get drunk, and watch the boys play football . . ."

"And then cop off with someone," Dot added, and she had to be winding me up, because it all sounded so low-rent that I was coming down with a severe case of scabies just thinking about it. "What do you reckon, Is? You up for it or you got something better to do?"

The silence that followed was so loaded with menace that every hair on my body stood up and danced the macarena. I peered at Dot through my lashes, but she just gave me the innocent smile of someone who hadn't spilled all my deepest, darkest secrets to the two douche-bags we hung out with.

"Yeah, Is, how about it?" Nancy drawled. "You too good to slum with us all of a sudden?"

"No, don't be ridiculous," I blustered. "Just hanging out in parks is a little, well a lot, juvenile. Why don't we watch DVDs and . . ."

"Because we want to go to the park," Nancy insisted, her eyes flashing while Dot and Ella sat there coiled still, like snakes about to shoot venom.

And this wasn't about going to the park. Not really. There was something underpinning this whole battle of wills that was making cold fingers of fear walk down my spine. All I could do was go for a little bit of damage limitation.

I shrugged, like the whole conversation was too boring for words. "What*ever*. If your idea of fun is going to the park when it's cold and wet then fine, count me in."

As if I hadn't told enough lies already, I then had to go home and play the devoted daughter, even though I didn't know my lines.

I perched on the arm of the settee as Dad waited for *Panorama* to start with my eyes going all Bambi of their own volition.

"Daaaaadddddd," I heard myself whine, and he stiffened.

"Oh, dear, I recognize that plaintive tone and nothing good ever comes of it," he said, peering up at me. "What do you want?"

"Why do you think I automatically want something?"

"Isabel . . ." he said with a warning note in his voice. "I didn't come down with the last shower."

"Fine," I sighed without any of my usual petulance. "I was wondering if I could go out tomorrow evening for a little bit."

"We don't have rules just for the sake of it. They're there for your own good."

That all depended on your politics, but I concentrated on pouting ever so slightly. "But if I absolutely promise that I'll do my homework before I go and I'll even show it to you, couldn't you bend the rules just this once?"

"Where on earth are you going that your presence is so desperately required?" he demanded, folding his newspaper so I could have his undivided attention. Wasn't I the lucky one?

"I need to go out with Nancy and Ella and Dot," I blurted out to my surprise, because I already had an excuse that I'd made earlier about an urgent school project. "Things have been weird between the three of us lately, and I think it will just make stuff worse if I don't hang with them."

I was expecting some savage observation about the herd mentality, but he was nodding his head sagely. "I take it this is because you and Dot have been spending so much time together?" he suggested, and it was sweet that he thought that, though he couldn't have been more wrong if he'd tried.

"Yeah, kinda," I hedged. "You know how bitchy girls can be."

"Thankfully, no. Boys are rather more straightforward—they just talk about football and steer clear of the emotional baggage." He frowned at the exact same moment that I did because, hey, we were having a talk that involved actual feelings and stuff.

"Friendship can be so complicated," I said cautiously. It was a relief to talk about it, even if it was in a completely guarded fashion. "People don't want you to be yourself, they just want you to be the person that they've decided you should be."

"So, your school days are not turning out to be the best days of your life?"

"God! I hope not!" I was so aghast at the horrific idea that Dad snorted with laughter and patted my arm.

"I want you back by ten-thirty at the very latest," he said in his sternest voice—but he must have been abducted by aliens in the middle of the night because his face softened and he absent-mindedly stroked the back of my hand with his thumb. "Or, just this once, if you wanted to sleep at Dot's, then I suppose I could allow it, though I don't want you to take advantage of my good nature."

I wanted to crawl into his lap like I did when I was little and just the feel of his crisp cotton shirt against my cheek, his hand rubbing circles on my back as he recited Edward Lear poems to make me laugh, made me feel safe.

"Thanks," I managed to choke out. "I don't think I want to stay over at Dot's."

He was still stroking my hand, and I could feel my whole body straining to lean in so I could have a proper hug. But then he let go of me and sat up straight. "Goodness! Is that the time? I don't want to miss my program." He picked up the remote and aimed it at the TV.

"You need to switch it on at the set first, Dad." I stood up and performed the necessary procedure.

"Does this mean you're out of your difficult phase, Isabel?" he asked teasingly, and if he stopped being so bloody nice to me then I wouldn't have to feel quite as shitty as I did.

"I'll get back to you on that," was all I said, but he'd already tuned me out and was engrossed in some political intrigue that was more than a match for my teenage psychodramas.

I'd been praying that it would piss down with rain so our little outing to Preston Park could be postponed. But no such luck. It was cold enough that my bright red, Amélie-style winter coat could have its first airing, even though the others were wearing the kind of clothes that owed very little to the elements or the imagination. Which was just as well because the four lads that were aimlessly kicking a ball about in the fading light looked like they were sharing a brain cell.

"Jesus wept," I announced witheringly. "What's that flapping around their knees? Oh, it's their trousers. Are they too good to wear belts?"

If looks could have killed, I'd have been in a lead-lined coffin. "Shut the hell up, Is," Nancy spluttered. "They'll *hear* you."

I flicked a glance at the four boys who were now shuffling the ball nearer and looking at us like we were red-hot Mamas shaking our collective booty in a rap video. "I don't actually think they have the coordination to kick a ball about and listen at the same time. Maybe they're the missing link between men and monkeys."

"Aren't they your type, then?" Dot said quietly, flicking back her hair with a coquettish move that didn't really suit her. "Got your eye on someone else?"

"Yeah, like that geek you keep getting off with?" Nancy sniped.

I crossed my fingers behind my back. "As if . . ."

"So are we gonna do this or what?" Ella wanted to know, thrusting her boobs in the vicinity of the boys who weren't even pretending to play football now but had gone into a little huddle—and I *knew* they were divvying us up between them. They should be so lucky.

"Well, go on then, Is. Go and talk to them!" Nancy demanded in a tone of voice that she was going to spend the rest of the week regretting.

"Since when did you become the boss of me?" I inquired

icily, putting my hands on my hips and stiffening my spine 'cause I knew it made me look taller and scarier.

"You usually go and do the boy-thing for us," Dot said plaintively. "But if you don't want to . . . I mean, if you're saving yourself for someone else . . ."

"Fine!" I snapped, making a mental note to reduce her to tears with some well-placed invective at a later date. "As you three are incapable of doing anything by yourselves?"

I flounced over to the boys, who were obviously not down with my whole Amélie vibe because they looked over my shoulder to where the Trio of Evil was obviously busting some particularly slutty moves. Up close, they were even less easy on the eye. Who'd told them that so much hair gel was a good look? That person should have been executed for crimes against fashion.

They were obviously waiting for me to stop with the filthy looks and say something, so I opened my mouth and said the one bomb-proof sentence that was guaranteed to get pikey boys really hot and bothered. "Hey, me and my friends go to the local grammar school. Do you want to chip in for two bottles of cider?"

An hour later I could still feel the taste of Rob's cidery tongue swirling around the back of my throat where he'd been trying to play a contact sport with my tonsils. I'd only managed to give him the slip by pretending that I needed to go and throw up behind the Crown Bowling Green because I'd drunk too much cider.

Instead I'd set off at full pelt and didn't slow down until I'd reached the Duke of York's cinema. I was sure that if you stuck me under a UV light you'd be able to see Rob's fingerprints all over me. And he'd managed to pull one of the buttons off my coat. When Smith kissed me, he cupped the back of my head, his thumbs massaging my scalp as he took his time. Like, the kissing was worth something. As if I was worth something. And once you've had that, you can never go back.

I pulled out my phone, kinda surprised that Rob hadn't lifted it during the make-out session from hell, because all he'd been able to talk about was his successful career nicking car stereos. Seemed like even I could get a break. Or two breaks because there was no one home and I could leave a message.

"Hey, Dad, Felix, it's me. I thought I'd stay around Dot's after all. You can call me on the mobile if you need me and I'll see you tomorrow after school. Bye!"

There was no answer when I called Smith, and I needed time to work on leaving a message that didn't repeat my pushy performance of Friday night. But five minutes later, when I was buying a metric ass-load of Freshmint gum so I could get the Rob taste out of my mouth, my phone started ringing.

I can't multitask in high-stress situations and some stroppy cow behind me was already muttering as I counted out the right change. I practically threw a pound coin at the shop assistant and dived for my phone, though it was probably Dad having a change of heart.

"Look, you said it would be okay and . . ."

"What happened to hello?"

"Hey, Smith," I breathed, grabbing my change and purposely bumping into the moaning bitch who'd dared to tut when my phone rang. "I just called you."

"I know, I couldn't get to it in time and you didn't leave a message."

"Yeah, hang on . . ." I tucked the phone against my shoulder as I unwrapped three sticks of gum and shoved them in my mouth. "Look, if you have stuff on it's cool, but if not, can I come around?"

Smith gasped. "But it's Tuesday evening. Doesn't that violate your wacky weekends-only rule?"

"Oh, don't you want me to come over, then?" It shouldn't have been humanly possible for me to sound that woebegone.

"I can actually hear you pouting, it's kinda freaky." Smith chuckled.

"What are you so happy about, anyway?"

"Well, you call and make it obvious you're desperate to get your hands on me."

"You were obviously dropped on your head as a baby," I growled, but I quickened my pace so I'd get to him quicker.

"Where are you?"

"I'm just at the Level, so am I carrying straight on to your place—or am I turning right and going home?"

"You're turning right," he said, and I almost dropped the phone in shock at the casual, cruel way he'd totally been toying with me like a cat with a poor little mouse between its paws. "Because I'm in The Great Eastern on Trafalgar Street. Wanna get some chips on the way back to mine?"

"If you're buying, I just spent my last pound on chewy."

I swung right and even though I'd be seeing him in two minutes, I couldn't hang up the phone if my life depended on it. No wonder I was broke. I was spending every last penny on top-up vouchers.

"Only if you give me a kiss for every chip. Might take some time, though, if you're planning on scheduling in one of your escape bids before the clock hits ten," he added.

"Oh, I thought I'd stay over if it was all right with you." I stopped under a street lamp so I could pull out my mirror and check my face for signs of stubble rash because I was the kind of skanky girl who had two boys in one night.

"Of course it is! Gotta get up early though." He sighed. "So no dragging me back to bed to do all sorts of rude things to me."

I rolled my eyes as I slicked on a coat of lipstick. "Dream on, saddo. Gotta be up at first light . . . JESUS CHRIST! Don't do that!" I screamed as two hands snaked around my waist and someone licked my neck. "Smith! I nearly had a heart attack!"

He stepped out of the shadows with an apologetic smile as I pressed my palm against my wildly beating heart. "You have no sense of fun, Is."

"I dropped my mirror," I wailed, sinking to my knees and scrabbling on the pavement. "If it's broken that's seven years' bad luck. Shit."

"Hey, that's just a stupid superstition," Smith said, crouching down and helping me hunt for it. "Look, here it is. It's fine."

I snatched it from him and held it up to the light to check for any hairline cracks. It looked okay. I, on the other hand, looked decidedly unokay. Why was it that my hair could never just lay all flat and docile on my head but had to make its tufty presence felt? I also had a slash of lipstick halfway up my nose, thanks to Smith scaring the bejesus out of me.

Maybe that's why he was frowning at me. Then he raised his eyebrows meaningfully.

"Okay, I'm sorry that I freaked out about my mirror but I need all the luck I can get," I muttered, wiping away the excess Lolita lipstick from my face.

"C'mere," Smith said gruffly, and I went into his arms to let him repair the damage. Or, if we're going to get technical about it, I let him kiss me until I couldn't think straight and my entire mouth was lipstick-free.

We ate vinegar-doused chips in Smith's bed and washed them down with this acidic red wine that made me squinch up my face every time I took a sip.

It was all kinds of romantic, curling up under the covers and feeding each other chips. Though the grease stains on the sheets were kinda gross, and mostly we'd got into bed because the thermostat was broken on the central heating and the flat was like an icebox.

Smith devised this ingenious way of keeping warm, which ironically involved taking off all our clothes, and then I wasn't worrying about grease stains or the current power struggle with the Trio of Evil. I wasn't thinking at all.

Afterward, I cuddled up against Smith, brushing his arm with my fingers and watching, engrossed, as an army of goose bumps marched across his skin.

"This is nice," I said. "Us, y'know, hanging out and stuff."

"Yeah, I particularly liked the stuff." Smith smiled, kissing my shoulder.

I rolled on to my back and gave him my best doe-eyed look. "Just the stuff?"

"I like you," he said gravely. "I like you even more than the stuff."

I was pretty relieved to hear it. But liking me a lot, well, it seemed a little lackluster when just being near him made me feel like it was the night before Christmas.

"I like you, too," I said carefully, and he beamed, snuggling against me so he could wrap his arm around my waist. It was all his fault for looking so happy that I liked him. He was practically daring me to say it. So I did. "In fact, I'm kinda in love with you."

It sounded so pathetic when I said it out loud. I shut my eyes, but that just made the silence even more unbearable. It wasn't like I expected him to say it back, except I did and he wasn't.

Suddenly, I was aware of everything: the sheet wrinkled up underneath me, the faint scent of vinegar and how my skin was going from warm to clammy as I waited and waited for Smith to say something.

"God, it's not like I want to get married or anything!" Of course I had to open my big, fat mouth and make a horrible situation a million times worse.

Smith tried to kiss my shoulder again, but I wrenched away from him. "Isabel . . ." he said imploringly. I gave him my heart and all he could do was whine my name after, like, half an hour.

"Don't Isabel me," I snapped, sitting up and clutching the sheet around me so he couldn't see the way every single inch of me was blushing. "So, like, is this just a sex thing for you?"

Smith sat up and I noted with some venom that the dim lighting from the lamp made his nose look bigger than normal. He tried to run his fingers through his hair, then remembered he'd cut it all off. "I thought you were cool with it," he said eventually with trace amounts of anger.

"Cool with what? That I thought we were having a relationship, and all you wanted was a no-muss, no-fuss hookup. And I don't love you, anyway, just seemed like the right thing to say," I backtracked and the hole I'd dug was so big now that I couldn't even see over the top of it.

"If I wanted a no-fuss fling, you're the last girl I'd have chosen," Smith snarled, getting out of bed and snatching his jeans up from the floor. "You're so high-maintenance it's not even funny."

"And, like, Molly's a little ray of low-maintenance sunshine," I hurled at his back as he started to get dressed. "I don't bloody think so!"

"What the hell's Molly got to do with it?"

"Everything," I burst out. "I know that you're in love with her. I heard these girls talking, and now you're just making do with me until she wakes up one morning and realizes that she can't live without you. Well, it's never gonna happen!"

Smith didn't say a word. Which I was getting really bored with. He could at least have denied the trumped up Molly accusation; instead he tugged on his T-shirt. "I hate it when you get angry," he said dully, striding over to the door. "You start talking a whole lot of shit about stuff you don't know anything about. Why can't you just be like other girls and start crying when you're mad?"

"Because I'm not like other girls," I reminded him icily.

"Don't I bloody know it," he said, slamming the door so hard behind him that I swear the whole building shook.

I sat there sulking for a bit, but there didn't seem to be much point when there was no one around to see it.

Getting dressed seemed like the best option, even though it was freezing cold outside of the covers. I dragged on my jeans and assorted top layers as quickly as possible, then sunk back down on the bed in despair when I looked at the time. It was almost midnight.

I was just cobbling together a story about having a row with

Dot that would explain my sudden appearance back home way after my curfew when there was a hesitant knock on the door.

If he'd got Molly, or God forbid, Jane, to come and have a girl-to-girl chat with me about the correct timetable for declarations of love, then I'd stab him through the eye with a fork before I made my excuses and left.

There was another knock, which made me wonder if I shouldn't just hurl myself out of the window, when Smith's head appeared around the door.

"Are you planning to throw anything at me?" he asked hesitantly.

"I was leaning toward blinding you with a fork," I replied with a sour look, but he must have thought I was joking because he sidled in, a cup of tea in each hand like that was going to make everything miraculously better.

I folded my arms and decided that it was about time for me to play the silent card.

Smith placed the two mugs on the bedside table and then held up the family-sized bar of Dairy Milk he'd wedged under his arm. "Peace offering?"

"Might work if I was *normal*."

"You couldn't be normal if you tried," Smith said gently, perching next to me on the bed and smiling faintly when I inched away from him. "And maybe that's why I meant it when I said I liked you." Smith brushed my forehead with his lips, while I tried to squirm away. Then he sighed so all my baby hairs lifted in the breeze. "I've only known you for a few weeks and I didn't think either of us wanted to get into some heavy relationship. And yeah, I'm into Molly and I know that she doesn't feel the same way, but it's not up for discussion. Not ever."

But before I could move seamlessly into my next monumental snit, he kissed the little patch of skin behind my ear, which has a gazillion nerve endings all waiting to go into sensory overload from a tiny smooch. "I'm not in love with you," he repeated to make sure I got the message. "But thank you for being brave enough to say it to me."

"I already took it back."

"You can't take it back."

"Says who?"

"There are rules and I made you tea and broke into the girls' secret chocolate stash that they think I don't know about, which is pretty damn lovable in anyone's book," he said, coaxing me out of my cardigan and under the covers in one movement.

Smith was the only person in the world who could chase away my woe-is-me mood with chunks of chocolate and silly jokes about my nose turning into an icicle. And I giggled and wriggled just like he wanted me to so we could simply pretend that this was just a casual, no-strings relationship/hookup/whatever. But we both knew that he was in bed with the wrong girl.

20

I'd had to be annoyingly vague when Smith asked why I was getting up so early when I didn't have a job or a place of higher learning to go to. I muttered something about a dentist's appointment, and he got distracted by wondering out loud if I'd be the first person in the history of forever to be told off for brushing my teeth too much.

Still, as I slunk into school five minutes after Registration, I knew that I'd have to come up with some bulletproof explanation for what I actually did all day. He was pretty fond of the whole master spy theory so maybe I should go along with that.

My first lesson was Art, which suited me just fine because it meant I could hang out in the back of the studio with some paint and my headphones. Even better, the Trio of Evil didn't take Art, so I had plenty of time to work on revenge tactics for making me get off with that delinquent lout—nothing like a little vengeance to take my mind off the sugar coma from all that chocolate last night.

I hadn't taken one step inside the studio, though, before Miss Hansen was bearing down on me. Usually she doesn't bear down, just gives me a vague smile and compliments me on what I'm wearing, so I was a little nonplussed.

"Isabel, there you are!" she exclaimed worriedly.

I gave a tiny shrug and tried to look apologetic. "Sorry, I'm late. My alarm clock didn't go off and er, I seem to have forgotten all my books and stuff."

She didn't seem remotely bothered about that, because she was an art teacher and being all heavy about punctuality would have got her kicked out of the cool club.

"Mrs. Greenwood wanted to see you as soon as you arrived," she informed me with a sympathetic smile. "I'm not sure what it's about but it would probably be best if you hurry along now."

It could have been so many things. Maybe Claire had ratted me out for missing the last four care and share sessions. Or I'd given one of the juniors a funny look, and she was too scared to come back to school. Or, hey, maybe I wasn't in trouble at all and she just wanted to thank me for being such a joy to have around the place.

The mystery was solved as soon as I walked into her secretary's office and saw my father pacing agitatedly in front of the door that led to Mrs. Greenwood's inner sanctum.

"What are you doing here? What's wrong? Is it Felix? Has there been an accident?"

The moment he heard my voice, his head swiveled around like it was completely independent from his neck. Which wasn't half as scary as the look on his face, which did nothing to reassure me that everything was AOK and he'd just happened to be passing and thought he'd pop in to see if I'd had a good time last night.

"We're going home," he said, each word carefully and precisely enunciated as if English was not his first language.

I wasn't going anywhere with him, not when he was in an inexplicably filthy mood. "I've got Art and a French lit test after that, so maybe this can wait till this afternoon," I said hopefully.

He was at my side before I could even blink. I didn't know he could move that fast. "Tell Mrs. Greenwood that I'll give her a ring," he barked at her secretary, who was cowering behind her computer.

"I have Art," I reminded him again, because my survival instinct told me it would be safer to inhale noxious paint fumes than go anywhere with my father when he looked like he wanted to hang, draw, and quarter me as a preshow.

"Not bloody likely," he gritted out, then he must have suspected that I was seriously thinking about doing a runner because he grabbed my upper arm in a circulation-crushing grip that didn't ease off until he was pushing me into the car.

"I bet you've left bruises," I started to say but was silenced by a skin-stripping look.

"Be quiet," he said pleasantly. "And do up your seat belt."

I'd barely clicked it into place before he rammed his foot down on the accelerator. I clutched onto the dashboard with white-knuckled hands. "I guess you're in a mood with me about something, but slow down, *please!*"

Either he didn't hear me or he didn't care. "I mean it, Dad! Slow down or I'm going to be sick!"

He huffed but eased off on the accelerator so I could breathe again.

"So what's all this about?" I tried again. "Not like you to have no respect for the book learning. And I've behaved perfectly at school. Well, not perfectly, but I haven't . . ."

"I thought I told you to shut up. I don't want to hear another word until we get home."

Unfortunately, it only took us ten minutes before we were pulling into the driveway and I willed myself to unbuckle my seat belt and get out of the car for my full-on yelling with surround sound for some dreadful crime I didn't realize I'd committed.

I followed Dad's stiffened back up the path and scampered through the door before he could yank me through it.

"I'll put the kettle on, shall I?" I offered brightly . . . but no. Steely grip on my shoulder and I was being frog-marched to the study. Must be really serious, then.

He pushed me down onto one of the uncomfortable wooden chairs that he likes to use for these occasions and loomed over me. I squinted up at him and started taking in all sorts of telling details. Like, the fact that he didn't get acquainted with his razor this morning and that was the shirt and tie that I'd ironed for him yesterday morning. Bloodshot eyes? Check. The same clothes that he'd worn yesterday? Check. Empty wine bottle on the desk? Check.

"Did you even go to bed last night?" I asked him sullenly, and it was so easy to slip back into my role as Isabel, the worthless wretch of a daughter while he was already assuming his role of the tyrannical Victorian papa.

"I might ask you the same question," he snapped. "Or I might rephrase it as exactly whose bed did you sleep in last night?"

I gasped at the unfairness of it all. "I told you! I phoned and left a message and said I was staying at Dot's, so don't blame me.

You probably managed to wipe the message before you'd even listened to it because you do that . . ." I was working myself up into a really righteous indignation because I had told him where I was going. Okay, I wasn't *actually* at Dot's but . . .

"Ah yes, the famous message, which was then followed by approximately fifteen other messages from Dot, who seemed to be unaware that you were tucked up cozily at her house, and those other two ghastly girls that you insist on socializing with, all extremely concerned about your whereabouts."

Those evil, scheming little bitches. Phoning and leaving incriminating messages on the family answerphone violated every rule of the friend code. But then, I kept forgetting—we weren't friends.

And if I'd thought last night's silence was bad, then the loaded menace of here and now when all I could hear was a rushing in my head, was going to make the final cut on the Worst Five Moments of My Life.

"You could have rung me," I eventually said, peering down at my bag. Really bad idea. Because he stopped standing over me like the Wrath of God and snagged the handles between his thumb and index finger.

"Oh, really. I wonder why I didn't think of that," he said with a sneer. "Next time you're trying to cover your deceitful tracks, I suggest you remember to switch your phone on."

I had a dim recollection of switching my phone off after Smith had scared the life out of me (and how sorry I was that he hadn't actually succeeded), but Dad was already finding that out for himself.

"Don't go through my bag!" I yelped, leaping up as he rummaged inside and hauled out my phone, but it was too late, he was already upending my bag and spilling the contents out onto the desk.

Condoms. Cigarettes. A printout of the infamous blowjob picture. The strip of photos that Smith and I had taken when we went to Eastbourne. A flyer from the Duckie gig. It was all there. Every lie I'd told over the last few weeks spelled out in the debris from my bag.

I was looking and he was looking and muttering under his breath. I started trying to cram everything back, because if it wasn't actually there, laid out before him, I could keep on pretending, but my hand hadn't even curled around the cigarettes before he was snatching my shoulders and whirling me around so he could shake me hard enough so I bit my tongue.

"What have you been doing?" he screamed. "All these revolting things in your bag . . . I want some answers right now!"

"Get off me!" I shouted right back, trying to pry his fingers off me. "You don't go through my personal stuff! I'm sixteen and I can do what I want, and it's got fuck all to do with you!"

"It's got everything to do with me. While you're under my roof, I will . . ."

I got away from him by kicking him in the shin so he let go of me with a strangled yelp and I was free to run for the door and up the stairs before he'd stopped rubbing his leg.

Even with my five-second head start, I'd barely made it to my room before he was in the doorway and preventing all my attempts to slam the door in his face.

"Let go," he said, all deadly calm and flaring nostrils. "Let go of the door this instant."

But the calm voice just made the mist even redder. So even though he was a foot taller than me and, like, five stone heavier,

I persisted in pushing and shoving at the door and screaming at him. It wasn't even words, just these angry, high-pitched cries like an animal caught in a trap.

He soon got bored with the tug-of-war and flicked me out of the way with a really insulting ease, before striding into my room, eyes darting wildly around for even more evidence of my misdemeanors. I'm not sure what he was looking for in my wardrobe: my own little vodka distillery, or a crack den. Maybe even a brothel full of barely legal teenagers. But instead he was rifling through clothes rails, snatching up garments, knocking hangers onto the floor, and this was the worst thing of all.

"Stop it! Stop it! Stop making a mess, you're mucking everything up," I screeched, scooping up armfuls of clothes that were scrunching under his feet.

"How could you?" He said in a choked voice that was so fraught with emotion, I stopped frantically trying to calm the havoc he'd caused in my wardrobe and looked at him helplessly.

He was clutching the black dress I'd taken out of his room, a couple of jumpers, a pair of shoes that I still hadn't worn because I couldn't walk in really high heels.

"Her things, you've been going through her things, *stealing* them. How could you?" He sat down heavily on the bed, gazing unseeingly at the stuff I'd borrowed.

"They're just clothes . . . I didn't think you'd mind," I ventured timidly, shocked out of my meltdown by the way he'd gone from furious to broken in five seconds. "Look, I'll wash them and iron them and I'll put them back and you'll never even know . . ."

"I want you to tell me what happened, Isabel," he said firmly, as if I hadn't even spoken.

I shut my eyes and breathed out heavily. "I've been seeing this guy for a little while and . . ."

He gave me a look of utter loathing. I'm not being dramatic. It was so venomous and laden with hate that I stumbled backward, bumping my hip bone against the edge of the dressing table. "I couldn't care less about the sordid details of how you've been spending your time. I want to know what happened that day, when she—I want to know what you were doing that made it happen." His face twisted up and he brushed the back of his hand across his eyes, and when he took it away, his face was damp. "It's not your secret to keep. She was my wife, she was my everything, and I have a right to know why she isn't here anymore."

He was properly crying now and it was awful. And I'm not made of stone, I'm made of flesh and blood and stupid, stupid emotions. There was no way I could make it better or turn back time so she'd still be here. It would have been a fair swap to have her back: on my case 24/7, nagging and bitching and letting me know what a deep disappointment I was, just so I didn't have to look at him with his head in his hands, shaking with sobs.

I shook my head, even though he couldn't see. "I can't. I'm sorry, but I can't."

He lifted his head and clutched his little handful of memories tighter. "Get out," he said quietly. "I don't want you in this house for another second."

It didn't take me long to scurry back into the study and retrieve my bag and all the secrets it had spilled out. I grabbed a bunch of clothes from the ironing basket, but then I heard his heavy tread on the floor and there wasn't time to fold them up neatly, just stuff them in a carrier bag, drop my keys on the hall table, and walk out.

Amazingly, it wasn't even lunchtime. It should take longer for what's left of your life to fall to pieces. I switched my phone on and listened to its angry beeping, but there were no calls from the girls, all worried about my sudden disappearance, which proved my theory that they were staging their piss-poor version of a military coup. And I couldn't bear to listen to the ten messages from Dad, each one of them probably a little more caustic and frantic than the next.

I cleared them all and then tried to call Smith, before I remembered that he always turned his phone off when he had lectures. I left him a plaintive message about needing somewhere to crash for a while, and then walked down to Western Road. Thankfully, I hadn't even had time to take off my coat before World War Three had kicked off, but it was cold out. Or maybe I was cold inside. I wasn't sure, but I wished I could stop shaking.

All the loose coins in my bag were probably still lying on the study floor and my ATM card was in my room, but I managed to find a two-pound coin tucked into a side pocket, which was enough for a bacon sandwich and a cup of tea in the Mad Hatter before heading to Topshop, so I could try on outfit after outfit because it was warm and it was something to do until the security guard asked me to leave.

My next destination was the pier, which might well have been the coldest place on earth after the Arctic Circle. I dived into the amusement arcade and surreptitiously poked my hands into the trays under the slot machines to see if anyone had left their winnings.

I scrounged up enough for another cup of tea and eked it out as I watched the seagulls swoop down onto the railings, scanning the wooden slats for discarded chips—and did I mention that during all these slow hours when I tried to kill time, I must have phoned Smith every ten minutes?

It was nearly 4 P.M. and I had no choice but to start heading for Dot's house so I could throw myself on her not-so-tender mercies. Once I was inside, though, I could swap her toothpaste for foot cream or something, but my evil plans were quashed when my phone started ringing and Smith's number flashed up.

"Finally!" I said by way of a greeting. "I've been calling and calling you."

"Hey, Isabel. Yeah, I got every single one of your many messages."

He sounded weird. Or maybe the whole day had been so horribly weird that it had leaked into everything. "I'm not stalking you or anything. I've just had a really bad day, like almost the worst day since records began, so do you want to hook up?"

"I'm not at home," Smith said. "But yeah. We should meet. Do you know that little park with the swings near the marina?"

"By the closed-down kiddies train thing?"

"Yeah. I'm there now. Needed to get some fresh air, y'know?"

"Kinda." I rolled my eyes at the irony. If I had any more fresh air today, it would fricking kill me. "I can be there in ten minutes."

"Right, well, see you then." He hung up abruptly enough that it gave me pause for thought. But not really. All I could think about was how much I wanted to see Smith. Not just because of the shitty day, which I couldn't tell him about, anyway. Just dying to see him because he was him and he might not love me, but he'd make everything all right just by holding my hand and giving me one of his crooked smiles.

Smith was already waiting for me on the swings, idly stretching his legs out and hanging onto the chains so he could sway gently in the breeze.

"Hey," I called, as I got closer, but he didn't say anything so I felt self-conscious and confused about how to put one foot in front of the other.

He fixed me with an unwavering stare. "How old are you?"

I expected the world to tilt off its axis. It felt like it had for a second, before it went right way up again and it was me that was wrong way around. "Eighteen," I said, like there could ever be any doubt. "C'mon, you know that."

"Bullshit," he snapped. "How old are you?"

I decided to fight fire with a flamethrower and a can of gasoline.

"I'm eighteen," I spat. "Are you, like, deficient or something? Eighteen!"

He placed his feet on the floor and stilled the swing so he could freeze me with a look that NASA could have used if they were ever doing research into killer laser beams. "You're sixteen."

"I don't know what this is all about, but you're completely wrong because . . ."

His hands bit into my arms, settling on top of bruises that were already starting to blossom, and he yanked me close in a parody of all the embraces we'd had. So close that I could see the tiny flecks of green in his blue eyes; the smattering of freckles across the bridge of his nose; the tiny scar just above his top lip that I must have kissed a thousand times. "Stop it," he whispered in my ear. "Just stop lying."

Then he pushed me away from him, like he couldn't bear to touch me, and I stood there, hands pushed into the pockets of my coat and I was on my own again.

"So how do you know what you think you know?" I asked him eventually, still clinging on to the vain hope that I could make him believe my version of the truth. Well, not the truth so much as the random sequence of stories I'd made up.

"Well, sweetheart, you've got mutiny in the ranks. I had a very interesting call from one of your friends this afternoon. Wasn't sure who it was at first because she kept giggling so hard she couldn't speak," he said, wrinkling his face as if the memory was deeply disturbing. "How could you?"

I was getting really sick of people asking me that. "How could I what exactly?" I asked.

"She told me that you've been stringing me along for weeks, then going back to your mates to discuss all the gory details. I understand it wasn't quite as good for you as it was for me?"

I covered my burning cheeks with my hands. "Oh, God," I whimpered, and Smith shot me a flinty look.

"I was prepared to cut you some slack because she also told me about your mum, but then she got on to the fascinating topic of exactly how old you were and all my goodwill suddenly ran out."

"It's not true," I insisted woodenly, because if I kept saying it then maybe he'd believe me. Well, it was worth a shot. "None of it is true."

"Yeah, she said you'd deny everything. Probably why I found this under my windshield wiper when I came out of my lecture.

I guess the mystery of what you do all day has been solved. Your friends really don't seem to like you that much, but I guess I can understand why," he said bitterly, pulling a crumpled and slightly damp piece of paper out of his pocket and handing it to me. I took a minute to smooth down the creases, but I already recognized the school crest at the top. It was my timetable with a handy *DOB: 08/08/1989* underneath my name. Damn Mrs. Greenwood's secretary and her attention to detail.

I was screwed. I kept going from hot to cold and then hot again, and the pinched set of Smith's features was all I could see. "I never lied about how I felt. About what you mean to me," I pleaded, but he turned his head away and my words were carried off by the wind.

"Just save it," Smith said, collapsing back on the swing, like his legs didn't want to hold him up. "I don't care about how you feel. I mean, Is, it was fun when you were in one of your rare good moods or all over me like white on rice, but most of the time? You were a grade-A pain in the arse."

He was just saying it to hurt me. He had to be. I grabbed the chains of the swing and tugged him close. "Will you just look at me?" I pleaded. "You have to look at me, Smith, please."

And finally he was looking at me and I had to force myself to stay still and meet his frostbitten eyes head on. "It got out of control," I admitted. "And I wanted to tell you the truth, really I did, and there were so many things I wanted to share with you and I couldn't because all the lies kept getting in the way. You'd kiss me and hold me and you did things to me that you'd never have done if I'd told you how old I was. And even though I'd lied to you, I was glad because the way you made me feel was worth it. It was the better end of the deal."

For one second, I thought I saw his face soften and his lips tremble, and I thought I'd reached him. Made him understand. But it was just a trick of the light.

"I don't need any more of your bullshit. I never want to see you again," he said, and I wished he would shout and scream and throw his hands in the air, but I just got this dull-eyed Smith-bot who waited for me to let go of the swing and step back, before he stood up and started to walk away.

I watched him go, his shoulders hunched against the wind, which was whipping up the waves and rattling through the boarded-up kiosks.

21

It got dark and I was still sitting on the ground, back propped up against the metal posts of the swing frame. Even I knew that I should be crying. Because Smith wasn't mine anymore. Never had been. Or I should be plotting the most blood-curdling revenge I could think of on those so-called friends of mine. But I couldn't feel anything, bad or good.

I got to my feet, trying to ignore the cramp in my calves after huddling into a tiny ball for so long. I staggered back to Montpelier Villas on autopilot because if I stopped to think about it, I'd have ended up spending the night fighting crack-heads for a comfy cardboard box and a well-appointed spot under some bushes. And even I wasn't *that* stupid.

Our house looked so homely and inviting. Chinks of light showed through the curtains in the front room and, if you walked past, you'd think that a normal family lived there. My fingers were doing a good impersonation of icicles, but I managed to stab at the doorbell and listened to the chime, listened for the sound of footsteps, the inner door opening, and his shadowy outline looming behind the frosted glass.

He had to let me in. It wasn't like he could phone Social

Services and tell them to take me away. Maybe he'd make me sleep in the porch or ...

"Isabel," he intoned in his most stentorian voice. That means loud, powerful, or declamatory. He managed all of them in the space of three syllables.

I opened my mouth to say something, God knows what, but he held up his hand warningly.

"Give me your phone," he ordered, which was kinda random but I showed willing, rummaging in my bag and hoping that he wasn't going to call Smith and bawl him out for deflowering me. But he just tucked it into his shirt pocket. "While you're in this house, you will speak only when you're spoken to. You'll refrain from lying and swearing. You'll stay in your room and be allowed down for half an hour in the evening to make yourself something to eat. In the morning, I will drive you to school and then you will come straight home and go upstairs. You will not see your friends or talk to them on the phone, and you're absolutely forbidden from seeing that *boy*. Do I make myself clear?"

I nodded dumbly, staring at the polished tips of his black brogues and only forcing myself to look at his frigid face when he coughed. "Yes, that's all clear," I mumbled.

"Very well, you may come in," he said magnanimously, holding the door open for me.

The central heating was going full blast and I allowed myself just the tiniest shiver as I connected with all that warm air. "I'll go to my room, then."

"Have you eaten?" He was standing there, arms folded as he watched me unbutton my coat with fingers that didn't want to cooperate.

"I'm not hungry," I said, because it would have killed me to be granted permission to shove two pieces of bread into the toaster. I was actually so starving it felt like my stomach was about to eat itself, but he tersely inclined his head in the direction of the stairs.

The first thing I noticed was that the lock had been taken off my door. Fine. What did he think I actually did in there? But whatever it was, I couldn't do it anymore because he'd obviously whiled away the afternoon by removing the TV, the DVD player, and my stereo. The computer was still intact, but the DSL cable was missing. Must have had to get a man in for that complicated procedure.

Okay, all privileges had been taken away. Bet he'd stopped my allowance, too. None of it really mattered, anyway. The only thing that had meant anything to me had removed himself of his own free will.

I made an executive decision that having a bath didn't involve getting any forms signed in triplicate, and after I'd scrubbed every inch of myself so my skin was practically raw, I dragged on my pajamas and crawled into bed.

It seemed like I'd never be warm again. And every time I shut my eyes, they'd snap open again because the voices would start...

"Grade-A pain in the arse..."

"I was prepared to cut you some slack because she also told me about your mum..."

"I never want to see you again..."

But it wasn't enough just to have the audio, no, I had to replay that look on Smith's face before he'd walked off. Like, he'd been smelling curdled milk or bad eggs. Like, I was a plate of food suddenly crawling with maggots. Like, I was, well, nothing good. And all because I'd stretched the truth so far out of shape that it didn't even resemble the truth anymore.

It all kept chasing around and around in my head while I thought about how if I'd just said this or touched him like that, it would all have been different.

Just when I was verging on the wrong side of sane and had about six miniature versions of Smith all looking at me like I was dirt, I heard a scrabbling at the door.

I poked my head out from under the duvet, just in time to see Felix creep in, like a little kid in a slasher movie. He kept looking over his shoulder as he very slowly shut the door, then timidly approached the bed on tiptoe.

"What do you want?" I asked him tonelessly, but he was already hurling himself at me.

Normally, Felix coming right at you is a cue to run as fast as hell in the opposite direction, but I was tangled up in the quilt and couldn't evade him. Turned out all he wanted to do was clutch his arms around my neck and burst into tears.

It was very disconcerting. At first, I thought it was a Felix Evil Trick™, but the sobs increased in volume and density until I had no choice but to wrestle a hand free and gingerly pat his quaking shoulder.

"There, there." I really needed to work on my sympathetic voice. Not that Felix seemed to mind. At my first touch, he began to cry even harder, burrowing against me like he was tunneling through to Australia as I groped for the box of tissues on the bedside table.

Felix smooched his face into my neck, making my skin soggy,

until I grabbed the collar of his jumper, gently tugging him up so I could mop at his cheeks. "I hate it," he wailed.

"Hate what?" I brushed the sandy hair back from his miserable face.

"Everything," he burst out. "Nothing is fun anymore and I miss *her*, Is, and there's no one who cuddles me or kisses me, and you and Daddy are always arguing and it makes my tummy hurt and I'm so unhappy . . ."

And I went from not being able to hug him to having my arms full of him, squeezing him so tight that rib breakage was a distinct possibility. But Felix just clung to me, as I rocked him back and forth.

"I'm sorry," I breathed, kissing his hot, damp cheek. "I'm sorry. I'm so sorry."

I don't know how long I held him, long enough that his sobs died down to the occasional hiccup, but when I tried to let go, he moaned piteously and I had to keep on cuddling him.

"You have to get ready for bed now," I whispered in his ear. "Otherwise Dad will come looking for you and there'll be another row."

I felt him nod, and then he was struggling free and wiping his snotty nose on the sleeve of his jumper.

"Ewwww, that's disgusting. Use a tissue."

Felix smiled ruefully. "I wish you weren't so mean to me all the time," he confessed. "Then I'd like you more."

"Yeah, yeah, you're going to have to get to the back of the queue on that one. And you give as good as you get, Monkeyboy." I sighed, propping myself up on the pillows. "So, what's been going on today then?"

There was a shrug and some lip biting. "Nothing."

"Pretty tearful sort of nothing," I said casually, and he went into this long, garbled explanation that was hard to follow without subtitles. The general gist of it was that he dropped the famous diorama on the way home from school and Dad had thrown fifty fits about it.

"And he made me eat broccoli," he finished in an aggrieved tone, pulling a 'yeuch' face like he could still taste it. "Then he was on the phone to Granny Hampstead for ages about you and how you were uncontrollable and he was thinking about boarding school, and then he laughed and said there must be one that wouldn't send you home for the holidays."

Yeah, bet that must have really tickled his funny bone, the thought of shoving me into some lockdown educational establishment where he could just forget that I ever existed.

"I don't want you to go," Felix said, getting up on his knees to give me another fierce hug. "Couldn't you just tell him you were sorry?"

That was such a loaded question. There were things I should apologize for that I couldn't even begin to think about. And then there were the other things, like Smith, which I'd never say sorry for because it would have been a lie, and I was never going to tell another lie ever again. I was going cold turkey on the whole untruth issue.

"It's not that simple," I said, reaching forward to cup Felix's pointy chin in my hand. "We're beyond sorry now. And you're beyond bedtime, so you'd better scram."

Felix slid off the bed, then paused. "I brought you this," he said, pulling something out of the pocket of his jeans. "I think it's melted a bit."

The Snickers bar had melted quite a lot and didn't even begin to make inroads into my empty stomach. I curled myself into a ball, licking the chocolate off my fingers and settled down to wait for morning.

I was wandering around a supermarket and everything was hyper-real and saturated with color, cartoonlike.

She was pushing the trolley around, humming under her breath as she dropped tin after tin on the floor, kicking them out of the way when they got stuck under the wheels.

I tugged at her sleeve because people were staring, and she looked down at me with a distracted smile.

"You know your father won't eat tinned food, sweetie." She shook her head sorrowfully. "You never listen, do you? We must have had this conversation a hundred times."

We turned the corner and now she was sweeping jars of jam off the shelves, letting them drop to the ground in an explosion of glass as they shattered. When I looked behind us, there was a trail of strawberry jam that looked exactly like blood.

It was blood. I could see it staining her hands, smearing on the handle of the trolley and dripping down her white skirt. "I must have cut myself on the glass," she said with a laugh, stroking my cheek, her touch wet and sticky. "I told you not to drop all those jars."

That wasn't true, but it didn't seem right to point it out when I couldn't speak and her face was getting paler and paler. . . .

"That's it! I'm waking up," I said out loud as I forced myself out of another dream that was going to end in exactly the same way as all the others.

I fumbled for the lamp switch and grabbed my copy of *Bonjour Tristesse* from the nightstand. Sleep was overrated, anyway.

22

The new regime kicked off bright and early the next day. I ate two bowls of cereal and a banana, with Dad's steely gaze doing its level best to ruin my appetite before we set off for school.

I thought that once Felix had been dropped off with a cheery wave and a note about the diorama in his blazer pocket, we'd move seamlessly into whatever chapter of the row we were on. But the rest of the journey was accomplished in a tense silence. As we pulled up outside the gates, I had the door open before he'd even finished turning off the engine. But his hand clamped around my wrist in an instant.

"I'm coming in with you," he insisted. "Mrs. Greenwood and I have a meeting."

He was spending so much time at my school, he should have set up an office in one of the supply cupboards. I kept my eyes straight ahead, not looking left or right, or listening to the giggles that accompanied us as he kept a deathly tight grip on my arm.

The meeting with Mrs. Greenwood was like this exercise in abject humiliation. After briefly recounting my many crimes—and no one should ever have to bear witness to one's father and headmistress discussing your sex life—I think she even started to feel sorry for me. But all she could do was flail her hands as he went through this list he had in his briefcase.

There was a lot of guff about my grades and homework, which she managed to deflect by showing him my spotless academic record, and then it got nasty. From this moment forth I was:

- To spend the lunch hour supervised by a member of the staff to make sure I didn't leave the school grounds.
- To be put into detention every afternoon until such a time as he could come and collect me.
- To sign up for some extracurricular activities, including the debating team, the school newspaper, and the loser squad who did do-gooding in the local community.

It was only when he started on the thorny topic of locker searches that Mrs. Greenwood dared to interrupt.

"I understand that Isabel could benefit from some additional discipline, but the school has a very strict policy about pupils' rights to privacy," she said sternly, peering over her glasses at my father who cocked an eyebrow and looked distinctly unamused.

"Of course, Mrs. Greenwood, I understand," he said mildly. "If you can't provide my daughter with the adequate supervision that she requires maybe I should look into removing her from the school."

Mrs. Greenwood gave me a sympathetic look before she could stop herself. "I would very much advise against disrupting Isabel's education at such a critical time," she said tentatively. "Continuity of care is a quality I feel we're able to provide, and if Isabel would only attend the counseling sessions that . . ."

"I want her locker searched," he said baldly. "I must insist."

He got his way. Of course, he did. And as luck would have it, the bell was ringing for morning break just in time for most of the school to witness the ceremonial unlocking of my locker. The only incriminating pieces of evidence were an empty cigarette packet and a couple of overdue library books, but by then it was too late. I was no longer, Isabel, the unrivaled queen of all she surveyed. I was Isabel, the biggest geek in the school, who had her dad bawl her out for smoking in front of everyone.

That was the high point of the day. Even having to eat my lunch with a bunch of Year Nines who all shifted their chairs away from me, couldn't come close.

The truth was that nothing could touch me anymore. Hurt is all relative. It's, like, if someone jabs a knife in your heart, then you're not going to notice a paper cut. So all the stuff at school was just bells and whistles.

The Trio of Evil didn't seem to have got that memo, though. It took them all day to get me on my own without a teacher hovering to make sure I didn't skip out. But even members of the faculty couldn't come to the loo with me.

I was washing my hands and composing version five of the letter to Smith, which would miraculously make everything okay between us, when the door opened and they trooped in. I was as cool as a refrigerator full of cucumbers, as they gathered around me in a little semicircle. My hands didn't even shake, as I tore off some paper towels and eyed their reflections in the mirror.

"So, Is, how have you been?" Nancy finally broke the silence, and I turned around so I could lean back casually against the sink.

"Peachy." I summoned up a faint smile. "On top of the world. Everything's great. How about you?"

Ella moved forward. "We've been really worried about you," she said, eyes wide. "Rushing off like that the other night . . . so we had to call your dad, it's what friends do."

I knew they had this whole scene planned out. They'd probably had a dress rehearsal. Nancy and Ella couldn't quite quell the cat-that-got-the-cream smiles, but it was Dot I couldn't take my eyes off. She looked different. Like, she'd got taller or prettier.

"It was you, wasn't it?" I shook my head. "'Course it was. Not like Nancy or Ella have the brains to plot this little *coup d'état*."

"Hey!" Nancy spat indignantly, but Dot made this little gesture with her hand and she shut up. Ella was trying to work out what *coup d'état* meant.

"You always underestimated me," she said simply. "You expected me to jump when you said the word and to know my place. Well, Is, I'm finished, and guess what? So are you."

"I'm trying out this new thing where I stop telling so many lies," I said, and I really wished that Nancy and Ella were someplace else because this was between me and Dot. "So, look, I'm sorry that I was a bitch on wheels, but I did it to survive this place and you're going to find out exactly what I mean. It's tough at the top."

Dot smoothed the edges of her fringe with a finger and gave me a smile that made the hairs on the back of my neck stand to attention. "It's worse at the bottom."

"Oh yeah, did your boyfriend get the note I shoved on the windshield of his crappy little car?" Nancy suddenly piped up. I so wouldn't miss her squawking voice.

"You shouldn't have dragged him into it," I said to Dot, who

234

all of a sudden didn't want to meet my eyes. "None of this was to do with him."

"Bet he dumped your sorry arse," Nancy chimed in.

"Did you phone him, Dot? I'm not gonna be angry, I just need to know what you said." I had this awful note of pleading in my voice, but I didn't care. "You can have it—all this power that you think is going to make your life complete—but if you have one ounce of respect for the fact that we used to be friends, then you have to—"

"I don't have to anything," Dot snapped, sliding forward so I wasn't leaning against the sink anymore but pressed right into the enamel. She wasn't looking quite so pretty right then. "It was all right for you to slag off every guy that we liked, but then you fall for some lanky student and . . . God, Isabel, it was embarrassing to hear you go on. 'Oooh, Smith, he's so dreamy. He's so thoughtful. He holds me all night long.'" Her voice rose up in this simper that sounded nothing like me, while Nancy and Ella came in on the chorus with these synchronized titters that made my skin crawl.

It took several long moments before I could resist the urge to rearrange Dot's smug little face with my fist. "Fine," I said at last, forcing myself to twist out from against the basin. Bad move. Then I had Ella and Nancy bookending me so I couldn't get to the door. "Okay, did you have this big finale planned where you flush my head down the loo? You'd better make it quick, I should be in detention."

"Let her go," Dot said graciously. "We can continue this tonight. I want you around at mine at—"

"No." I was already at the door. "I'm grounded until I'm thirty, which, I'm sure you'll be pleased to know, is a result of your evil machinations, but see, we don't have to pretend to be friends now."

"Oh, we don't hate you." Ella sounded pretty sincere, but then it was hard to second-guess Ella—she never seemed to be playing with the full set of cards. "You're, like, on probation so we can still hang out and stuff, but you have to be the new Dot now."

"But you're still the old Ella," I pointed out. "Sucks to be you, eh?"

"Not half as much as it sucks to be *you*." Nancy glowered.

"Ella's right," Dot said smoothly, cutting through Nancy's angry mutterings. "We wouldn't want you to be all on your own. Not after all the crap you've pulled on other people. It would be really unfair. So we had a big talk about it last night and we decided that you can still be one of us if you agree to a few little rules."

I looked at their eager faces; they were waiting for me to throw myself at their feet in supplication, literally. I thought back to all the fun times we'd shared, all the fond memories of hanging with the gang—and I couldn't come up with anything. Not one single happy moment when the four of us were in perfect harmony about anything that didn't include making someone's life utter misery. It was quite a revelation.

"You know what?" I said conversationally, making sure my fingers were already on the door handle. "It's really nice of you guys to be looking out for me, but I think I'll pass. When have we ever been there for one another, without some nasty ulterior motive?"

Dot shifted uncomfortably like she had itching powder in her pants. "You'd have done exactly the same, Is."

"Maybe I would. Guess we'll never know. But my point is that we're not friends, we never were, and I certainly don't want to waste any more time with a bunch of retarded, wannabe sluts like you."

And the matching expressions of utter disbelief on their faces were almost worth every indignity I'd had to suffer in the last twenty-four hours. Almost.

23

School was rapidly becoming my favorite place in the whole wide world. At least it wasn't home, where I was on intimate terms with every inch of my bedroom walls and had to choke down dinner under Papa's ever watchful glare. I put my elbows on the table one night and he almost had an apoplexy. Fun times.

At school it was easier to ignore six hundred people who hated my guts. I clamped on my headphones, and rose above the threats and the smirks to a sound track of angry-girl music. Being chaperoned every minute of the school day was a big help, especially as one of the Year Nines on my lunch table told me that some of her classmates had put a contract out to have me pushed down the steps. It was like *The Sopranos* meets *Bring It On.*

I've bullied enough people to know that the minute you show them that they're getting to you, you've signed your death warrant. But if you can weather the storm, sooner or later someone who isn't you will fuck up and the attention will shift. It was taking a long time. A week went by, then another one, and I could live with the shoulder bumping and the Diet Coke that someone poured into my open bag. The grafitti in the loos that said: "Isabel Clarke is a big, skanky ho. Stop her and ask her how," was a nice touch, but what didn't destroy me made me stronger. Repeat to fade.

So I kept my face blank and didn't let anyone know what was going on inside. Inside there was this ache right where my heart used to be. It was Smith-shaped. And all those pages of A4 lined paper I covered with my crabbed scrawl had nothing to do with the extra homework Dad had insisted I was given. I was now on version nine of the Smith letter.

The first six versions lacked poetry. But what they lacked in rhyming couplets, they made up for in dogged, not-getting-a-clueness. I was in the denial stage then, so they were all variations on "I miss you," "I love you," "I'm sorry," written out over and over again in my best handwriting, like I'd been set lines to prove my contrition.

Then I went into grief mode, which involved scrawling out achingly relevant song lyrics on Post-it notes, which I was going to make into this emo-tastic collage, scan it on my computer, and e-mail to him from the school computer lab.

But now I was edging into anger. It was starting to dawn on me that his entire motivation had been about getting me naked—he was everything those girls had said he was and I'd been too lame to see it. So, version nine was hopelessly stalled on the opening sentence: *You really are an utter bastard, aren't you?*

I screwed the piece of paper into a ball and chucked it in the general vicinity of the garbage bin, when there was a cursory knock and my father stepped into my room. Hey, thanks for knocking.

He looked around suspiciously to make sure I hadn't constructed a bong out of graph paper and string. When he was satisfied that I was living within the letter of the law, he folded his arms and subjected me to his gimlet gaze. To be honest, I'd looked better. My roots were starting to come through in all their dirty-blonde glory and, as I had no money for luxuries like black hair dye, they just had to stay like that. Plus, the whole pale and thin angle I was working screamed 'teen crackhead' really loudly.

His nose wrinkled, so I guess he was thinking more or less the same thing as I sat cross-legged on the bed and waited for him to say something. At least not speaking until I was spoken to meant I didn't have to make polite conversation.

"I can't come and pick you up tomorrow afternoon. Felix got top marks for his diorama and I promised I'd take him to the cinema."

Typical! When I turned in 95 percent on a test, there was always a pained inquiry as to what happened to the other 5 percent. "Okay," I said uncertainly. "What do you want me to do?"

I was sure he'd devised some scheme that heavily featured a private security firm, but his shoulders slumped. "I'm trusting you to come straight home after school. If that's going to be a problem, then you can explain to Felix why our outing has to be canceled."

I airily waved a hand. "It's fine. I'll come straight home. I won't pass go, I won't collect two hundred quid . . ." but I was talking to the empty space where he'd been standing, and the rest of my sentence was drowned out by the door slamming.

Friday was a very painful day. Mostly because I repeatedly got hit with hockey sticks by Ella and Nancy during Games. They apologized profusely each time Mrs. Harris caught them, then walked back to Dot so she could pat them on the head. I'd never have pulled such a cheap trick in my day. I'd had, like, *style*.

I was hobbling to my Art History with an incomplete homework assignment when I realized there didn't seem much point in turning up. There didn't seem to be much point to a whole lot of things, so I kept on walking. There was no one about, just the faint scrabble of pens, a distant voice reciting one of Shakespeare's sonnets, the whooshing flame of a Bunsen burner. And I couldn't breathe from the faint smell of disinfectant and school dinners leaking up from the canteen and the sly looks and the head tilts and just the endless, relentless sameness of it all, which was choking the life out of me.

I walked out into the yard, through the gates, then ran to catch the bus that was just pulling into the stop.

I liked the sensation of uncertainty. Of not knowing where I was going, but as the bus headed along the coastal road, I began to recognize certain landmarks: the burger bar with the stupid dinosaur outside it, the row of mint-green beach huts. The café where Grandpa made the driver stop so he could buy Felix an ice cream to stop him crying on the way home from the funeral.

The bus dropped me at the cemetery gates and although I was sure I didn't know the way, my feet carried me along the rows as if the rugged path through the serried ranks of graves and tufted grass was a familiar one. I hadn't been there since that day when the sun glared down on me through the thin black cotton of the dress that my aunt Pam had bought me, and I'd stood at the back, concentrating on the tips of my toes in my one pair of nice shoes and pretended not to notice the looks and the whispering.

The grave was tucked away in this quiet little corner. She'd have hated that. She'd always liked to be the center of attention. Always had to know what was going on, even when it was nothing to do with her. There was a little glass jar of daisies, so Dad must have been here sometime in the last couple of days because the flowers were still fresh, petals milky white as they fluttered in the breeze.

And the stone was up now.

FAITH CLARKE
1967–2005
BELOVED WIFE OF DAVID,
DEVOTED MOTHER OF ISABEL AND FELIX

I love you without knowing how, or when, or from where,
I love you simply, without problems or pride:
I love you in this way because I don't know any other way of loving.

The last lines are from a poem by Pablo Neruda that they read to each other at their wedding. On their anniversary, Dad would always get her a bunch of daisies because she'd had them in her bouquet, and he'd go down on one knee and recite the whole poem to her, and she'd blush and tell him not to be so ridiculous. But secretly, you could tell she was pleased that he hadn't forgotten. They were like that a lot—always teasing each other, locked into this private world where there was only room for the two of them.

Not that it had done either of them any good. Because now he was miserable and fucked up and she . . . she was lying in the ground underneath my feet.

But as I stood there, listening to the seagulls circling overhead and the distant sound of the waves, felt the long grass brushing against my ankles, I couldn't understand why. I looked down at my hands flexing and stretching nervously and I just couldn't understand how you could go from being alive, from having molecules and blood cells constantly shifting around inside you, and thought processes and a mind full of memories and dreams and love and hate, and in just one tiny second these miraculous things stop and you're dead. How could all that disappear? What happened to your soul, your essence, your wonder? Just because a muscle stops beating? It made absolutely no sense.

After the funeral, the vicar had cornered me while I sat in the garden and embarked on this long speech that I'm sure he always pulled out on those kind of occasions about how when someone dies, they're not really gone. You might not be able to see them but they're always with you and you carry them around in your heart.

It was a filthy lie. She wasn't all around me. She'd gone for good. She was in the ground and she wasn't ever coming back. And it made me so mad that I reached down, scooped up the jar with the flowers in it, and hurled it as far as I could.

My iPod battery petered out as I walked slowly back into town. I toyed with the idea of storming over to Kemp Town so I could give Smith version fifteen of the letter in audiobook style. But as that would mostly have involved screaming, "You chickenshit wanker," it was best that I followed orders and scurried home like a good little girl.

When I felt the hand on my shoulder, my immediate thought

was that it *was* Smith, because our thoughts had telepathically collided and in that split nanosecond, my whole body came alive. But then a familiar voice said, "I want a word with you," and I turned around to face Molly and the really belligerent look on her face.

"Oh, hey . . ."

"Don't 'oh hey' me," she snapped, wagging a finger at me, which would have been funny except she meant it. "How could you do that to Smith?"

Even though it was Molly and I did have a teensy case of hero worship, she was just another person grabbing me with hard hands and looking at me with that perfect blend of disgust and disappointment.

"Why don't you just piss off?" I spat out.

Molly's eyes opened Bambi-wide. "God, you look dreadful," she breathed and, yeah, she had a point. There was the swollen cut on my face, stringy hair, and the crumpled jumper that I'd been wearing for four days, which really helped with the whole Little Orphan Annie thing I was working. But she stiffened up again pretty quickly, because obviously after the way I'd treated poor, defenseless Smith I deserved to look awful. "Smith told me what you did."

That was big of him. I didn't realize I'd said it out loud until her eyes narrowed and she jabbed her finger against my collarbone, which hurt.

"What are you going to do? Write a song about it?" I taunted, because I knew she couldn't wait to rush back and tell Smith that I was obviously pining for him. Well, she could tell him how I was still the biggest bitch in the 01273 area code while she was at it.

"I wouldn't give you the satisfaction," she said haughtily. "I only write songs about people I like."

"Well, somehow I'll manage to get over that crushing blow. And you can tell Smith, from me, that he's . . . he's . . . a . . ." I couldn't really summon up the words to convey exactly what Smith was. It wasn't even straight in my own head, whether I loved him or hated him or any of the million shades in between.

Molly wasn't exactly waiting with bated breath for me to get to the end of my sentence, anyway. She was too busy gathering me up by my coat lapels so she could get right in my face. "You stay away from him," she warned me, nose wrinkling up in distaste. "He doesn't need a psycho-queen like you trying to fuck with his head."

I wrenched away from her with a ripping noise as the collar of my coat gave up the fight. "I bet it suits you to have me out of the picture," I shrieked, demented-harpie-style, causing shoppers to turn around and stare. "So then you can have him all to yourself because, like, you know he's totally in love with you and you're just stringing him along. Must remind you of your rock 'n' roll days."

"What the hell are you talking about?" Molly stopped contemplating how she'd ruined my very expensive, very lovely coat and tried to look innocent. "Me and Smith? God, that would be like incest or something equally gross. Who told you that?"

"He told me himself," I said with grim satisfaction. "You'd know, too, if you weren't so tragically self-involved."

"I'm self-involved?" she gaped indignantly. "What about you?"

"What about me? You don't know anything about me and it's none of your business, anyway," I choked out, pressing the heel of my hand against my pounding head.

"Isabel, are you all right?" It was unthinkable, but she was curving her arm around my shoulders and trying to hug me.

"I'm fine," I snarled, my teeth snapping together as I pushed her away. "You can fuck off and so can he!"

But I wasn't fine. I was about as far from fine as it was humanly possible to be. I ran all the way up the 180-degree gradient of Montpelier Road before I could get home, lock the door behind me, and slide to the floor. It took a while to persuade my body that it didn't need a triple bypass, and then I looked up and saw the note stuck to the banister.

Isabel: (he'd written in his perfect copperplate script)
Felix and I will be back at approximately nine-thirty.
There are some eggs and cheese in the fridge so you can
make an omelet for your evening meal.
I expect to find you in your room when we return, and then
I'd like to have a talk with you about your future plans.
DC

He was even more pompous via the medium of the written word. I had five hours to watch TV, use the phone to call every single one of my many friends, and gorge on any junk food I could find.

So I wasn't amused to find that he'd *locked* the living room door so I couldn't get near the telly. And as I wandered down the hall toward the kitchen, the future plans that he'd mentioned seemed to take a sinister turn that didn't involve UCAS forms and what I wanted to do on the weekend.

The study door was unlocked because why would I want to go in there? It didn't take me long to find what I was looking for.

They were in the second drawer that I looked in, a clutch of glossy brochures from places that all started with "Saint."

Saint Mary's. Saint Augustine's. Saint Ignatius's. Saint Mary's again. We weren't even Catholic. I flicked one open and began to read: . . . *emphasis on academic excellence in an environment free from the distractions that can lead impressionable adolescents astray. We pride ourselves on learning through discipline and prayer and have many years of experience in dealing with students who have special emotional needs.* That was from the prospectus for Saint Mary's the second, but they all said pretty much the same thing.

He was going to send me away. For real. Away from Felix. Away from Brighton. Away from any chance of making things right again.

I ripped the first brochure, the second, and the third and the fourth, until there were little pieces of colored paper floating around my feet like confetti. Then I looked at all his books, standing to attention on the shelves, all lovingly alphabetized and stroked while he searched for the right reference.

"You love those damn books more than you love me," she used to say pitifully when she was trying to coax him out of the study to, like, engage with another human being. And he'd smile really sweetly, in this way that he's forgotten how, and say, "I don't love anything more than you, but the books do come a close second."

And now she was gone and it was just him and his books and anything that wasn't right, that couldn't be filed away or put on a shelf where it couldn't get into any trouble, was just parceled up and sent somewhere else.

My hands were bleeding by the time I'd finished. I didn't even know you could cut your hands from tearing up books.

From ripping their spines apart and sending their covers hurtling into the far corners of the room. From slashing pages and stomping them underfoot. It looked like a hurricane had torn through the study, and it was only when I saw the havoc I'd wreaked that I realized that there was no coming back from this. Maybe that's why I'd done it.

I didn't bother packing a bag this time. All my clothes were dirty, anyway. I just went back into the desk for the fifty pounds he hid there for emergencies, which he thought I didn't know about, and headed for the only place where there was a chance I'd get a welcome.

24

Dot made me beg for it. I stood, shivering on her doorstep, while she asked Nancy and Ella, standing behind her, what they thought she should do. She turned back to me with determination quivering from every pore. "I'll let you in, but there's a few conditions."

I stood there for at least another ten minutes until the three of them were satisfied with my rendition: "I'm really sorry for being such a colossal bitch. I'm also very grateful that you're prepared to give me a second chance, even though I have a lot of work to do to make things up to you." Finally, my complete lack of sincerity passed muster and I was allowed to cross over the threshold. I was amazed that they hadn't filmed my comeuppance on Nancy's camera phone.

"Is your mum in?" I asked Dot, who didn't seem as ecstatic about my capitulation as I thought she would be. She shook her head emphatically and then started evaluating my sorry state.

"God, you look like shit," she declared. "Did they do that to your face?"

I made a noncommittal noise, but even that pulled at the

tightening scab on my cheek. "Guess I'm not ready for my close-up, huh?"

"She can't go out with us looking like *that*." Nancy was completely unrepentant about trying to maim me. "We're not going to get any action if she's tagging along like our special-needs friend."

I knew that Dot was mentally counting to ten because she bit her lip and shoved her hands behind her back. Seemed like the responsibilities of leadership were starting to get to her. Ha!

"Go upstairs and have a shower and do something, anything, with your hair." It was so much easier when someone else was making the decisions for me. I obediently headed for the stairs. "You can borrow some of my clothes but not my Miss Sixty jeans and not my new black skirt or my green jumper with the beading and . . ."

I was wearing two T-shirts, a jumper, Dot's third-best pair of jeans, and was drying my hair when she sidled into her room, glancing over her shoulder like she wanted to make sure we were alone.

"They're driving me mad," she growled, crouching down on the floor next to me so she could push a plate of pizza at me. "I never realized what a couple of nasty ho-bags Nancy and Ella really are."

I wasn't sure if she was playing me or not and if I agreed with her, Nancy and Ella would suddenly burst in and start giving me ten shades of hell. I settled for a nonspecific grunt.

"We can still be friends, you and me," she continued, steadying herself by putting a hand on my knee. "Like we were before, away from those two. I wanted you to know that." She was watching me carefully for signs of extreme gratitude that I was getting the chance to be her bestest friend. Never going to happen.

"Okay, cool," I said, fingering the ends of my hair to see if they were dry. "Thanks for letting me borrow some clothes." Then something else occurred to me. "My dad's probably going to call in a couple of hours and demand that you send me home for some light torture."

"You've had a pretty crappy couple of weeks, haven't you?"

I had, I really had, and Dot was responsible for most of it. Gotta love the irony. "Well, I've had better, I've had worse. It all depends on your politics. You know me, I'm tougher than I look."

Dot and I shared a deeply significant look as she processed the subtle warning. But it wasn't true. I was starting to get the nagging suspicion that I wasn't tougher than I looked. Inside, I was as fluffy and insubstantial as a marshmallow.

"It wasn't personal, Is. Well, not much. I just saw an opportunity and I went with it." My lack of official approval for her new dictatorship was really bothering Dot. "I'm not going to apologize, but I just wanted you to know."

"Look, it's fine. I'm fine. Everything's fine." I waved the hand that was clenching the brush so tightly I was amazed it didn't snap in half. "So what have you got planned for tonight?"

When she gave me a rundown on the social itinerary, I almost considered going back home to face Dad's spectacular fury. Instead, I pulled on my ripped coat and listened to Nancy and Ella witter on about the loser boys from the park, like they'd miraculously transformed into sex gods since I'd last seen them.

"I think Rob will give you a second chance if you tell him you're sorry," Ella explained doubtfully as we trudged down the road. "He thinks you're tight."

"Yeah, he doesn't know you only put out for fugly students," Nancy added tartly, and was shushed by Dot.

"That's all in the past now, right, Is? Ancient history."

"Yup," I assured her. "It's practically Paleozoic."

All three of them turned to glare at me. "Don't start using long words that nobody understands. Jesus!"

That pretty much set the tone for the rest of the evening. We met the boys in Churchill Square and trailed around after them as they eyed up candidates for happy slapping. It was like being in the middle of a documentary about delinquent youths on Channel Four.

"They're not actually going to attack someone, are they?" I hissed at Dot as they swaggered toward some hapless little nerd who was standing outside Borders.

Dot gave me an incredulous stare. "They're just acting hard to impress us. Lighten up, Is!"

After they'd jostled the nerdy kid for a few seconds, two security guards appeared and I found myself being pulled along by Rob, our sweaty hands clasped together as we stumbled down Silkwood Road.

"That was fun, huh?" he bellowed at me, when we came to a halt and I could catch my breath.

"More fun than I've ever had," I agreed gravely as the others caught up with us. "You really know how to have a good time."

My sarcasm didn't register. I don't think Rob even knew what sarcasm was, but he'd obviously decided that despite my tightness, I was worth another go. He slung his arm across my shoulder so one meaty paw was almost swiping at my breast and leered at me.

"Wanna go halves on some booze again, then?"

Rob behaved like a perfect gentleman. He held the door open for me and stumped up a bit extra for some Stella Artois in order to woo me. All I knew is that if I had some alcohol, then maybe I could forget about the utter crappiness of everything for five minutes. If I had a lot of alcohol, then maybe I could forget it for even longer.

The next thrilling installment of our evening was cozying up in one of the rain shelters on the seafront drinking lager. We sat on the boys' laps and chucked the empty cans over the railings that led down to the beach. I was feeling buzzed enough that I didn't want to poke Rob's eyes out every time he squeezed my thigh. I could even ignore the encouraging looks the others kept giving me.

"This is boring!" Rob announced, aiming the last can in the general direction of the nearest trash bin. It missed by a mile. "We should do something really exciting."

There were murmurings of agreement, but I just sat there with a smile so fake it made my face hurt. I didn't want to be freezing my butt off on the seafront on a cold November night with people I didn't like. I wanted to be warm and safe . . .

"Yeah! Fuck, yeah!"

"Good one, Roberto!"

I looked up in surprise as Rob punched the air and I nearly fell off his lap. "Huh? What did I miss?"

"It's a surprise," Nancy said, lifting up her mouth from where it had been sucking on Ratboy's tongue. Her lipstick was smeared all over her chin, which I didn't bother telling her about. "Come on, let's go!"

Our big evening of fun involved far too much walking in subzero temperatures for my liking. I shivered slightly, which was Rob's cue to wrap his arm around me while his other arm, well . . .

"Okay, this might be a really stupid question, but what are you doing?"

He smiled goofily. "You always get one stupid twat who doesn't lock his door," he informed me, trying the handle of the next car.

Aw, sweet. He wanted to show me his expertise at nicking car stereos, in some throwbacky way to killing a woolly mammoth and dragging it back to the cave to prove his hunter-gatherer skills.

"Riiiigghhht," I said uncertainly, hoping that no stupid twats *had* left their doors unlocked. I might have been queen of the five-finger discount, but even I had my standards.

"Got one!" There was a shout from farther down the road and a big whoop! We were off and running *again*, the wind stinging the cut on my face and making my eyes water.

Rob wriggled into the driver's seat and fumbled under the steering wheel, as we all peered into the Nissan Micra's dark interior to see what he was doing.

"Well, this is fun," I said brightly to Ella. "I knew I needed to get out more."

"It is fun, isn't it?" she agreed happily. "Pity Dot's missing it."

"She's gone back to Gary's," Nancy said with a terse shrug of her shoulders. "Said she was cold. Lightweight."

There was a spluttery engine noise before the car purred into life. "Get in, quick!"

"I thought he was just going to take the CD player," I protested, but Rob was already yanking me onto his lap, ignoring my squeak as the steering wheel jabbed into my tummy.

Nancy, Ella, and Ratboy were climbing over the passenger seat into the back, then pushing the seat upright so Ella's guy could make himself comfy.

"There isn't room for me," I said, trying to struggle free. "We can't get the seat belt around both of us."

"Just chill out." Rob laughed. "I've done this a million times."

"Yeah, Is, don't be such a whiny little baby," Nancy snapped, but it was okay for her, all snug and comfy in the back.

Rob kept hold of me with one hand and slammed the door shut with the other. "Right, let's see how fast this thing can go."

I could feel panic welling up in my chest, blocking my airways so I had to start panting hard. "I wanna get out. Let me out, now!"

"Shut the fuck up!" one of the boys said, and I was wedged against the door as Rob put his foot down on the accelerator and pulled away from the curb in a screech of tires that made me flinch.

"It's all right. We'll just go up to Rottingdean and see the lights," Rob called over the roar of the engine, and he thumped my arm in what he probably thought was a comforting gesture. I wormed my hand down toward the floor so I could grip onto the edge of the seat.

"It'll be okay," Ella agreed. "Here, have some more to drink."

I grabbed the can from her, closed my eyes, and downed it in three nervous gulps. It helped, and the buzzy feeling was back so that as Rob picked up speed I started to like the sensation of going too fast, of watching the road blur in front of us, and the way the streetlights seemed to melt. It was like flying.

"Cool, innit?"

I squinted at Rob. "It kind of is."

"Want me to go faster?"

"Yeah, go on, then."

We were high above the town, climbing up past the posh girls' school and on toward Saltdean. I thought that the road would never end and the petrol tank would never empty and we'd stay in perpetual motion forever. Not getting anywhere, just going faster and faster and faster and the lights coming toward us were so bright, so pretty, so dazzling . . .

"Shit!"

Rob suddenly swerved to the left, throwing his whole body behind the wheel as we veered onto the wrong side of the road. I heard the frantic beeping of a horn, and we smashed through a fence. Then a sickening crunch as we slammed into something that hurled me forward so I smacked my head against the steering wheel, then snapped backward as Rob managed to stop the car.

I should have passed out. Drifted into this heavy, velvet blackness so it didn't hurt. But my body never did anything I wanted it to, so I slumped against Rob and moaned because there were so many shooting pains stabbing into me I couldn't begin to separate them.

"Oh, my God, is everyone okay?" I was dimly aware of Ella crying. There was something wet on my forehead, dripping into my eyes, and I tried to lift my hand to brush it away.

"I'm stuck," I said, but it didn't come out right because I'd bitten my tongue and it was hard to maneuver the words out. "My hand's stuck."

My arm was trapped between the seat and the door, and when I tried to pull it free, I really wished I hadn't because there was this tsunami of agony. I looked down at my arm. It was still attached to my shoulder, though I couldn't be a hundred percent certain about that. I tentatively tried to flex my fingers and the agony upgraded to this piercing burn that started in my elbow and shot down to the tips of my fingers. But pain was good, right? Pain meant . . . it meant something. I knew it did from biology, but I couldn't remember exactly what.

"She's bleeding. Isabel's bleeding." Rob shifted under me so my arm was pinned even further into the door. "She's banged up her head."

"It's my arm." No one seemed to appreciate my poor hapless limb, which was being crushed past the point of no return. I squinted out of the window, but all I could see was grass and hedges. "We're in a *field?*"

There was a blast of cold air as the boy sitting next to us opened the passenger door and scrambled out, pulling the seat forward so everyone could climb over. Each tiny movement sent a jolt of pain ricocheting through me, which was nothing compared to the OMG-I'm-going-to-fucking-die-ness of Rob beginning to wriggle out from under me.

"What are you doing? Keep still," I whimpered, clamping my other hand around his wrist.

"Gotta get out," he muttered. "We can't stay here. Someone will have called the police."

"I don't care."

There was a banging on my side of the car as Ratboy struggled to open the door, and Rob took advantage of my momentary distraction to slide himself free. I plunked down on the seat, jarring my arm just enough that if I'd had a big knife I'd have cut it off—it couldn't have hurt any less.

The door was finally pried open, and I turned my head and

tried to smile. Why was I trying to smile? Ella was still crying, but Nancy peered at me curiously before her eyes widened in alarm.

"Is, you need to get your hand out," she said urgently. "Just pull it out."

"That's a good idea," I muttered thickly. "Wonder why I didn't think of that."

"She's covered in blood," Ella sobbed, before Ratboy pushed her out of the way and peered in.

"Man, you look really fucked up," he breathed.

"I'm fine. Just . . . I've got blood in my eyes—and could someone wipe my face? Please?"

He scrubbed at my forehead with the sleeve of his jacket, and I guess I was cut up because it felt like millions of tiny needles pricking into my skin. It took my mind off my arm for at least five seconds.

"We need to call an ambulance," Ella spluttered, hiccuping gently. "She might need to be cut out."

"She's fine," Rob insisted, coming up behind Ratboy. "I'm going to get your arm free."

"Oh no, no, I'm fine. Don't worry about me . . ."

"Look, it might be broken and she shouldn't be moved." Nancy tried to pull him back, but he shook her off.

"Right, Isabel, hold Sean's hand," he ordered me, and I frowned.

"Who the hell's Sean? Do you mean Ratboy?"

"Bitch . . ."

"Just hold her hand, mate, and let me just . . . this might hurt a bit."

No good ever comes out of those five words. It didn't hurt a bit. It hurt a lot. It hurt so much that I squeezed Sean's hand so hard that the bones crunched together, and then I threw up this acidic flurry of vomit all over myself as Rob pulled my arm free.

SNAP!

Your body shouldn't make snapping noises. There should be a law against it. "Well, it's broken now," I said, and then their shocked faces were receding into the distance and the darkness was licking away at me.

25

I really didn't want to, but someone was telling me to open my eyes and I was kinda curious to see what the afterlife was like.

Peeling my eyelids back took a considerable amount of effort, and I needn't have bothered because the afterlife sucked. I was flat on my back on wet grass with Nancy and Ella looming anxiously above me.

All these things occurred to me at the same time: the ammonia stench of sick; the cold, wet feel of the grass penetrating through my coat; the aching cut on my forehead; the bruised tenderness down my right side. And I found that if I thought about all of them, then I didn't have to think about my arm. It was like I could flick this switch and turn off the part of my brain that dealt with arm stuff. It was actually pretty cool.

"Get me up," I croaked. "Get me out of my coat, it's gross."

"You shouldn't move, you might have a concussion," Nancy said hoarsely, but I was already groping with my good arm for Ella's hand.

"I'm fine," I repeated for about the seventieth time that night. "What's happening?"

"Oh, Is, the boys have just left us!" Ella gasped indignantly.

"They got you out of the car and then they were worried about the police so they ran off, but Sean said we should call for a taxi but then we thought you might need an ambulance and then I got really worried that you were dead, and in the end we didn't know what to do."

I concentrated on her inane chatter as she and Nancy carefully pulled me upright. As I put all my weight on my feet, the blood rushed up and I staggered. Nancy's arm shot around my waist to stop me from toppling back to the ground.

"Oooh, wow, head rush." I shut my eyes and waited for the spinning to stop and wondered whether I should throw up again. I decided against it. "Let's hear it for my endorphins, they rock."

"Is, are you sure you don't have a concussion?"

"So . . . God, look at the car." I stumbled toward the buckled Nissan, which was leaning drunkenly against the wall we'd smashed into. My side of the car was completely dented in. "It's always amazing when you see the wreck and you're all, like, how did I manage to survive that? Can we take my coat off now?"

Nancy and Ella were in this little huddle, but I snapped my working fingers at them and they hurried over. At least they knew that I was back in charge.

"Coat. Off. Now! And don't touch my right arm or I'll puke all over you."

I was actually starting to feel good about stuff. I hadn't been killed, which was a definite plus in the pro column, and I couldn't feel my arm and judging by the "ewwww's," Nancy and Ella got sick on their hands as they unbuttoned my red coat. I held myself very still as Nancy worked it over my arm, biting down hard on my lip as I felt something pop, but I was too fascinated by what was emerging from my sleeve to worry about that.

"Okay, I'm calling an ambulance now, Is." Nancy's voice was operating at batlike sonar frequency. "What the fuck is that lump?"

It looked like my elbow had shifted about ten centimeters, because there was something that must have been a bone jutting out beneath my skin. "It's all right, it doesn't hurt," I said breezily, letting my arm dangle. "So, hey, what's the plan? And it had better not involve the emergency services because we're wanted fugitives."

"I don't know," Nancy said helplessly.

"Which is why you're always destined to be the sidekick, Nance," I told her kindly. "We're in a field, so I guess no one can see us from the road. We need to call someone to take us back into town."

I raised my eyebrows at them because did I have to do everything? "We could call Nancy's brother, I s'pose," Ella suggested. "And he could take us home."

Nancy nodded. She seemed a bit subdued after my sidekick dig. "Yeah, we could do that."

The stars, which I'd been staring at, morphed into a million pieces of fluttering paper. "I can't go home. He'll ship me off to God-botherers' school."

He would, too, wonky arm and all. After he'd made me glue every single one of his books back together. And when I thought about how my life had descended into this cruel practical joke, my mind turned to Smith as it invariably did because he was the only one who could explain the punch line.

Nancy already had her phone out. "Hang on! Wait . . . did you call him? Did you call Smith and tell him about me?"

"Is, I don't . . . this isn't the time, okay? Do you know how much I wish I could just take it back and . . ."

I cut right through the historical event that was Nancy actually trying to apologize. "Because if you did, you've still got his number in your phone, and I need him to put me back together again."

Nancy huddled into her coat and she seemed smaller, diminished. "I can't get a signal."

"Well, start walking until you can."

"Yeah and I could just call an ambulance . . ."

"Which I don't need, and if you do then they'll call the police and I'll . . . I'll tell them it was all your idea—and my arm looks like there's a freaking alien in it waiting to bust right through—and who do you think they're going to believe? I want Smith! Call him right the hell now and get him to pick me up!"

"Whatever, Is," Nancy snapped, and that was okay. I could handle her hating me more than her shop-soiled version of sympathy. "Christ, you've got a broken arm and a concussion and all you can do is order me around and be a bitch."

"Why are you still here?" I asked her testily, and she turned away with a flounce, her phone held out in front of her like she was divining for water. "And my arm is not broken!"

She was gone for ages but, thankfully, Ella was far more conciliatory. I made her toss my coat in the back of the car and retrieve my bag.

"I found these, too!" she panted, running back to me with two cans of lager. "Maybe you should drink some for the shock, like brandy."

I wasn't in shock. I was thinking clearly—for the first time in ages—that all of this was some wonderful form of provenance to bring Smith back. But if I stopped concentrating on not concentrating about my arm, I could feel this sharp, angry throbbing that made me catch my breath.

"Yeah," I agreed. "But I should have a toothbrush and some Colgate in my bag."

Ella helped me brush my teeth with lager and toothpaste, which made me want to hurl again. Then I got her to hold up my mirror, even though it was practically pitch-dark, so we could try and lose a little of the car crash victim vibe.

"Maybe if I put some lipstick on you, he won't notice the gash on your forehead," Ella said helpfully.

I was all ready for my close-up and swigging back lager as fast as I could, when Nancy came back.

"He's coming to get you," she said before I could even form the question. "And no, he's not happy about it, and yes, he's still really pissed off with you and you shouldn't be drinking!"

"I'm in shock," I said smugly, but the throbbing was getting harder to ignore. If I got drunk again, it would help. Couldn't hurt, anyway.

"If you die because you've been drinking alcohol while you're concussed then don't come crying to me," Nancy said darkly.

"Then I'll come and haunt your ugly arse and move your furniture about and scrawl things on your bedroom wall in blood," I added. It was just like old times. Also, being vile to Nancy gave me something to do that didn't involve wondering if my arm was, like, torn. "Someone light a cigarette for me."

Climbing up the ditch that separated the field from the road was excruciating. I couldn't see where to put my feet and nearly fell over. In the end, Ella pushed and Nancy pulled and they managed to get me up on to the pavement with the can of lager still upright.

That was more than can be said of me. The head-rush thing was happening again, but it didn't feel quite so good. "I need to sit down." My voice was coming from a long way away.

"You can't. You need to stay on your feet until that freak of yours turns up," Nancy snarled, folding her arms. "It's bloody freezing."

The cold was just one other thing to deal with that I couldn't. "I could just lie down on the verge for a bit," I murmured to myself.

"You look really weird, Is," Ella said, glancing at me. "You've gone really pale. Maybe you should drink some more."

Nancy snatched the can out of my hand. "She's not drinking! Grab hold of her!"

They stood there, one on either side of me as I swayed unsteadily and groaned at the gnawing sensation, which traveled down from my armpit. There was nothing to do but look up expectantly each time we caught sight of a pair of headlights coming toward us. Only one car stopped, but that was just this old guy who wanted to know if we were okay, until Nancy told him to piss off.

I couldn't bear it any longer—pulled under from pain and the certainty that Smith wouldn't show up. Then I heard a faint *put-put-put* noise and we were lit up in the glow of headlights as a car crested the brim of the hill.

"He's here," I whispered, and saying it made it true because his little car was slowly coming toward us. "I look okay, right?"

Nancy snorted incredulously, but Ella was smoothing back my hair. "You look great," she said without an ounce of sincerity.

I took a step forward—so it didn't look like Nancy and Ella were holding me up—and waited patiently for him to open the door and uncoil himself from the driver's seat.

"If this is one of your sick little jokes and you just need a lift back to town then I'm gonna leave you here," he said savagely, walking around the car but not looking at me, like I was Medusa and the sight of me would turn him to stone.

I waggled the fingers of my good hand feebly. "Hey, hi, you." I thought Ella and I had done a damn good job with our scene of the crime makeover, but he lifted his head when I spoke, then put one hand on the back of the car to steady himself.

"Bloody hell," he growled, whipping around to glare at Nancy. "You said she was okay."

"I said she was sort of okay," Nancy replied haughtily. "Look, you have to persuade her to go to the hospital."

"It's, like, so rude to talk about me as if I'm not here," I said to Ella, who patted my shoulder comfortingly.

"Get in the car," Smith commanded, yanking open the passenger door.

"Why are you so angry with me?" I whined, shrinking back against Ella because his most withering expression was worse than when he wouldn't look at me at all.

There was the toot of a horn and Nancy abruptly let go, so I had to cling to Ella. "It's my brother—come on, Ell."

Ella yelped in relief. "Gotta go, Is. Smith's here now, and he'll probably look after you," she added doubtfully. "Can you come and get her, because I think she's about to fall over?"

Smith's face twisted darkly as he walked over. "You're not going anywhere until you help me get her into the car," he said in his most menacing voice, and Ella obviously wanted out because she was yanking me toward him with indecent haste, each step making me whimper in pain.

"Stop bumping her," Smith hissed, lowering me onto the seat as gently as a doddery maiden aunt. Once he was sure that I was in, he shut the door very carefully, then said something to Ella, which made her burst into tears before she ran off.

I leaned back against the headrest, with a hand to my frantically beating heart, and shut my eyes as he opened the door and got in. There was a small click and I could feel the overhead light come on. Then his fingers on me, as he tilted my chin and brushed back my hair, which was sticking to my forehead.

"Looks pretty deep, I think you need stitches," he said calmly. "Where else are you hurt?"

I opened my eyes with a superhuman effort and tried to lift my hand so I could touch him. He was too far away. "I just want to go back to your place and sleep. I'm so tired."

"Where else are you hurt, Isabel?" he repeated mechanically, and I knew then that the only way to get him back was to be so broken that he'd be scared that he couldn't make me right again.

"My arm," I whispered, and it worked because he looked down at it in all its mangled glory and sucked in a breath. I couldn't even look at it anymore—in fact, amputation was starting to seem like a valid lifestyle choice.

"It's broken," he said finally. "In about fifty different places, apparently. Right, I'm calling your dad, because I'm guessing that was pretty low on your list of things to do, and then I'm taking you to the hospital. Now remind me of your number."

"I'm not telling you."

"You are un-fucking-believable, you know that?" He was leaning over me, trying to snag the end of my seat belt without putting any pressure on my arm, and his breath hit the side of my face like a kiss.

"I know I lied to you about practically everything, but when I said I loved you, I meant it. I still do."

"I'm going to put this down to a concussion," he said, winding the seat belt around me and under my arm. "I'm taking you to the hospital, which is nonnegotiable, and we'll take the issue of calling home under advisement, right?"

"Right. But you promise you won't be mad at me . . . hate it so much."

He didn't say anything, just turned the key in the ignition.

I don't remember much about the drive to the hospital, but every time I managed to drift off, his hand was on my knee, shaking me out of sleep, and he kept talking all the time, asking me stupid questions and prodding me when I didn't answer.

Then I was on my own in the car, and it was like this battle between the tiredness and the pain, and finally I was on a trolley, the strip lights on the ceiling whizzing past as I was wheeled down a corridor. Someone jostled my arm and I cried out thinly, shutting my eyes because the brightness stung.

When I opened them again it was because there was a light shining in my eyes with a doctor attached to it.

"Ah, you're back with us, that's good. Now, I need to know exactly what you've been up to?"

I might be a congenital liar but the doctor at the Royal Brighton Hospital almost had me beat. He wouldn't buy any of my bullshit. Not the falling off my bike story I conjured up on the spur of the moment or my legal status as an eighteen-year-old or, well, any of it really.

He just held up a syringe full of yummy painkilling liquid and refused to stick it in me until he got parental consent.

"What part of 'I'm eighteen' don't you understand?" I demanded, and he and the nurse exchanged exasperated looks.

"I'm not giving you any of this until you start telling me the truth."

I bit my lip and was just about to try out a different story about being a homeless street urchin when Smith pulled back the curtain. "I'm her brother," he said tonelessly. "Our parents are overseas—do you want me to ruin their twenty-fifth anniversary cruise and call them?"

I didn't even care that I'd brought Smith over to the dark side, because whatever was in that needle made everything stop hurting, except my heart.

Yeah, my heart ached and broke into millions of little pieces all the way down to the X-ray department and then all the way to the treatment room, where two doctors popped my elbow back, emphasis on the pop. They wrapped my arm in gauze and started plastering—and Smith hadn't left my side, but he looked like he wished he were at the bottom of the ocean. Like the distance between us was too great to be overcome.

All that was left was to apply butterfly plasters to the cut on my head and to hand Smith a prescription and a leaflet about plaster-cast care.

"If I told you that I wanted you to stay in overnight for observation, would that register with you?" the doctor asked me as one of the nurses went to find me a jacket out of the lost property.

I shook my head decisively.

"She doesn't listen to anyone," Smith said quietly from the chair he was slumped in. "You get used to it after a while."

"I just want to go home," I said, wriggling down off the trolley. "Thank you for looking after me," I added politely.

"Oh, don't mention it," he said dryly. "I hope your parents enjoy that *cruise*." He had the nerve to do air quotes, but I didn't call him on it, because Smith was standing up and wrapping his arm around me because I needed him.

26

I knew it was 2:27 A.M. because the clock on the wall of the hospital canteen said so, but it felt much later. I was that kind of wired that you get when you're dog-weary but feel like you'll never be able to sleep again.

There was a mirror on the wall opposite me, taunting me with its shiny surface, so all I could do was rubberneck my own reflection. I looked exactly like I'd been in a car crash. My hair was clumped in these blood-soaked rattails, my skin was a strange shade of putty, and my eyes were sunken. Then there were the millions of little cuts all over my face, the angry gash marching across my forehead, and that nasty little scab on my cheek.

I forced myself to look away and watched Smith walk toward me with a tray positively laden with calorific goodies, which was a far more pleasing treat for the eyes.

Smith shunted a mug toward me and then gestured at the pile of goodies on the tray. "What do you want? Biscuits? Crisps? The muffins look good . . ."

"Tea's fine," I said, taking a sip, then pulling a face. "Gross! I know I like my sugar, but how many spoonfuls did you put in this?"

He gave me a pale imitation of a smile. "Stopped counting after six. Meant to be good for shock, isn't it? Sweet tea."

"I'm not really in shock anymore. Reality's settling back in." I paused for a second. "It sucks."

"Does your arm hurt?" He was so good at that note of concern that I could almost believe that he meant it. "And that thing on your cheek . . ." Smith pointed to my hockey wound, which was scabbing over nicely. "That didn't happen tonight, did it?"

"Sports injury," I said shortly. "So, I was meaning to ask you . . ."

"And Molly said that she saw you this afternoon."

The afternoon seemed like it had happened years ago. "Oh . . . She caught me at a bad moment," I said delicately, experiencing an entirely different twinge of agony. She must have rushed home to give Smith a blow-by-blow account.

If she had, he didn't show it, just blew slightly on his tea. "She's sorry about ripping your coat, by the way."

"A rip is the least of that coat's worries." I thought of my poor, puke-stained coat in the back of the totaled car and shuddered.

"So is this how it's going to be?" Smith asked me suddenly, his expression resolute.

"Is this how what's going to be?" I snatched up a packet of biscuits and ripped open the plastic with my teeth. I still felt nauseous, but I needed something to do with my mouth that didn't involve talking.

"Same old Isabel, even now . . . Getting good and evasive about the truth? Answering a question with another question?"

"I'm afraid so," I told him sadly because it was so good, so unbelievably good, to be sitting across from him, watching the curve of his bottom lip and the flutter of his eyelashes as he blinked, to have his undivided attention. "Why did you lie for me?"

He looked up from his contemplation of a bag of fluorescent orange cheese crackers. "Because you were in pain and you needed a shot and he wasn't going to give you one."

So he still cared about me? Or else he knew that the sooner they shot me up, the sooner he'd have me out of what was left of his hair.

"Well, thanks. Sorry you got dragged into all of this, but I didn't know who else to call."

"Don't mention it," Smith said shortly, and I had the good sense to go back to nibbling along the edge of my biscuit, which tasted like cardboard.

I knew that I was putting off the inevitable. He was going to leave me again. Maybe he'd give me a lift first, but he didn't want to be with me. Couldn't bear to be in the same room with me, because it made his brow wrinkle up and his fingers twitch nervously as he sorted through the cup of condiment sachets.

"Excuse me, darling?"

I looked up into a vaguely familiar face, but it was the faint Irish lilt that made my stomach lurch and beads of sweat blossom along my forehead.

"Oh, hi," I muttered unwillingly.

"You've broken your arm? That's a pity. And how's your Dad and that little brother of yours?"

"They're fine, y'know. Everyone's good." I could tell that Smith was watching this exchange with great interest, like it was another piece in the puzzle. And God, she was pulling out the chair next to me.

"I've got five minutes before my break's over," she said, and I wanted to punch her stupid kindly face in. "You and I can have a nice little chat. Is this your boyfriend?"

"No!" Smith and I snapped in unison and he didn't have to sound quite so emphatic about it. "He's just a friend who happens to be a boy. Allegedly."

Smith raised his cup in a mocking salute and the nurse, what was her name (Mary? Margie? Maggie?) shot me a conspiratorial look, like we were just having a lover's tiff.

"I'm Marie," she said to Smith. "I looked after this young lady's mum this summer, didn't I, poppet?"

"I'm Smith." They solemnly shook hands. "I looked after Isabel this autumn, didn't I?"

Then he winked at me like he knew that I needed to be mad at him, just a little, to be able to deal with Marie sitting across from me.

"I thought about you," she was saying, her hand creeping out to pat my cheek, until I shifted back. "You got yourself into such a state. Never seen anything like it."

"Yeah," I muttered indistinctly, inching my chair sideways so I wouldn't have to look at her pity head on.

"I didn't mean to upset you," Marie said, folding her arms over her buttresslike chest. "But we all felt sorry for you, losing your mum like that—and your wee brother, poor little thing, we just couldn't get him to stop crying."

"He cried for, like, weeks," I said, remembering Felix shuddering with sobs that sounded as if they were being wrenched out of him.

"And you didn't cry at all, poppet. We were all worried about that."

It was time for this horrific scenic trip down memory lane to end. Didn't the hospital provide their staff with tact training?

"Yeah, well, aren't you going to be late?" I asked her rudely.

She didn't look that pissed off because she was so big with the understanding. Just gave me another one of those "I get you" looks, which were starting to make me want to gag, and got up. "You take care of yourself, darling—keep that arm elevated."

"Well, it was nice to meet you," Smith piped up when I made it plain that I wasn't going to say anything.

I waited until she waddled to the door, then shoved away my half-empty cup and stood up. "I hate this place, I've got to get out of here," I spat. "I can hardly breathe."

He caught up with me by the exit, 'cause I could move pretty fast for a banged-up girl in a plaster cast.

"Is! Just hold on!" he pleaded, seizing my wrist and pulling me toward a deserted row of chairs.

Whacking someone with your plaster cast hurts you a lot more than it hurts them. I really wouldn't recommend it.

"I mean it!" I shouted, struggling in his arms and making no effort to lower my voice, despite the goggle-eyed looks from a couple of cleaners desultorily mopping the floor. "I can't bear it! This place . . . the smell. The walls are closing in on me."

"Stop it!" Smith said, giving me the tiniest of shakes. "Just stop it and come here."

He pulled me down onto a seat and held me tight so I couldn't wriggle free. I stilled instantly; it had been so long since he touched me like that. But his words weren't as soft as his hands, which gently turned my head so I had no option but to stare deeply into his pretty blue eyes.

"You tell me everything right now. Or I'm going to leave you here and I'm never going to see you again." His voice crackled with ice, ready to break under the slightest pressure.

So I started to talk. It was hard at first—the truth. I was rusty. But I found that it got easier and easier. I started on the small stuff. School. From bullied to bully and back again. That led on nicely to the Guantánamo regime at home, the school brochures, my study-trashing exploits and why I could never go home again.

It was as if Smith had sneakily arranged for that doctor to inject me with a truth serum, so I even told him about Rob, and his hand tightened painfully on my shoulder, but he didn't say anything; just let me carry on with the whole digging-my-own-grave soliloquy.

". . . and I threatened her until she agreed to call you, and then you were there and now you're here and that's everything," I finished miserably, my throat aching from it all.

"It's not everything," he reminded me, shifting me in his arms again so he could get another look at my face; so I couldn't hide. "Haven't told me about your mum, have you?"

"Please, don't . . ." I begged, shutting my eyes so I wouldn't have to look at him.

"Tell me."

So I did.

What I remembered more than anything was the beep of the monitors and the blinking numbers that measured her heart rate and her blood pressure. The plastic drips arranged next to the bed. One for drugs, one for fluid, and one containing this sickly-looking brown liquid feed that was connected by a tube to her stomach.

She couldn't feed herself because she wouldn't wake up. But she wasn't asleep. Sleep was peaceful and she wasn't. Her mouth was stretched wide open for the tubes, her eyes open and unseeing, although we told Felix that she was looking at him.

We told Felix a lot of stuff. That she could hear him when he said that he loved her. And we told him that when she had one of the periodic fits, she was squeezing his hand tight because she knew he was there.

I don't think she knew anything. I think she'd already gone and all that was left was a body that had become a battlefield, that was fighting itself for each minute, each second that she stayed.

And Felix and Dad . . . it was like that bit in Peter Pan, "Clap your hands if you believe in fairies," because they were so sure that she was going to get better. Even as her kidneys weakened and her liver packed up so her pretty face became a gruesome shade of yellow that clashed with the purple bruises dotting her skin.

They wanted him to sign a DNR—Do Not Resuscitate. Do not recover. Do not return. He said, very calmly, that they wanted him to sign her life away and he wouldn't. Not even when those numbers on the monitors kept dropping, and the fits became more frequent, and she didn't open her eyes anymore.

I couldn't even sit in the Intensive Care ward. Couldn't watch her try to die. So I hung out in the relatives' room with its stale gray carpet, nicotine-colored walls, and the faint smell of rotten food from the fridge. Marie gave me a pile of magazines and I waded through them, filling in every crossword and puzzle I could find with a leaky felt-tip that Felix lent me. There was this lame picture of a sunset on the wall, with a verse from the Bible scrolling over it in a cursive script: "To every thing there is a season, and a time to every purpose under the heaven."

He sat there with his head in his hands after another showdown with the doctors and I read it out to him. "It's pointless and cruel, what you're doing," I said. "She doesn't want to be here anymore and you have to let her go."

I was right, but it didn't give me any satisfaction. Not even when he bor-
rowed the leaky felt-tip because he'd left his fountain pen at home and
signed the forms with an angry flourish and a bleak look.

But still she lingered on, and my whole world narrowed down to hurried
meals from whatever takeaway was open when we left the hospital. Snatches
of sleep. Grabbing clothes out of the laundry basket. Sneaking outside the
main exit for sly cigarettes and nicking packets of gum from the hospital
shop. The phone ringing and ringing: her blood pressure was up, her clotting
rates were down . . . "We just called to see how Faith is, any news?"

He almost didn't make it. He had to go into the University to see the
dean when the numbers on the monitors went into freefall. They made me
go and sit with her and hold her hand because they were still pretending that
she could hear my voice. That she could feel my hand clutching at her fin-
gers as her body shook with involuntary tremors. I had to keep asking
Marie to give her another injection to make it stop.

Felix was clinging to my arm, hiding his face in my shoulder and crying,
when he stumbled through the big swinging doors, tie undone, jacket half
on, half off.

"Is she . . . ?"

"No, she's still here," I said, and he darted off to find a chair because there
were never enough chairs.

We sat there, three wise monkeys, with the curtains drawn around us,
the monitor beeping and occasionally stuttering, which didn't mean any-
thing because a nurse would always come and reset it.

The numbers kept dropping, and the doctor came and told us that the
kidneys and the liver "were no longer viable" and her heart simply couldn't
take the strain. She didn't even look like her anymore—she was exanimate,
which means without animation. It means dead. Almost.

I could hear two people talking outside our cubicle, laughing about their
plans for the weekend. I turned my head away from the monitor, started to

rise so I could tell them to shut the fuck up because there was someone dying and we didn't want to know about their ten-pin bowling tournament, when the beeping became one long, continuous punctuation of noise.

It was a terrible sound. Not the worst, though, because he moaned, this gut-wrenching exhalation, and gathered up her broken, no longer viable body and started to cry. "My darling girl, my love, my love, don't leave me."

I think Felix was huddled under the bed, because I could hear him sobbing, and then there were doctors, nurses swooping down, but it was too late and I couldn't stand it for another second.

The big swinging doors made this satisfying bang as I sent them crashing back into the wall. All the way down that long, cruel corridor were more and more doors and they all banged as I pushed through them. It wasn't enough. There was a neat row of chairs lined up outside the relatives' room, but they scattered like birds flying south for the winter as I kicked them—picked one up and sent it hurtling into the air.

All I could feel was this suffocating, blinding rage, which made me want to lash out and scream because it was too big to be contained.

But when I got out of the ICU there was nowhere to go. I crawled into this tiny alcove behind the lifts, and that's where Marie found me an hour later, banging my fists into the wall.

"And she took me back to the relatives' room, and Dad and Felix were in there because they were tidying her up, and I just sat in this chair, next to him, and I couldn't speak. 'Cause I knew that if I opened my mouth, I'd start screaming and I wouldn't ever be able to stop." I paused to take in a few, deep breaths. "He was sitting next to me, hunched over, and I remember thinking that he hadn't shaved in days, and then he turned and he said in this really quiet voice so Felix couldn't hear, 'I will never forgive you for this.'"

Smith had been silent up until then, holding my hand and squeezing my fingers, but now he let go and I was adrift. "Why wouldn't he forgive you? For making him sign the DNR form?"

I shivered inside my borrowed jacket, which was this horrible shade of puke green. "I guess, it didn't really feel appropriate to ask him to go into details, y'know?" I sat up straight because I didn't have him to lean on. "So is it my turn yet?"

He slumped back in the chair and stretched his legs out in front of him. "Your turn for what? Do you want a tissue or have you still given up crying for Lent?"

"Don't change the subject," I hissed, because if he thought he was going to get tears on top of everything else then he could bloody well think again. "It's my turn to get you to be honest with me!"

"I have been honest with you!" he protested indignantly, but I wasn't going to let him get away with that crock of shit.

"Did you get some freshman pregnant so she had to have an abortion? Is it true you've shagged half the campus? Did you ever see anything in me other than some skanky little ho-bag who'd let you get some touch because Molly wouldn't?" I could have carried on until it got light, but he clamped his hand over my mouth.

"You meant more to me than that and you know you did, so don't rag on what we had," he said harshly, and I could have pushed out my lips so I'd be kissing his palm, but I didn't. "If I take my hand away, will you shut up and listen to me?"

I raised my eyebrows meaningfully, but Smith wasn't fluent in eyebrow, so I had to give him a muffled "yes."

"I love Molly," he said, and I realized my heart still had a bit of breaking left in it. "I know it's never going to happen, but she's my friend and I care about her deeply and if you can't handle that, then it's your problem. And for what it's worth, Is, despite all the crap you've piled on me, I care about you, too, despite what I said that day by the swings, but I'm not going to help you destroy yourself."

I opened my mouth to demand a retraction, but he held up his hand warningly.

"Thank you," he said ironically when I pouted but kept my lips together. "As I was saying, I won't be that guy. And really you deserve better than me. You really do." He smiled faintly. "Okay, you can say something now."

"I don't want anyone but you, why can't you see that?" I tugged at his shoulder so he had to look at me, even though I was wailing loud enough to be heard in Hove. "You hate me!"

"I don't hate you . . ."

"And I don't care what my so-called friends think of you, I never did and even if all those stories were true, they didn't stop me, did they? I still loved you."

I wouldn't have thought it possible, but he smirked a little at that and his arm crept around my shoulders. "Is, I don't know who you've been talking to, but I'm not the low-rent, coffee-bar Casanova that you seem to think I am. Sorry about that."

"I don't believe you," I insisted doggedly. "I mean, you said you'd only wanted this no-strings hookup with me . . ."

"Yeah, because you blew hot and cold the whole time," he snapped. "You didn't exactly act like you were after a relationship, and then you're declaring your love for me and going into a full-blown hissy fit when I won't say it back. I should have known you were only sixteen, you sure acted like it."

It was really mean of him to twist the facts like that, especially when I wasn't at fighting weight. "When will you stop hating me because I told you some stupid lies that I regret more than anything?"

We were locked in this verbal Ping-Pong match and just when I thought I'd slammed the ball over the net and had the advantage, he snatched it away from me.

Smith cupped my face in his hands, and because I was a sucker for all the things that weren't to be, I leaned forward so he could kiss me. But kissing wasn't on his agenda. Instead he moved in for the kill. "And when are you going to stop hating your mum because she left you when you needed her most?" he whispered right in my ear.

I guess he thought it was game, set, and match or whatever you have in Ping-Pong. But he should have known better. Should have known *me* better.

Now it was my turn to stroke his cheeks, rub my thumbs over the sharp planes of his cheekbones so I could get close enough to . . .

"Fuck you, you bastard," I said sweetly, and while he was still reeling from that blow, I swung out my hand and slapped his shocked face hard enough to make him jerk back from the impact.

Smith touched the hot red mark on his cheek wonderingly and then shut his eyes like he was exhausted. "You know something, Isabel?" he asked in a gravelly voice. "You make it impossible to love you."

27

I don't think I'd ever felt as unlovable as I did at that moment. I felt ugly, inside and out.

Smith slid one seat over to make absolutely sure that I wouldn't accidentally touch him, and yawned as if all the drama of the last half hour had wiped him out.

I craned my neck to look at the clock. It was edging toward three-thirty A.M. "It's late," I muttered. "You should go." I'd learned my lesson now. Blabbing out your darkest secrets just gives people the knife they need to stab you in the gut. First Dot, now Smith ...

He pulled a face. "You'd love it if I just left you here, wouldn't you? Then you could work your martyred routine a little bit more, instead of asking for help."

"I don't need you to help me," I sniped. "I don't need anyone."

"Yeah, well, you'd still be standing by the side of the road with a compound fracture if that was the case," Smith pointed out, before giving a resigned sigh. "Come on, I'll give you a lift."

A lift to where, though? That was the question. Maybe I could ...

"Before you even say it, you're not coming back to mine."

Smith could read minds now, which was just beyond irritating, if I could have mustered up the energy to actually be irritated. The drugs were starting to wear off, the adrenaline had exited stage right, and I'd reached rock bottom.

In fact, if there was someplace that was lower than rock bottom, then there's where I was. I ached in places where I didn't know I had places. My head was throbbing, my eyes were dry and itchy, and I had this awful metallic taste in my mouth that all the Freshmint gum in the world wouldn't cure.

I was starting to cobble a plan together. It wasn't great as plans went, but it didn't involve going home or having to spend any more time with Smith and his insightful observations into my psyche.

"Where to, princess?" he asked, jangling his car keys impatiently as I hoisted myself upright and began to hobble toward the exit.

I stuck my chin out defiantly. "I'm going to find a hotel in town, and before you get pissy about that, even though it's, like, none of your business, I'm going to call my grandparents in London tomorrow, or later today, whatever, and ask them to come and pick me up. Happy?"

"Not remotely," he hissed, shouldering the door open for me. "But, hey, that makes two of us."

It was a relief to collapse onto his majorly uncomfortable passenger seat. I closed my eyes as he started the car and let the rhythmic putter of the engine lull me into a doze.

"C'mon, Is, wake up, we're here," Smith said, nudging me gently with his elbow. "And promise you won't get too homicidal with me."

"Too tired for long words," I mumbled, snuggling a little further into the seat. "You'd better have picked me a nice hotel."

I opened my eyes and started struggling with the seat belt, until Smith pushed my hand away. I couldn't see anything but his face and the worried way he was gnawing his bottom lip.

"Look, hey, I'm fine," I insisted, almost keeping the tremor out of my voice. "I said some stuff, you said some stuff, it's been the longest night of my life, let's just agree to disagree."

"I'm sorry but I think this is for the best," he said, and he didn't just look worried, he *was* worried, and as I looked over at my house, all the windows ablaze with light, the front door open, and—oh, look—a police car parked right in front of us, I knew why.

"How could you?" My breath hitched in my throat, because there was someone standing in the doorway, hand shielding his face from the porch light so he could see out into the street.

Smith was already opening my door, hand under my elbow so he could help me out. My body was being way too obliging and stepping onto the pavement so it could walk the necessary distance toward the shadowy figure still standing in front of the house.

"He's going to kill me," I said under my breath. "He's going to chop me into little pieces, sauté me, and *then* send me away."

"I'll come in with you, it will be all right," Smith said soothingly, but it wasn't all right, because he was coming down the steps onto the path, and I was trying to use Smith as a human shield.

"Isabel!" he thundered, and my insides turned to liquid and whooshed down to my feet. He reached us in three long strides, face blazing with fury, and only Smith grabbing my hand and tucking it into his stopped me from turning tail and fleeing.

I had time for one heartfelt "Oh, God" before the Brighton Inquisition started. Except it didn't. He just stood there, staring at me, wearing his disgust like cheap aftershave. If it had been humanly possible to shrivel away from the force of someone's loathing, I'd have fitted inside a Dustbuster.

"What the *hell* have you been doing?" he asked quietly. Shouting would have been better, not that gossamer growl that made my blood go cold. "Give me one good reason why I should even let you through the front door."

He grabbed hold of my arm, my broken arm, as a prelude to probably putting me in the back of the police car himself, and I squealed in pain as he let go and Smith stepped between us.

"Sir, I'm Atticus Smith," he said politely, holding out his hand. "I'm a friend of Isabel's."

And it might have been the dumbfounded expression on my father's face as he shook Smith's hand or the whole Atticus thing, but he let go of my arm and I started to giggle. And then I wasn't giggling but almost bent double with laughter.

"I think she's still in shock," Smith said loyally, and I straightened up, still tittering feebly, and decided I'd be okay if I didn't make eye contact with my father.

And I didn't have to because there was a policewoman hurrying down the steps, holding something, while a pajama-clad Felix peered out of the front window.

"I take it this is Isabel?" she asked my father, who turned at the sound of her voice.

"Yes, yes," he said heavily, like he wished it wasn't true. "She's back."

She held something up—something red and bedraggled in a see-through plastic bag. "So, Isabel, is this your coat, and could you tell me exactly what it was doing in a car that was reported stolen earlier tonight?"

Spending the night locked up in a police cell seemed to be the lesser of two evils, compared with the way my father was still staring at me like he was already sizing me up for a coffin.

But when she started haranguing me before my arse even connected with the sofa, he turned and gave her the full effect of his most glacial expression. Think frozen tundra and you'd be halfway there.

"My daughter's been through quite enough for one night," he said in his most "Don't mess with me, I'm a professor of English" voice.

"I need Isabel to answer a few questions about what she's been—"

He cut her right off with an impatient flick of his hand as Smith collapsed next to me on the couch. "Bet you're regretting your misplaced chivalry now," I hissed out of the corner of my mouth, and his eyebrows pulled together in a ferocious scowl.

"I think what Isabel needs is some food and some sleep. If you leave me your number, then I'll arrange a mutually convenient time for you to come around and . . ."

"We'll need you to bring Isabel down to the station, sir." She shot me a look to let me know that I was a thoroughly bad little girl.

"As I was saying," he drawled slowly, and Smith shuddered like he was starting to believe everything I'd told him, "you can come around when Isabel's feeling better. I'm sure she just happened to be in the wrong place at the wrong time."

It was really nice of him to stick up for me like that. But he was sly and tricky. It was probably just a cunning ruse to ship me off to reform school before sunup.

She was still spluttering away about procedures as he walked her to the door.

"He doesn't seem that bad," Smith offered uncertainly, fidgeting against the cushions.

"Whatever," I whispered. "You haven't seen his game face yet."

There was a muffled squeak as Felix came in, holding a brimming mug in front of him. "I made you tea," he announced importantly.

Smith jumped up and took it before he could slop any more over the carpet, and once he'd been relinquished from his burden, Felix was hurling himself at me in one of his infamous "tackle hugs."

"Hey . . ." I protested. "Watch the arm!"

"We thought you'd run away," he exclaimed, eyes wide and bottom lip already quivering. "And then he called the police and she came around with your coat and I thought you were dead!"

"As if!" I scoffed, tugging on his cowlick. "Just a little battered. Look, you can draw something on my cast."

Felix gave it a good rap with his knuckles. "Does that hurt?"

"Yes," I snapped in unison with Smith who'd been gazing at Felix with amusement.

"Who are you? Are you Is's boyfriend? Dad said he was going to horsewhip you," Felix recalled gleefully as the man himself came back into the room.

"I'm sure I said no such thing." He ran his fingers through his hair and looked thoughtfully at Smith, who squirmed deliciously. "I trust you weren't involved in tonight's debacle?" he asked pleasantly.

"He wasn't..." I started again. "I called him after the accident and..."

"I took Is... I mean, Isabel to the hospital and oh, yeah ..." Smith rummaged in his jacket pocket. "There's a prescription for some antibiotics and some painkillers and instructions on how to take care of the cast. It's not meant to get wet, so she needs to wrap it up in a plastic bag when she has a ..."

"Thank you," Dad said calmly, taking the papers from him and giving them a cursory look. "Felix, will you please go to bed?"

"But Dad...!"

"It wasn't a suggestion, go!"

Felix went, grumbling with every step, sure that he was going to miss all the action. Lucky Felix.

Dad walked over to me, brushing past Smith, who looked like he was planning an intervention, then crouched at my feet. "Let me look at this arm of yours," he ordered softly, and I stuck out my plaster cast for his perusal. "Can you move your fingers?"

I wiggled them feebly, staring at the spot on the rug where Felix had spilled the tea. He turned my head toward the lamp so he could see the damage for himself and I could see myself reflected in his pupils.

"Well, you've certainly managed to wreak havoc everywhere you went tonight," he remarked. "A-plus for effort, Isabel."

"I'm sorry about your books," I said in a tiny voice. "I just went, like, crazy when I found those brochures and ..."

For someone who was practically on his knees in front of me, he could still do the dour papa like no one else. "Do you have any idea quite how angry I am with you?"

This was familiar ground for us. I knew my lines perfectly.

"So what else is new? Even if I hadn't got medieval on your stupid books or got myself half killed, you'd still be angry with me. You're always angry with me!" My lips settled into that tight line where they felt most comfortable. "I bet you wish I had been killed, that would have sorted out the Isabel problem in one fell swoop, wouldn't it?"

"Shut up!" he shouted at me, standing and snatching up one of the cushions and throwing it across the room because he couldn't do that to me. "Shut the hell up!"

I was trying to get to my feet, but it was proving impossible; my hand kept sinking into the sofa and I was putting too much weight on my bruised leg. Smith looked warily at my father, who was clenching his fists at his side and doing the stary thing again.

"You wanted to know the truth?" I said to Smith, because no one had asked him to come in here and watch Act Four, Scene Five of my miserable existence. "All my terrible secrets, yeah?"

"Is . . . don't," he begged me, finally holding out his hand so I could yank myself up. "You're really tired and freaked out and you don't know what you're saying."

"No! You were the one who was obsessed with the truth," I insisted, jabbing him in the chest with my finger. "I thought it was so terribly important to you."

"You're incapable of telling the truth," said my father from somewhere behind me, poison dripping from each word. "You've destroyed this family with all your lies and your dirty little secrets."

I wobbled precariously in Smith's hold. There was this strange prickling at the back of my eyes and I couldn't see too well. I held up a hand to my face and it came away wet because the tears were coursing down my face, getting into all those cuts and scrapes and making them sting. Guess I could cry, after all.

"He wishes it had been me, not her," I choked, slapping Smith's hands away from me. "That's why he really hates me."

"I'm sure it's not like that," he said helplessly. "It's not your fault that your mum died."

"That remains to be seen," my father bit out, running his finger over the picture of her on the mantelpiece. "Isabel has been remarkably unforthcoming about what happened or didn't."

Smith shook his head. "I'm sorry about your wife, but it's not fair to blame Is when she wasn't . . . you didn't have to sign the form but . . ."

"You don't get it!" I shouted, and it was like a dam bursting in my chest because these sobs were coming up from the bottom, and I suddenly slid to the floor because my legs decided that they didn't want to hold me up anymore. "You don't get it. I didn't tell you because I don't want to remember . . ."

"What the . . . ?" Smith exclaimed, and I had to say it because none of it would make sense until I did.

"I was with her, you idiot! I was in the car with her when she crashed!" And I was crumpling in on myself, curling into a little ball, and someone was picking me up, cradling me against crumpled cotton as he sat down and rocked me back and forth, rubbing circles on my back, like he used to when I was little. "Ssshhh, Belle, don't cry," he said, brushing my wet cheeks with the pads of his fingers. "It doesn't matter."

I buried my face into the crook of his neck and wept harder. "I'm so sorry. I'm sorry it wasn't me. I wish it had been."

"It wasn't your fault, Belle," he murmured soothingly, kissing the top of my head. "She was going too fast and she didn't have her seat belt on, and I told her a million times, didn't I? And you always put your belt on because I drummed it into you and that's why you only had a few scratches. Not like now."

I rested my aching head against his shoulder and let him settle me more comfortably on his lap. "We had a fight, a horrible fight, and she wasn't looking and I told her to . . . And, like, if I'd got out of bed earlier or if I'd packed my bag the night before, it would have been different and that lorry wouldn't have come out when it did and . . ."

28

She was a major pain in the arse when Dad was away at one of his boring old conferences on the importance of the novel in the computer age. They were always about stuff like that. She'd embark on these little projects, like painting the front room eau de nil, then decide that she hated it, so Felix and I would have to breathe in paint fumes while it got restored back to white with hint of a tint of rose pink. Then there'd be the hours spent calling him and having what sounded like completely inappropriate phone sex, judging from her end of the conversation. "Oh, David," she'd simper, sitting on the stairs and giggling. "You're being very naughty."

What was even worse was that she'd try to be my new best friend. I didn't need a new best friend, I already had three old best friends who worked my last nerve without her barging into my room and asking me what music I was listening to and wouldn't it be the best fun ever if we watched DVDs, ate ice cream, and painted each other's toenails? Actually, no, it wouldn't.

That's when she wasn't getting riled up about me staying out late and coming home with love bites dotted over my neck. She was worried that I'd get myself knocked up before I hit my twenties—just like her, pregnant at nineteen. She'd been the bright-eyed first year who wore a lot of black and too much red lipstick, and Dad had been the dashing postgraduate student *teaching her twentieth-century poetry, and before you could say Sylvia Plath, she'd had to drop out because the morning sickness was really getting in the way of all those essays she was meant to be writing.*

Never let me forget that. She'd sigh in this really annoying way when Dad was helping me with my homework and say, "You know, he's not the only one who's got smarts. I do have four A-levels."

He'd immediately push me and my books away so he could take her in his arms and murmur sickly sweet nothings in her ear. "You've got smarts, too, my darling girl. You picked me after all."

"I thought you picked me," she'd say with this tiny little frown like they didn't have this conversation every fricking week. "I was just the shy, innocent waif . . ."

"You were neither shy nor innocent," he'd say throatily, and then they'd disappear upstairs, and it's no wonder I learned to cook from an early age.

But this time he'd gone away just as the shit hit the fan, and Mrs. Greenwood and Lily's mum were baying for my blood and we had to schedule in a meeting so they could slowly pull off my fingernails and make me confess or whatever.

She'd loved to scream. Not like Dad, who'd wait for an explanation, then make me fall over my perfectly crafted alibi. Like that last afternoon, when she'd heard my key in the lock and tripped over her feet in my pink Birkenstocks, so she could start in on me.

"I'm going to kill you!" As opening lines went, that one was pretty predictable. "Give me your phone, now!"

I'd slowly unbuttoned my cardigan and made her wait while I hung it up and admired my blonde highlights in the hall mirror, then turned to her with the innocent expression I'd had years to perfect.

"Say 'please.'"

It was easy to send her free-falling into a hissy fit. She said that I was more like a bratty little sister than a daughter, but that was just to make her feel good about herself. You should have seen her preen when someone in Topshop asked her if we were sisters.

"I will not bloody say please," she'd shrieked, going from zero to ear-splitting in nanoseconds. "I want to see the picture and how do you even know what a blowjob is?"

"Wouldn't you like to know?" I'd smirked, holding out my phone so she could snatch it up and start fumbling with the buttons. "Do you actually know how to use that?"

She'd thrust it back at me. "Show me the picture!"

But there was no picture because I wasn't stupid enough to have incriminating evidence on my phone. So I'd stood there, scrolling through my photos until even she had to admit defeat.

"I've had to cancel my Pilates class so I can have your headmistress imply that I'm a bad mother," she'd wailed, following me up the stairs. "And just wait until I speak to your father tonight."

By now we'd reached my bedroom, so I could get one parting shot in before I slammed the door in her face. "I have to review for my Maths GCSE. Unlike some people, I actually plan on having a career."

She'd sidled into my room later as I was trying to cram as much trigonometry into my head as possible.

"Belle, c'mon, don't be such a cow," she'd wheedled, sitting down on my bed and picking up a copy of my textbook. "We do we always end up bickering when we should be friends?"

I'd put down my notebook with an angry little huff. "You're not my friend, you're my mother."

She'd tried to stroke my hair then, but thought better of it when I yanked my head back. "You never talk to me anymore, you just do your angry teen queen act and it's getting really tired."

"It's not an act. I am an angry teen queen, it's like, this whole phase I'm going through."

I have such a vivid memory of her sitting cross-legged on my bed, in jeans and one of Dad's shirts, the sleeves rolled up and her hair long and loose cascading down her back. She was really pretty, maybe she was even beautiful with her creamy skin and her wide mouth, which usually quirked upward into a smile, but not now. Not when she looked at me and I gave her my blankest expression and pointed at the door with an imperious finger. Then her mouth drooped down and her shoulders slumped because I didn't want to be her bestest friend anymore.

"Get out, Mum! Go and bug Felix or phone Dad and bitch about what a disappointment I am, just leave me alone," I gritted out, and I didn't see her until the next morning, when I'd fallen asleep over my textbooks (I used to be able to drop off standing up in those days), and she was tugging and yelling at me.

"I'm not going to tell you again," she'd shouted right in my ear. "Get up! We're going to be late!"

And because she'd distracted me and because I'd stayed up too late cramming, I didn't have my stuff packed for school. I had to have a running commentary on how utterly useless I was.

"Why do you always leave everything to the last moment? Why do we have to go through this every morning? It's not enough that you're already on Mrs. Greenwood's shit list, now I'm going to have to listen to a lecture on my shoddy timekeeping."

We were only five minutes late when she'd shepherded me and Felix into the car. I'd munched a piece of toast with peanut butter, went over my notes, and told Felix I was going to rip him limb from limb if he kept kicking the back of my seat—just another normal morning chez Clarke. We'd dropped off Felix and she'd switched on the radio, so I had to listen to not only her inane chatter but the inane chatter of the DJ while I tried to memorize algebraic formulas.

"Turn it off!" I'd snapped, hand reaching forward to hit the button, and she'd slapped it away, not even taking her eyes off the road.

"I'm listening to it," she'd mumbled. "You managed to study last night with your stereo going full blast."

"That was good music, not this crap," I'd sneered over the drone of Mum-rock.

"I'll have you know that I'm the authority on good music," she'd hissed. "In fact, I took you to see Nirvana when you were in utero, before they ever got famous." She'd sighed dreamily. "Four months pregnant and in the mosh pit. God, your Dad was furious."

"Yeah, well I'd never be so stupid as to get myself pregnant," I'd said witheringly, rustling my notes for emphasis. "And if I did, I wouldn't even tell you, I'd just go and have an abortion."

I was just talking crap because it's what I did. It was practically in my job description, but she gave this tiny, angry hiss and glared at me.

"You really are horrible sometimes, Belle . . ."

"Maybe you should have had an abortion yourself then," I'd flung back at her. "And then you wouldn't be wasting away as some stay-at-home mum who's got nothing better to do than relive her fucking glory days and make my life a misery."

I don't think I'd even realized that we were picking up speed as we hit the Lewes Road. I had this sense memory of running my hand along my seat belt, adjusting it slightly because it was digging into my neck.

"I nearly did," she'd suddenly snarled, quirking her eyebrow at me as I nearly dropped my toast. "You didn't know that, did you? I was eighteen and the last thing I wanted was some squalling brat who was going to grow up and hate me . . ."

"Oh, shut up!" But deep down, I'd always known that that was how she really felt. I'd known it every time I'd caught her looking at me out of the corner of my eye with this malcontent expression. "And you're going too fast."

"I'd even made the appointment, but he came around the night before and asked me to marry him," she'd recalled with a bitter little laugh, beeping the horn furiously at someone she'd overtaken who wasn't too happy about it. "Said he loved me and promised me we'd be happy."

"Well, I never asked to be born!" I screeched like every teen cliché wrapped into a one-size-fits-all sentence. "And I know that you wish that you'd had the abortion..."

"When you're acting like this, then yeah, I do," she'd hurled back at me, and she'd started to spew out something else that I'd totally asked for but she'd never said it because this truck had suddenly pulled into our lane and she was slamming on the brakes and swerving to avoid him.

Everything went slo-mo, so I could see the back of the lorry coming toward us in minute detail, see her hands gripping the wheel as she wrenched it to the right and then the bonnet of our car crumpling up like a concertina as we plowed into it.

It made a terrible noise. Like someone crunching ice or running their nails down a blackboard but amplified a million times. I'd put my hands up as the windshield shattered, showering us in a cascade of broken glass, and we were both screaming and the car was still moving forward, then we'd stopped.

All the wind was knocked out of me as I was yanked back by my belt, the air bags exploding into life so I was struggling not to black out. Then everything was still and she'd let out a shaky breath.

"Jesus, Belle, are you okay?" she'd asked me, but there was another screech of brakes and the car behind slammed into us, pushing us further forward into that unrelenting wall of metal.

I did pass out then. Like, I'd willed it to happen because I couldn't cope with the here and now of being shoved against the billowing plastic of the air bag so hard that I could feel the edge of the dashboard knocking into my chest. She was screaming, and it was such an awful sound that I didn't want to hear it.

It was only for a few seconds, and then I'd opened my eyes and the whole world had changed. There were people gathering around the car and she was caught in the gap between our seats, lying on her side so I could see her face, if it hadn't been covered in blood.

They'd got my door open, but I wouldn't leave her. She was still there, then. She'd moaned faintly, and I'd unbuckled my belt so I could touch her, have my fingers come away sticky.

"It hurts," she'd whispered. "Belle, hurts so much."

"Mum? Are you all right?" I'd asked even though she'd looked like a broken doll, limbs arranged in a crooked pattern. "Mummy?"

"I'm so scared . . . want David . . . don't want to go," she'd mumbled, and I figured it was good that she was talking. Wasn't that what they said? In accidents they always treat the silent ones first because the people that are moaning and yelling are well enough to moan and yell. "Don't leave me."

So I didn't. Even though she'd stopped talking, stopped moving, I stayed there, stroking her hair and saying her name, while they hosed down the car with this foamy stuff so the smoking engine wouldn't catch fire. And I'd stayed there through every awful vibration of the cutting machine they'd used to cut through her door and get to her.

I had this theory that if I was touching her, connecting her to this world then she'd know, on some level she'd know, and it would keep her here.

"But it didn't work, did it?" I sobbed and his arms tightened around me so he could pepper my face with frantic kisses. "And she didn't want to go, Dad! I promise you, she wanted to stay with us."

"Sshhh, shhhh," he soothed, hands jerky as he kept rubbing those comforting circles against my back. "I know, Belle, I know."

"It was all my fault, and you'd have all been better off if it had been me. It should have been me."

"You're not to say that ever again," he whispered fiercely. "My God, Belle, why have you kept that all shut away?"

"Because if I didn't think about it then it didn't happen. It was a bad dream and I'd wake up and she'd still be here, but I couldn't sleep and I wanted to because then I could wake up," I stuttered over the words, fisting the tears out of my eyes. "Dad, I'm sorry, I'm so sorry that she left you."

"Thank you for staying with her so she wasn't alone," he said so softly I had to strain my ears to catch the words. "She didn't like being by herself."

"She was always bugging me to do stuff with her when you weren't here, and it used to really get on my nerves that she'd never give me any space, but now . . ." I started crying again, hopelessly, helplessly, because suddenly it hit me every bit as hard as that final slam into the back of the lorry that she was gone.

He didn't say anything; just let me cry until my head felt like it had been packed in cotton wool and then when my throat was too sore to cry any longer, he put a finger to my lips. "If anything had happened to you tonight . . ." he began, then smiled wryly. "Anything worse than this . . . I wouldn't have been able to live with losing both of you. Even when I've been so very angry with you, with the way you've acted as if her loss was this minor inconvenience, I love you too much, Belle, even when I don't like you."

"You want to send me away to some school where they're going to make me pray all the time." I sounded a bit like my old self. "I saw the brochures. I saw them!"

He met my accusatory stare without flinching. "I'll admit, I've given it serious consideration. You didn't seem to want to be here, and I can't endure this situation any longer, Belle."

"I don't want to go, I want to stay here with you and Felix, but everything is so messed and I don't know how to fix it. Not just Mum, everything, and I'm so unhappy," I finished on this desperate wail, and I was gushing out saltwater again and had my good arm around his neck in this complete stranglehold.

He took it in very good humor, snagging a tissue from the box on the side table and telling me to blow my nose in a stern voice that shocked a giggle out of me.

"I will not lose you, Isabel," he said gravely. "Not to car accidents or your self-destructive behavior. We'll sort things out, but I will not have a repeat of these last few months, do I make myself clear?"

I nodded. "I am sorry, Dad. I know it was my fault . . ."

"It wasn't," he insisted bleakly, choking on the words. "I needed . . . wanted to blame someone because if I hadn't gone away, if I'd been here . . . and I've been trying to hold everything together, make us a family again, but I feel like I lost you as well as her."

"No! You're not to say that!" Now I was comforting him, planting millions of tiny kisses across his cheeks. "I did get lost but I wanted someone to find me, you know that, right?"

"I'm beginning to." I reached out my hand so I could trace the lines etched around his eyes that never used to be there. He turned his head so he could kiss my fingers. "I think you're responsible for some of those wrinkles and at least 75 percent of my gray hairs."

"They make you look distinguished." I frowned. "Kind of."

"I love you very much, Isabel, even when you make me utterly furious," he said.

I could feel my eyelids drooping and I yawned hard enough to dislocate my jaw. "Right back at you, Dad."

"Bed," he said firmly, helping me stand up, his arm around me for support as I staggered to the door. "You must be exhausted."

"I passed exhausted a few hours ago," I said, yawning again and then I looked around. "Hey, where did Smith go?"

Dad coughed delicately. "He very diplomatically excused himself from the room when you started crying. He seems . . . nice enough for someone who's been leading you astray."

"It was more like the other way around," I said, and there he was sitting on the stairs with Felix as they both tucked into bowls of cereal.

They both looked up, and then Smith got to his feet, clutching his cornflakes and looking like it was his turn to burst into tears.

"It's quite all right, Atticus," my father demurred. "I don't happen to have my shotgun at hand."

The flush started at Smith's hairline and if he hadn't been wearing his Jack Purcells, I bet even his little toes would have been blushing. "Yeah . . . um . . . look, I'm sorry . . . I didn't . . ." he stammered while Dad smiled faintly. He could be one scary fucker sometimes. "I'll go, if that's okay with you, sir?"

"Are you all right to drive? It's very late and you've had rather a stressful night."

I don't think Smith could have got out of our house fast enough. "No, it's cool. I might walk, clear my head."

"Thanks for everything," I said, and it seemed so lame after he'd been all rocklike in the face of everything I'd thrown at him. "Sorry for being . . . well, sorry for everything."

And even though I was leaning against Dad, Smith walked away from the door so he could find the one unmarked spot on my face and press his lips to it. "Don't mention it." He smiled. "Remember not to get your cast wet."

"I think we have it covered," Dad said silkily, putting his hand on Smith's shoulder and flexing his fingers ever so slightly. "And you should stop for tea when you come around to collect your car."

"There might be cake," Felix chimed in hopefully.

Smith edged toward the door with one wary eye on Dad, like he expected him to break out the horsewhip and/or shotgun. Then he was giving me a halfhearted little wave and a lopsided smile before Dad shut the door behind him.

"He's been really good to me," I offered, but he shook his head.

"It can all wait until you've had some sleep."

"So should I go to bed or shall I just stay up because cartoons will be on soon?" Felix asked as we shuffled up the stairs.

"We're all going to bed," Dad said firmly. "And we're going to sleep until at least lunchtime."

My leg gave out before we reached the top and he swung me up in his arms. "What if I can't sleep?" I whispered. "What if tomorrow just keeps on sucking?"

He nudged open the door of my room with his foot and placed me gently on the bed. "One day it won't," he said, tugging at the laces of my sneakers. "One day you'll wake up and find that the pain's still there but it doesn't hurt quite so much."

I shrugged out of my borrowed jacket and decided that if I

was going to sleep it might as well be fully clothed. "But it doesn't ever really go away, does it?"

He tucked the quilt around me, nice and tight, and then straightened up. "No," he said, eyes shadowed. "It doesn't ever really go away."

"Good," I muttered, and I was asleep before he'd even switched off the light.

Epilogue

So, I'm sorry that I haven't been here for ages.

A lot's happened but I guess you probably know that. I'm not sure how it works. Like, can you see me all the time? If you can, that's weird and slightly icky, especially if I'm doing something rude. But, anyway, things were bad for quite a while. Disaster movie bad. I don't even want to get into it, not because I'm being avoidy but it's in the past and I've moved on.

I got into another car crash a few months ago. I've really screwed up my arm so I guess that I'm not going to be a brain surgeon or a concert violinist. I think I needed to be really hurt on the outside so the hurt on the inside would realize that it wasn't on its own and that it had to come out.

Dad was amazing. I told him everything, and he didn't get really cold and sarcastic like he does—you remember? He pulled me out of school immediately, wouldn't take any crap from Mrs. Greenwood or the governors. I'm going to go to college in September and maybe I'll squeeze my A-levels into one year, maybe I won't.

I haven't seen the others. Even Dot. She kept calling, and Dad said I had to be straight with her and tell her why I didn't want to see her ever again. I miss her sometimes but I don't want to be that girl any more. I never did. Not deep down.

It's been really nice to just chill. Grandma's talking to me again, she taught me how to knit because it's good therapy for my hand, and I made a cover for my iPod and I made one for Smith, too. I'll tell you about him later. But mostly this year, I've been working with Dad. Or, like, I've been working for Dad because, yeah, he's been amazing but he was really pissed off that I hurt all his books and he wanted compensation. And a new filing system. Payback's a bitch.

I go to the university with him some days and sit at the back while he lectures and hear his students moan about him. Then I come home and make these really exotic meals. And I taught Felix, who says hi by the way, how to bake so we've been having a lot of cake.

What else? I did some volunteering at an old people's home, but I gave it up because I didn't like the old people. They smelled funny and most of them were loopy. Oh, come on! I haven't suddenly sprouted wings. I'm still me.

Dad's taking the summer off and he's rented a place in Devon with a swimming pool. He says he's going to write a book about some dead American novelist, no surprises there, and that Smith can keep me out of trouble. Yup, Smith's coming, too. As my sort-of-not-boyfriend.

I'm not sure what he is, but we kissed the other night for the first time in ages and maybe I've finally wriggled back into his good graces. It's taken a lot of effort, not just in knitted iPod covers or Victoria sponges. Takes more than that to make someone trust you again. Dad was easy compared with Smith.

All his friends hated me for making him miserable and lying to him. Even when I was at my most forlorn with my plaster cast accessory, they'd walk out of the room when I walked into it. I guess I deserved it, but I think they're warming to me. Well, Molly is and she might come down to Devon while we're there. Jane is always going to hate my guts and the feeling's pretty mutual and Smith . . . he's like my best friend, and maybe now that we're getting kissy again, he might be my best friend with, like, benefits.

Should probably stop getting fixated on one kiss. Smith says that we went too far and too fast last time and that we have to slow down—*I* have to slow down. I think I'll be eighty before we ever have sex again. And I still love him. I can't help it. I wish I could sometimes, because it hurts when he won't say it back. He says that he needs more time. I wonder if he sneaks into my room when I'm asleep and whispers it in my ear while I dream about you.

Yeah, I always dream about you. Good dreams. I wish I didn't have to wake up. But I always do and the pain's still there, but I don't ever want it to go away because then it means that you've gone away. But you're not ever going to leave me, I know that now.

Everyone was right when they said I'd carry a piece of you in my heart and I do. And it burns so bright, the tiny corner of my heart that's exclusively yours, that it's turned all the terrible things we said that day into ash and all that's left is the good stuff.

I see you all around me. I see you in Felix when he's concentrating on his homework and his tongue pokes out the corner of his mouth. I feel you in the way my hands rub the butter and flour together when I'm baking, like you taught me. I hear you every time Dad calls me "Belle," like you used to. A million times in a million different ways, you're there in my heart. Don't ever stop. Don't ever leave.

I love you, Mum. Always.

a note from the author

I started Let's Get Lost *about three months after my mum died. I never got a chance to say good-bye to her, so I wrote this book instead. Three years and about ten different drafts later, I finished it and hope that it's a fitting tribute to an amazing woman who nurtured my love of reading and gave me all the opportunities she never had. Without her, I'd never have become a writer.*

There are no words left, so I'll just point out that Isabel's badges came from the wonderful http://mymy.girlswirl.net/ and that "Anthems for a Seventeen-Year-Old Girl" is by Broken Social Scene from their very brilliant album You Forgot It in People.